# MILLENARIANISTIC
# CHRONODYKE

Copyright © 2024 by Johannes Paine
First Print Edition
All Rights Reserved

Published in Canada by Matt Payne
Cover designed by Johannes Paine

ISBN: 978-1-7750835-3-5

pattmayne.com

# MILLENARIANISTIC CHRONODYKE

**Prologue: The Sailor**

Thunder crushed the air and neon lightning flashed against the purple-black sky like a stormy rave. A lone boat with a lone occupant was tossed upon the frothy waves, but even in this turbulence the sea man was serenely hunched over the desk in his cabin. He transcribed a typed document into calligraphy by flickering candlelight using a featherpen, a sturdy parchment, and his own steady hand. His penmanship was so exquisite that nobody would guess it was scrawled by a lowly sailor, and certainly not under such tumultuous conditions.

When the message was copied in full he double-checked each letter to make sure he'd been true to the original:

> *"My sweet princess. Free 2sday nite. Bring that sweet budgie. I betray my city but never betray my heart xoxo."*

Only when his accuracy was doubly confirmed did the slightest hint of a satisfied smile tug at one corner of his mouth, for that's all the indulgence this grizzled *sailor-turned-messenger-pigeon* would allow himself. Then he rolled up the parchment and slipped it into a waterproof plastic tube, labeled and dated it, and put it in a slot on the shelf with all the others, behind their tiny little doors. With the original back in his rain slicker and his bright yellow hat set firmly on his wise old head this man of the sea went out onto the deck to behold the great spectacle of Mother Ocean having one of her many beautiful fits.

### Chapter 1: Jay Dean I

The afternoon air offered a salty freshness and the playful ocean wind tousled Jay Dean's brown hair. The man stood atop a stone parapet, a leftover fortification from a previous age, and looked out at the ocean where a bearded ship bobbed upon the waves. He recognized this ship as belonging to the navy of Ethelcrest's rival island-nation, *GX Island*. Their ships were decorated to reflect the national manly hairstyle of a rough pointy beard and a big topknot. Theirs was a mongrel fleet composed of vessels purchased at auctions or pirated from less aggressive seafarers. The beards and topknots gave the ships a sense of common identity to make up for their lack of uniform structures.

The ship's beard parted and a little square mouth opened up. A much smaller boat was ejected from this orifice and travelled among the waves toward the shore. This smaller boat also had its own smaller beard and topknot. You always knew when a GXer was approaching on the water, but it was impossible to know how many of their bearded submarines were milling about beneath the waves.

The smaller boat reached the shore. Jay watched three men disembark and walk up the path from the beach to the cliffs and the stairs. Finally the men arrived on the wall beside Jay. Two wore navy-blue woollen jackets and the beard and hairstyle dictated by their culture, while the third and tallest of the trio sported a black jacket and extra medals on his chest. Their eyes were wide, but thin and slanted. Their pale skin was roughened by their seafaring lifestyles.

The tallest of the three visitors stepped forward and spoke. His accent was very proper, aggressively throaty, with a strong focus on the consonants. "I am Admiral Ivan Spuknit. We received your message. What is your offer?"

Jay smiled what he thought was a disarming smile, although his guests offered no kind of disarming gesture in return. In fact they were physically armed with scimitars and machine guns, both of which were outlawed on Ethelcrest. Jay turned away from the ocean and pointed inland where the visitors could see that this wall surrounded a small village, making it a fortress.

Jay said, "This fortress is Ethelcrest's oldest building."

"And who are those people?" Ivan pointed a long finger down into the village where several hundred naked, hairless, blue-skinned humanoids stared up at them in patient silence. Within the shadows of the fortress-walls they glowed slightly like radioactive blueberry-people. "I thought this was a secret meeting!"

"They're just the natives," Jay said dismissively. "They don't speak and they never leave the fortified safety of the reserve."

"I don't like them," Ivan complained. "Why are they looking at me? Why did you bring me here where they can stare at me like that?"

"The natives are the spirit of the island," Jay explained. "We signed a pact with them hundreds of years ago, and they've been living in peace within this fortress ever since. I brought you here so you can see the history of Ethelcrest, because we are about to forge an alliance that will usher in the next phase of that history."

"Tell us your plan," Ivan grumbled.

"My uncle, Mayor Dean, wants to overthrow our municipal democracy and take his rightful place as king," Jay Dean explained. "Our family are the rightful rulers of this island, but we can't trust the voters to make the right choice this year. They're still upset about the whole balloon fiasco. It shouldn't be hard to conquer these domesticated plebs. We have no standing municipal army to defeat, since each burb has its own police and military reserve, and Mayor Dean can summon his own army from the Banking Burb where he's burbmaster, plus a few other burbmasters will surely join the cause when they see how the tables have turned. But our municipal navy is loyal to the whole island and will oppose our bloody coup. The mayor needs your navy to crush our navy. We have a couple navy captains on our side who will help you against the rest. Then our armies will conquer Parliament Hall. We'll murder any opposing burbmasters and replace them with allies. And we will transform this corrupt democracy into a glorious kingdom."

"Some of our men will die in this naval battle," Ivan countered. "Why should we sacrifice our men to help you? What do you offer in return?"

"We'll give you one burb. But not one of the good ones."

Ivan stroked his beard and paced back and forth on the windy stones. "Your mayor, he was elected, and your island is vibrant and healthy. I do not see how democracy has been bad for you. Tell me again how your city elects a mayor. On GX Island we do as our women command, and your political system is strange to us."

Jay said, "The island is divided into burbs. The citizens of each burb elect a burbmaster, who goes to Parliament Hall to represent their burb in municipal parliament. Then the burbmasters vote among themselves to name one burb-master as mayor. This works in conjunction with a party system, where most burbmaster-candidates are members of political parties, which are like private clubs representing certain interests such as magicians' rights. If the voters all elect a burbmaster from The Magic Party, for instance, those burbmasters will all vote for their party leader, who is also a burbmaster, to be mayor. I work for the current mayor, but his father was also the mayor for twelve years, and *his* father was mayor for thirty-two years."

"Thirty-two years?" Ivan repeated incredulously.

"He was a hypnotist and a murderer," Jay added. "My point is, these elections are a farce. The people are idiots. Only a king can rule! Or a queen, of course. Or non-gendered monarch, or whatever."

"But a king can be an idiot too," Ivan argued. "How do you know that a king will truly be better than an elected mayor?"

"It's just more badass," Jay insisted. "Mayor Dean has a

warhammer and a composite bow that he never gets to use, but as a king he could use them all the time. Now I'm not gay, but when I see the mayor swing that warhammer, there's a deep part of me that submits to him sexually."

Ivan grimaced. "Your uncle?"

Jay took out a tattered photo and handed it to Ivan. The photo depicted Mayor Robert Dean wearing blue jeans, and no shirt or socks. He had a great brown beard and a barrel chest. The picture caught him halfway through swinging a massive warhammer. The hammer's head was arcing towards a wooden box upon which somebody had stencilled the letters, "HIGH TAXES."

Ivan nodded. "Yes, this is a very sexy man." Then he turned to his companions and they conversed in their harsh language, so full of sharp consonants, and Jay didn't understand anything they said.

Finally the guest returned to Jay and said, "We will help you, but we want the Moon Burb, and we want one of your blue people."

Jay gazed down at the natives who were still staring up at him in silence. "Why would you want one of them? Didn't you say you didn't like them?"

"The more they stare at me the more I want one," Ivan said with a sense of troubled curiosity. "There is just... something about them."

"I don't think I'm allowed to give them away, but maybe we can appoint one as an ambassador or something."

"What should we feed them?" Ivan asked. "I do not know their customs."

"I've never seen them eat," Jay answered. "Except there's a soup factory nearby and sometimes the factory's exhaust creates soup clouds, and the natives get a nice nutritious rain, free of charge."

"You are truly a man of the people."

"I don't think they're people. I don't think they even procreate."

"But there are hundreds of them!" Ivan protested. "If you conquered their island centuries ago, and they don't procreate, then how are there so many of them now?"

"I think they live forever."

"They just keep staring at us."

"They scare the shit out of me," Jay admitted. "If you want one, go ahead and take one. As an ambassador."

Ivan and his buddies took a set of stairs down into the village. He threw one of the natives over his shoulder, then came back up to meet Jay.

"I take this as down-payment," Ivan said. "We will take the Moon Burb after your mayor becomes king, with the help of our navy. But if you betray me, Jay Dean, I swear by my beard, I will scrape your face off with your own teeth."

"That's a deal," Jay said, and they shook on it. "Our fortunes will all be made on election day. Now can I have my photo back?"

"I keep the sexy photo," Ivan grumbled. "No man should carry such a sexy photo of his own uncle. Maybe your island is as corrupt as you say, if this is how you think of your uncles. Maybe you do need a king."

The GXers returned to the beach and loaded the blue native onto their little boat. Then the little boat motored up to the big boat and was swallowed in its beard. Jay tried to figure out whether he had just betrayed his home, or saved it. He turned back to the natives, the spirit of Ethelcrest, for answers. But they just looked at him, possibly judging him, but maybe not, and Jay filled up their silence with his own hopes and fears. Finally he resigned himself to fate and went to find his uncle, to tell him that the deal was struck, and their hour of ascendance was that much closer.

## Chapter 2: Henry I

Breaking out of prison had been no easy task, but it was nothing compared to the dark days that followed.

Henry Ecgherht wandered through the labyrinth of sewers that permeated the island-nation of Ethelcrest. After his map was stolen by a sewer-dwelling hobo, and his flashlight carried off by a surprisingly well-organized rat-swarm, the escaping convict was immersed in absolute darkness with no way to find fresh air and sunlight. He chased the wayward flashlight's traitorous beam through so many side-tunnels that he lost track of his position, and finally the dancing light disappeared around a corner and taunted him no more. Henry had been a prisoner but now he was a rat in a maze, betrayed by his own figurative kind. Yet every setback only strengthened Henry's resolve, his will to be free.

He went without food for three wandering days, and it wouldn't be proper to describe what he drank down there, hidden from the free-range electorate.

Deprived of light his other senses were heightened. Henry was able to sniff out the slightest lingering freshness that infiltrated this world of stench. He followed that freshness upstream until a soft glow announced his proximity to freedom. Finally he rounded a corner and beheld the end of the tunnel, where a stream of refuse spilled out into a gorgeous grove beside a waterfall.

After all that darkness the light nearly blinded Henry. And after the gray desolation of his prison-home, to see the leaves flutter with a green so rich and pure brought a tear to Henry's eye. The very bushes seemed to wave at him in welcome and the pond's water sparkled like fireworks in his honor. Butterflies chased each other all about the grove. A fabulous peacock pranced along the water's edge clucking and chittering.

Henry dove from the drainage pipe and splashed into the pool. The cold water shocked his filthy skin and brought a new level of wakefulness. He pulled himself out of the pond, keeping a safe distance from the peacock, and proceeded to strip off his clothes and scrub his skin clean with some moss and dirt.

He had a very special item stashed in his pants. It was a red wig he'd fashioned from hair he'd stolen from his red-headed cell-mate. Over the months he'd been locked up Henry took every opportunity to stash away strand after strand of those long, healthy red hairs. He placed the wig on his head and beheld his visage in the wavy surface of the pond. He liked what he saw: a lean, muscular body strengthened by boring months of extra exercise, and a chiseled handsome face rendered unrecognizable by the thick cluster of red hair.

The peacock also seemed interested in that red hair and started making its way over to Henry's position. He was too hungry and fatigued to fight off a full-grown peacock so he started hauling on his pants.

All he had to do was make it to the docks, where a boat should still be waiting for him, though he was late and approaching the end of their agreed-upon window. If he could evade capture for a few more hours then he'd be on his way to join the pirates of Coal Island, and the freedom of the high seas.

That's when he caught a patch of blue moving amongst the greenery at the top of the cliff beside the waterfall. It was a cop!

The cop turned and shouted back to his unseen buddies, "I found him!"

Henry bolted, still naked save for the wig. He abandoned his clothes and the curious peacock. He ran away from the prison and those who would return him to it, ran through the woods and toward the dock, toward *freedom*.

But then he heard a gunshot and a bullet nicked his left ear. A second gunshot, and a second bullet nicked his right ear. Then a voice said, "Third one goes right down the middle!"

Henry stopped and put up his hands. He didn't want to go back to jail, but he even more didn't want to die.

"Turn around," the voice commanded. Henry obliged and beheld his captor. The cop's uniform was pristine and crisp. His dark mustache was the perfect decoration on his plump and pale face, and he had a grin to match the sparkle in his eye as he kept his pistol trained on Henry.

"Henry Ecgherht, fugitive," the cop said.

"Guilty," Henry admitted.

"Convicted for fraud and impersonating foreign royalty."

"Guilty," Henry repeated.

"Guilty of breaking bylaw eighty three in the Moon Burb."

"That's such a stupid law," Henry said.

"Guilty of attempting to blow up the space station."

"I was framed!" Henry bellowed, trying not to lose his composure.

The officer took out a pair of handcuffs which jingled as they dangled from his hand, and he tossed them over to Henry. "Now put these on, and let's take you home."

Henry caught the cuffs, but hesitated to comply. "I would really prefer to not go back to jail."

The next bullet nicked Henry's dangling dick, not enough to draw blood, but just enough to put tiny painful little burn-marks on his foreskin.

"You win," he said. Henry held out his left arm and prepared to cuff himself, but then he heard an awful screech. It was like a monkey's cry crossed with a rooster's crow, and the trees above the cop exploded in a flurry of feathers and leaves.

"No!" the cop screamed. He aimed his gun up at his assailant and fired three shots, but they passed harmlessly between the great peacock's feathers, and the avian beast landed on his face. Cop and bird fell to the ground. Henry couldn't see exactly what was happening with the man's upper body occluded by the bird's plumage, but the sounds of tearing flesh and diminishing sobs told Henry all he needed to know. All hope for the officer disappeared when two more peacock's emerged from the foliage, and joined in the feast.

Henry inched forward to steal the officers' pants but he almost lost a finger when a ravenous peacock snapped at his outstretched hand. More of the birds were coming, attracted by the smell of blood, and it was clear that there wasn't enough meat for them all. Henry might be next on the menu. Plus he saw more scraps of blue further back among the greenery. The law was hot on his tail. So he turned and fled once more.

Twigs and leaves scraped at his unprotected body but Henry paid no mind. He heard the thudding footsteps of his pursuers and the fluttering wings of hungry birds.

A glistening body of water made itself seen through the trees ahead. He had almost reached the ocean! But he stopped when he slammed into a chain-link fence. With his fingers wrapped around the metal wires Henry peered through to the other side, to see what he could see. And what he saw was a basketball court, surrounded by this fence, and it was jam-packed with people. Just beyond that court the ocean waves sloshed lazily over a beach of boulders, and Henry saw his getaway boat, complete with its getaway driver smoking a cigarette on the deck. The driver wore one of those little wool hats. Henry knew the small motorboat was his intended target because of the green flag all aflutter upon the flagpole's tip.

His goal was in sight, but he was naked and there were a hundred people blocking his path. He could pass around the basketball court, but on the right was a big open park and on the left he saw the open space of wharves and parking lots, where the cops could easily see him.

Henry crawled along the fence looking for a place to hide, or maybe a way to sneak around the court without being seen. What he found instead was two people in the bushes making out.

"Can I touch you here?" a man's voice pleaded.

A woman whispered her consent: "Yes but only with your left hand."

Henry sneaked up closer and tried to mimic the man's

voice. "Can I take my pants off?"

The woman acquiesced and a moment later a pair of blue jeans came flying from the bushes. Henry caught them and put them on. Next he said, "Can I take off my shirt?"

"No," the woman said. "I like it with your shirt on."

Weirdo. "Well can I take off *your* shirt?"

A pink blouse came flying from the bushes. It was tight around the shoulders, but still better than nothing. "Can I take my shoes off?" he asked finally.

"No," she snapped. "We discussed this before! You keep your fucking shoes on!"

"Please," Henry begged. "I'll do anything!"

"Let me punch your face while you fuck me!" the woman hissed menacingly. "Then you can take your shoes off!"

"Deal!" Henry agreed.

"What?" the man said. "No!"

But it was too late. The smacking sounds of punching and fucking mingled with the groans and grunts of pleasure and pain as two battered sneakers flew from the bushes. Henry caught them and put them on. Now he felt like he might be able to blend in with the crowd, and soon found a hole in the fence that let him into the basketball court.

After slipping in through the hole Henry tried to lose himself in the crowd which was composed mostly of college-aged people, many of whom had stylish haircuts and dark-rimmed glasses. Even more of them held up signs proclaiming such political slogans as, "Eschewing Hyerbolic Mainstreamism," and "Retrofreeze NOW!" So this was some kind of political rally, and the air was charged with anticipation as they all conversed excitedly and quietly.

They seemed to be waiting for the rally to begin in earnest. Henry pushed his way through the crowd toward the opposite fence. Risking a look over his shoulder Henry saw several cops searching the fence outside the court. There was no turning back. He almost made it to the other side when somebody turned on their megaphone and started preaching.

"What will the future look like?" the megaphone called, wielded by a tall and skinny curly-haired man.

The crowd compressed upon itself as everybody moved closer to the megaphoner. Together they answered, "Millenarianistic Chronodyke!" Then there was a big cheer and everybody waved their signs in the air.

The cops were now inside the fence studying faces in their search for Henry the Fugitive. Out on the ocean the boatman impatiently checked his watch. So Henry kept moving toward the fence even as the rally picked up intensity.

The megaphone continued in a more moderate tone. "Everybody can see that our species is approaching a trans-formation vector," the speaker proclaimed. "And when that vector doubles back on itself through recursive mimetic paradigm shifts, then we'll literally be in the unknown."

Henry had no idea what this speech was about, or what kind of political ambitions these people had. But that didn't matter now. What mattered was that he was a few feet away from the fence, the final physical barrier between himself and the open sea. He shoved aside a pretty young woman who frowned at him (but then raised a curious eyebrow at his pink blouse). Then he grabbed the fence in his fingers, and pulled himself finally to the edge.

The speech continued. "We're not just here to win an election. We're transforming the oscillation of economic unpredictability into a substrate for a new kind of trans-social matrix!"

Henry started climbing the fence. The cops would spot him, but maybe by then it would be too late.

A hand grabbed his shoulder and pulled him down. Henry turned and froze when he saw a cop. The officer pointed at a sign that said, "KEEP OFF FENCE."

"Sorry officer," Henry said sheepishly. Apparently his disguise was working. "I was looking for a better view."

The cop crouched down. "Wanna hop on my shoulders? You'll be able to see everything then!"

"No, thanks."

"Come on!" The cop insisted, patting his shoulder with a hand.

Henry walked away but then somebody grabbed his elbow. It was the same woman he'd so rudely shoved a few moments ago. She said, "What's got you so agitated? You must have read the updated manifesto. Isn't it just the worst?"

The cops were everywhere in the crowd now so Henry decided to keep the conversation going for a little while, to help him blend in. Unfortunately he hadn't read any manifesto, and he had no idea what the rally was about. He listened to the speech for another moment to try to gain some contextual clues about this party's platform.

"Clitorial umbrage doesn't irradicalize the linguistic logic gates of agent-agnostic integrated systems!" the megaphone absolutely screeched, and the crowd cheered.

Henry's head hurt from trying to decipher what he'd just heard, so he just said, "To be honest, at this point I have campaign fatigue."

"Oh my God, I know!" the girl exclaimed. "They've all been campaigning ever since the balloon scandal. It feels like it will never end!"

"Well I think we have a real chance," Henry offered. He kept scanning the area, looking for any escape route. But the cops were smart. They set themselves up at each corner of the court while a couple more searched the crowd.

Out on the boat, the driver checked his watch one last time and threw his cigarette into the ocean. Henry's ears couldn't hear the distant sizzle of that extinguished smoke, but his heart heard it loud and clear. He had to get out there quick, but he was trapped and surrounded.

Somebody cried out in a girlish voice, "I found him! I found the fugitive!"

Henry's heart jumped and his eyes darted to the speaker. It was a cop standing outside the fence, in the bushes from where Henry had so recently emerged. The cop was a burly man and he lifted up two persons (a naked woman and a man wearing only a shirt), holding them by their wrists. Then he spoke in that same girlish voice, "Busted outta jail and he's already gettin' laid!"

The shirt-wearing dude wriggled in the cops' grip and said, "I'm not a fugitive!"

The red-headed woman screamed, "He was assaulting me!"

"What? No I wasn't!"

"I said he could fondle me with his left hand, BUT HE USED HIS RIGHT HAND!"

The crowd booed and two cops began beating the creep with their batons. The rest of the officers broke up the rally. "Okay everybody, party's over, time to go home." The megaphone went silent and people shuffled toward the exits.

The boat had turned and was chugging away over the waves. Henry moved to make one last assault on the fence, but the woman was still holding his arm. He noticed now that she also had a finger on his wrist. She didn't seem concerned with personal boundaries. She gave him lots of eye contact, which was unnerving and enticing at the same time. Henry noticed that one of her eyes was higher than the other and he couldn't decide whether that made her more or less attractive. But the more he looked at her the more he wanted to wrap himself up in her asymmetry.

"Your heart rate increased when they caught that fugitive," she said.

"That's just what happens when I see naked people," he said.

"Interesting."

"I gotta go," he said, and tried to pull his arm free.

Before he reached the fence again Henry heard the blood-curdling screech of a little girl. "It's not him! He's not the fugitive! Henry Ecgherht is still at large, and he's somewhere in this crowd! Let's find him, boys!"

Henry instantly reoriented his attention back to the woman who hadn't let go of his arm anyway. She asked, "So, what's your name?"

"Johnny," he said.

"Johnny what?" she inquired.

Henry's frazzled brain tried to think of any collection

of sounds to use as a fake last name but for some reason came up blank. All he could think of were names of shapes. Square. Triangle. Trapezoid.

"Tetrahedron."

"Hmm," she said as she studied his face. "Interesting. Well, Johnny Tetrahedron, I'm Lauretta Spice. Are you going to the after-rally?"

"I don't have a ride," he said.

"I'm going with some other volunteers," she told him. "We have a spare seat in the car. Maybe you can meet Malcolm's campaign manager, Immanuel, and some other volunteers."

Henry took one last, wistful look at his departing getaway boat, followed by a tense glance at the vigilant police officers who were scrutinizing everybody as they left, and he submitted to the winds of fate.

"Sweet," he said, forcing a grin. "Lead the way."

## Chapter 3: Nico I

On the surface it was a familiar scene. The same seven people, the same five guys and the same two gals, all sitting around the same picnic table under the same old sun. They all ate the same kind of hamburger from the same hamburger stand, out here in the same sports park in the Dirt Burb. From the far end of the field they could hear the same old ringing smack of a bat striking a softball, and the cheering crowd, just like every other time before. Even their seven dirt bikes were the same. Sure, some parts had been replaced, but your dad can replace a few skin cells and he's still your dad. Yes, they were the same old gang in their same old stomping grounds. They'd even just finished whooping the ass of the South Side Marauders in this week's endurance race, the same as they'd done so many times before.

And yet, everything had changed.

Beneath the same old dirt that covered their same old bodies and bikes alike, beneath Nico's sleeveless shirt and beautiful blue eyes, even beneath Bjorn's crusty scowl and worn leather jacket, the team was broken.

"You can't do this, Nico," Bjorn said simply, and uselessly. He shrugged his shoulders, wobbled his head, and held his hands out like a supplicant demanding water from his sovereign lord, gestures Bjorn had learned by watching his dad argue about politics. "We can't win the tournament if we're down one man."

"One man *and* one woman," Stoya corrected. She sat beside Nico and held his hand beneath the table. "I stick with my man wherever he goes because he's the strongest man on the island."

Bjorn was holding his hamburger and now he dropped it loudly on the table with disgust, and gesticulated like a Parkinson's patient. "Well that's just great! We have always been there for each other, but I guess those days are over! How will we win the tournament without you? And without the tournament money, how will we afford to repair our bikes?"

Now the rest of the table chimed in.

"I sold my kidney for new spark plugs!"

"I've been using my own piss for coolant!"

"I carved my own carburetor from my dead dog's skull!"

Nico finished meticulously chewing his burger and then dusted off his hands. The blond young man nodded to acknowledge the concerns of his companions, swallowed his meal, and looked them each in the eye. "When we win a competition, the only people we defeat are our fellow bikers," he said. "But who really wins? You all said it yourself. We can't afford to take care of our own bikes, and we're the best team on the island. But people pay good money to watch the competitions. Where does all that money go? Into the pockets of the fatcats, that's where."

Bjorn threw his hamburger passionately on the grass. "You and your fatcats! Always with the fatcats! Why don't you focus on biking instead of fatcats?"

"It doesn't matter how many competitions we win. We

could be perfect at biking and we would still get screwed. And the fatcats are doing it to everybody, not just us. Sylvi, your dad is a shoemaker but he can't afford his own shoes. Holmes, your mother is a whore, but she can't afford her own whores. But the fatcats get to have all the shoes and all the whores, and they didn't produce any of them."

"So what?" Bjorn rejoined. "So you abandon us? Bah!" He hurled his French Fries on the ground with his burger.

"I'm not abandoning you," Nico said patiently. "I'm helping you. The elections are soon and there's one political party who is on the side of artists and performers. The Dancing Party. I'm going to join them, to help them win, and they'll demand that the fatcats pay the workers and performers fairly."

"You can't even dance!" Holmes said.

Stoya defended her man. "The Dancing Party is about more than dancing. They're about all performers, including whores like your mother, and even certain types of burglar."

Holmes nodded. "It would be nice if a political party represented my whore mother, instead of just my pimp father."

Nico stood up and stretched, and nobody could keep their eyes off his beautiful body as the sun shone off his blond hair even through the dirt. His filthy blue jeans and stained sleeveless t-shirt did nothing to hide the perfect glory of his lean masculine frame. Yes, his chest was strong, but not so strong as to suggest he'd put any effort into building it. His was a casual, natural strength borne of genetics rather than the gym, the kind of power that others had to work for. And that supple ease made him all the more desirable to all who beheld him. It was impossible to not fantasize about resting your head on his bare chest and smelling his sweat as he held you.

He swung a leg over his bike and straddled his machine. "And you're wrong about another thing, Holmes. You know I can dance, when I'm riding my bike!"

He started the bike and revved the engine. "I'm joining The Dancing Party so I can give something back to Ethelcrest. So I can give something back to the sport, and all performers. I know you don't understand, but this is something I have to do. And I beg you, all of you, to join me! Let the South Side Marauders win this tournament! And we will go fight the real war! The war with the fatcats!"

Stoya mounted her own bike and revved it in support of her sexy boyfriend. The grease and dirt on her face looked like warpaint and her blond hair fell over her shoulders in braids. "True glory!" she screamed over the bike's engine.

Bjorn was not convinced. He jumped up and stomped on his burger and fries, smashing them into the ground. "I forbid it! Politics is for nerds and liars. It is the fatcat game, and you can never beat them!"

Stoya spit on the ground. "Your despair is weakness, brother! You humiliate yourself with your words."

"No," Bjorn said. "You humiliate us all with your abandonment. Hear me now and heed my words. If you abandon us like this then you are cursed, and your whole lineage is cursed until the end of time."

Nico's face turned dark and sour like a blackberry candy. "Don't say that," Nico told him. "After all these years, don't let this end with a curse."

"Then don't end it at all," Bjorn responded. "Come to the tournament, one last competition, and show the world one more time how you can make your bike dance. Do that for us, and we will be there on election day to vote for your stupid party."

"I don't half-ass things," Nico said. "I don't want to be half-biker and half-politician. Yesterday I was fully a biker, but today I am fully a politician and a servant to all of Ethelcrest."

"And on the day of the tournament you will be fully a biker again," Bjorn said. "Otherwise you are fully cursed."

Nico wanted to argue more because he knew that he was right. But he also knew that his soul would rot if he didn't ride with them at this final tournament.

"I'm joining The Dancing Party, but I'll be there for the tournament," he said. "I swear it!"

Bjorn and Nico gripped hands so tight that they could feel each others' pulse. Their nostrils flared and their eyes burned with the cosmic passion of their fraternal bond. But there were no more words to speak, so Nico and Stoya revved their engines once more and blasted off into the unpaved parking lot and the dirt road that led back to the center of town.

A team was broken, a promise made, and a new political journey begun.

### Chapter 4: Henry II

Henry sat at a card table surrounded by curious eyes and furrowed brows. He was very much the odd-man-out at the after-rally party, even though he was keeping quiet and trying to blend in. Maybe they subconsciously recognized his face from the television broadcast, but couldn't quite make the connection consciously because of his clever wig. Maybe they were thrown off by the tiny stolen blouse he was wearing, whose buttons struggled and strained to keep the pink fabric stretched across his chest. Maybe they were jealous of how Lauretta had been hanging off his arm all night, feeding him drinks and dragging him to dark corners for frustratingly short make-out sessions. Maybe they were still wondering whether "Johnny Tetrahedron" could possibly be a real name. Or maybe they were suspicious of the massive pile of winnings that Henry had somehow collected while playing their confusing card game.

Henry was also suspicious of his own winnings because he had no idea how to play. His goal for the moment was to earn their trust and learn anything he could about their political party, Millenarianistic Chronodyke. That was a necessity if he wanted to avoid getting caught, but ultimately he needed to get off the island. So far Lauretta was the only one who approved of him and everybody else seemed to grudgingly accept him out of respect for her. If he asked about the rules to the game then they might know that he was an imposter, so he had been playing random cards all night, and winning almost every round.

So now, with all the hateful eyes on him (plus those two beautifully asymmetrical blue eyes just to his right), Henry confidently placed two cards down on the table and leaned back to see how the other players would react.

"A bold move, Johnny," Immanuel said, to his left. Immanuel was the campaign manager for Malcolm Sneck, the party leader, Henry had learned. Immanuel was a lean, curly-haired man in his fifties and he wore a shirt and tie. He laid down two of his own cards, and so did each subsequent player in clockwise rotation around the table.

After the rally Lauretta had ushered him into her friends' car in the parking lot, and they joined a caravan of vehicles that took him to this two-story office building nestled in a cluster of trees. Someone had to punch in a security code to let the caravan through the barbed-wire gate, and then they'd all flooded the basement and proceeded to party. The basement had offices, janitorial closets, two rec rooms with wet bars, some server farms, and a robotics workshop. Every room was triangular, including the halls. The whole place was filled with drunken activists arguing about politics, except for these four drunken card players who were intently focused on their game.

The game was called *Ransack's Hegemony* and it made no sense to Henry, just like everything else he'd seen from these incomprehensible nerds. The cards all displayed holographic images. Depending on your angle of view each card would either show you some writing in a strange character set, electrical drawings, or a picture of a dessert.

"You had me scared for a minute, Johnny," said Vij from across the table as everybody compared the hands that had just been laid out. "That power source birthday cake combo is a real whopper, but I bet you never suspected that I had the doorbell cherry pie!"

"That's exactly what I was afraid of!" Henry lied. "Oh well, I have to let someone else win a round sometimes."

Vij collected his winnings. Instead of poker chips the

players in *Ransack's Hegemony* used five-sided dice to tally their profits, and Henry had the biggest pile. Vij studied Henry as he sorted his dice. These five-sided dice wouldn't stack, so they all had big messy piles. "Yes, if you won every single round, somebody might suspect you of stacking the deck."

"Don't be a sore winner," Lauretta said to Vij. She looked up at Henry with those pretty eyes through her dark-rimmed glasses, and the smell of her hair made him smile. He got tingles every time her soft blouse brushed his arm. His prison time had kept Henry away from women for too long and he was trying not to let it effect his judgment. His primary mission for the evening was slowly shifting from escape to getting Lauretta alone and getting rid of her clothes.

Immanuel shuffled the cards and started dealing but Vij's eyes were still locked on Henry.

"So Johnny," Vij said with forced casualness. "Where did you say you worked again?"

"I'm a consultant," he said offhandedly while pretending to study his cards.

"Hm," said Vij, also pretending to study his cards. "What kind of consultant? Financial? Legal?"

"General."

"Hm!" Vij almost barked. He laid down two cards. "What a coincidence! I happen to need a general consultant, you know, for my general affairs. Do you have a business card so I can hire you?"

Henry patted his chest pockets. "I must have left them in my other blouse."

When his turn came Henry played two more random cards and Vij and Lauretta immediately got pissed off and threw their hands down.

"Don't fold yet guys," Henry said. "Immanuel still has to play."

Immanuel scowled, the first time that evening that he'd expressed any unambiguous negativity. "Don't be facetious. No amount of cake can decouple those transistors!"

Henry almost apologized for his alleged facetiousness, wishing to smooth over the endless social disturbances arising from his total ignorance regarding the values and behaviors of his hosts. He kept putting his foot in his mouth because he had no idea what anybody else was talking about. But since he was doomed to keep blundering until he could escape these freaks Henry decided that obnoxiousness would be a better bridge than endless apologies with diminishing returns. So Henry grinned at Immanuel as he scooped up his bounty.

It was Vij's turn to deal. Vij had short, messy blond hair and a receding hairline. His head was slightly egg-shaped and his eyebrows were so thick that they looked like caterpillars. Whenever he raised or lowered a brow it looked like the caterpillar was arching his back to wiggle across his face.

As everybody reviewed the cards Vij had dealt, Vij continued his casual interrogation of the new guy. "So Johnny, what burb did you say you were from?"

Henry forced a chuckle. "As a traveling general consultant I pretty much live out of my suitcase. You could say I live in all the burbs, or none at all."

"Ah, so that explains why we haven't seen you at any meetings or rallies before," Vij said. But now his tone was unnecessarily loud and other people in the room were turning their heads. "I guess you just go to the rallies and meetings of whichever burb your job takes you."

"That's right."

"When you visit the other Millenarianistic Chronodyke factions in the other burbs, do they all agree with Malcolm Sneck's stance on transdermal mathematics? Or is anybody ready to accept Immanuel's quasi-random mathematronics?"

At the mention of his name Immanuel brushed away the idea with a wave of his cards. "My formulations are purely theoretical," he said, though he couldn't suppress a proud smile. "They don't belong in a political platform."

"That's not what I asked though," Vij said. He hadn't taken his eyes off Henry and Henry refused to break the gaze first. "I'm asking Johnny his opinion on Sneck's transdermal mathematics, and what he's heard in his alleged travels."

Henry barely even know who Malcolm Sneck was, nevermind trans-something mathematics. He needed to say something vague and general enough that it might sound correct.

"The general consensus in the other burbs is that Sneck's mathematics are expedient," Henry said, and he was pretty sure that he hadn't even drunkenly slurred any of the words. "But some people agree that Immanuel's formulations in a virtual environment could offer up interesting data points."

"That's exactly my intention," Immanuel said. He seemed very pleased to hear that people were discussing his ideas all across the island and he looked at Henry with gratitude. Henry in turn was pleased with himself for using so many syllables to say absolutely nothing and make it sound like something.

But Vij still wasn't convinced. His scowling frown intensified to the same degree as Immanuel had warmed to Henry. But then Vij relaxed completely and casually asked, "So what burb are you headed to next?"

"The Moon Burb," he blurted out.

"We only have a small faction there, don't we?" Vij asked. "Not a lot of support for Millenarianistic Chronodyke over in the ol' Mon Burb, eh?"

"Ah, no," Henry said.

Lauretta elbowed him. "Your turn to play, Johnny. And hey, Vij, lay off the interrogation, okay?"

Vij shrugged. "Who's interrogating? I'm just asking some questions of my new friend Johnny Tetrahedron, that's all. I'm not suggesting that he's a spy from a rival political party, I'm not suggesting anything like that, just because he shows up out of nowhere one day and acts like he's been here all along. No, we're all brothers here, no suspicions or anything like that. Alternatively, I also don't suspect that maybe he's a spy for the government trying to root out radicals or anything like that, or maybe some kind of extra-terrestrial chimera learning our habits so they can infiltrate our society, our very political parties. No, of course I don't suspect anything like that from our good friend Johnny Tetrahedron who travels around non-suspiciously doing general kinds of work and who doesn't know anybody who we know. Nor do I suspect him of being any kind of pagan trickster-god sent to disrupt our party before the first debate, no, that would be paranoid, and I'm not paranoid, so I don't suspect any of those things from our good friend Johnny Tetrahedron."

"Well good," Lauretta said. "Because he's not any of those things!"

With a great sweep of his arms Vij knocked all the cards and dice onto the carpet. "He's an imposter! And you brought him here!"

Now Immanuel stood and stared down Vij. "Show some restraint, Vij! Lauretta vouches for him, and that's good enough for me."

"Do you?" Vij demanded of Lauretta. "Lauretta, do you vouch for this man?"

Lauretta had wrapped an arm around Henry's and he felt her trembling with rage as she hissed, "Yes! I invited him here and I vouch for him, and he hasn't done anything wrong!"

Henry was uncomfortable with this. Everybody was gathering around now to see the drama at the card table, which meant that everybody could see Lauretta pinning her reputation on the credentials of an escaped convict. He rubbed her back lightly to comfort and calm her. Hopefully that would prevent her from making any more rash statements about Henry's moral character.

"He's twice the man you are!" she snapped at Vij.

"Well maybe he won't mind if I join him in the Moon Burb when he goes to visit their next rally," Vij suggested. Now he was completely calm and cheerful, surrounded by the wasteland of cards and dice that he'd created in his rage. "And we can talk about politics for the whole car ride over. What do you say, Johnny?"

"I'm sure he'd be delighted," Lauretta said. "And I'll go

with you too, right Johnny?"

Henry dug deep into his soul and conjured up a great big smile. "That would be fucking awesome, guys."

"And we can hand out flyers on the street and spread the word about Millenarianistic Chronodyke," Vij continued, glaring.

"Fine, great," Henry agreed. "I can't fucking wait."

"Me fucking either," Vij said, nodding.

"Me fucking too," Lauretta joined in, but her anger was gone now that they'd compartmentalized the confrontation and pushed it off onto a task for a later date.

"O-fucking-kay," Immanuel said. "Let's gather up these fucking cards and dice and have some more drinks before we all kill each other."

As Immanuel and Vij poured fresh drinks Lauretta hauled Henry into an unlocked office and kissed him hard on the lips. Then she whispered, "When I saw you wearing that blouse, Johnny, I knew you'd understand me. I knew you'd accept me with my crooked eyes. I don't even care if you're a spy. Just don't betray me."

Instead of answering her, Henry pulled her close and kissed her lips. Soon they were naked on the desk, two lonely humans merged into one sexual soul. He would abandon these lunatics as soon as he could get beyond the barbed-wire fence of this weird compound, but until then he must play the part of Johnny Tetrahedron, and that meant enjoying this woman's company.

### Chapter 5: Nico II

Nico showered off all the dirt and changed into a fresh pair of battered jeans and a sweatshirt with the arms torn off so people could see the natural swell of those creamy smooth muscles. Then he got a haircut, an undercut. Finally he visited a tailor's shop called *Tyler the Tailor's*. If he was joining The Dancing Party he had to look good. He wasn't sure if he had enough money for a decent suit, but he went in anyway to at least get an estimate.

"I'm joining The Dancing Party," he told the tailor, "and I need to look good."

Tyler the Tailor was a broad-shouldered, brown-bearded beast of a man with a twinkle in his eye. When Nico entered the shop Tyler was reclining in a high-backed swivel chair with his feet up on a sewing table, filing his nails and inspecting his handiwork. He stood up to greet his new customer with a welcoming *please-the-customer* smile, but it immediately transformed into a more genuine *pleased-by-the-customer* smile when he saw how heart-breakingly handsome this particular customer was.

Nico knew about this shop from ads in the newspaper, but Tyler's own ensemble exceeded those advertisements in style and grace. The tailor's jacket was somewhere between indigo and navy blue, with an elusive glossy sheen that disappeared as soon as you noticed. The lapels were a deep orange-red and pointed like a dual arrow at the spot just below his sternum. The big shoulders tapered down to his waist so perfectly, as did his pant legs down to his ankles, that he looked like a low-polygon vector graphic overlaid with the richest of textures. A puffy pink cravat exploded from between the lapels, and his socks had a rich brown-on-darker-brown criss-cross pattern. Tyler's pants were black and he studied Nico through smart-looking glasses before saying, "Honey, if you want me to make you look good, then my job is done." He dusted off his hands in an exaggerated fashion and sat back down in his chair. "Now you can strut on out of my shop so I can take a gander at that sweet ass."

Nico assumed that this was Tyler's usual sales pitch, engineered to boost confidence and lubricate wallets. But the big man's eyes hungrily roamed Nico's body, and he bit his lip and shook his head, and Nico began to wonder if perhaps Tyler the Taylor had designs not just for the latest fashions in men's wear but also for men generally, and Nico in particular.

"My girlfriend says that I need new clothes if they're going to accept me into any political party," he told the tailor. "She said I should get something elegant and modern, yet simple and professional."

Tyler stood once more and continued to eye-conquer Nico's sweet bod. The tailor strutted around the customer like a thoughtful peacock, drinking in his contours and mentally undressing and re-dressing Nico for reasons that mixed sexuality with professionalism. Nico graciously allowed the lustful giant to peer at every bulge and swell, every nook and cranny, because he recognized that Tyler the Tailor's skill at designing suits could not be decoupled from his animal lust. That lust was the engine of this enterprise, so Nico struck a confident pose with one hand in his pocket, the other stroking his smooth chin, and he put one foot slightly ahead of the other to give Tyler a full view of his manly contours, all with the purpose of revving that engine.

"Mmm, mmm, *mmmm!*" Tyler grunted and slapped Nico's ass, making him flinch. Tyler had a voice so cavernously deep that it could fill a valley of gods with soul-wrenching terror, but his mannerisms and choice of words were more like a madam running a burlesque show. "You have so much to work with, my sweet little pumpkin, that it would simply be tragic to let you walk out of here in a plain professional suit. Your body should be the centerpiece for a great work of art, exploding with flair the way your cute little smile makes my loins explode with delight."

"My girlfriend," Nico repeated, "thinks that I'm handsome enough that a really fancy suit would only distract from my natural good looks. I really just want to look professional so I can blend in with the other people at The Dancing Party. I don't know if they'll even accept a no-good biker like me. They're all professionals from nice homes, but I'm just a dirtbag from the outskirts of town, and to be honest, I doubt I can even afford anything more expensive than a basic professional suit. I spend all my money on my bike and my girl."

"That's a lucky girl and a lucky bike," Tyler said, "but this might be your lucky day. I've been looking for a male model to showcase my latest designs. If you'll be that model then I'll make any suit you want, no charge."

"Singing for my supper, so to speak?"

"Sexy for you supper is more like it."

Nico looked in his dusty wallet and then glanced at the price tag hanging from the cuff of a nearby mannequin. The vast chasm between those numbers triggered a defeated sigh in Nico's gorgeous chest. He grinned humbly and said, "I guess I'm your model, then. But let's be clear about the trade. How many suits do I have to model before you'll cut me a simple one for myself."

Tyler stroked his beard. "I was hoping you wouldn't put limits on it. I just want to dress you and undress you and take pictures all day."

An idea suddenly clicked in Nico's brain. "If I agree to be your model all day, wearing whatever you want, then I also want you to make some badass suits for my whole bike crew, so we can all look good on the day of the big bike race." This might help make up for him abandoning them.

"Sweetheart, that's a deal and a half. And I'll be there on race day taking photos of you and your crew, and they'll all go into my newest catalog."

Well into the afternoon Nico allowed himself to be measured and manhandled, prodded, cupped and fondled, squeezed into leather and silk, bound and strapped and slapped, tied up and spun around, folded like origami, caressed like pottery clay, and all the while the camera flashed and snapped greedily.

When the ordeal was over Nico was given a fine suit, gunmetal blue with a light gray shirt and black tie, a fancy napkin in his breast pocket, and shiny black shoes. He stepped out of the tailor's shop looking like a high-powered professional, but he felt like a cheap whore. It would all be worth it when his bike crew dazzled their audience and opponents alike with their own flashy new garb.

He met Stoya at a little restaurant where she proudly admired his clothes but also straightened his collar and fixed a stray hair. "Now The Dancing Party will surely accept us." She had bought herself some sharp business attire.

They called a taxi to take them to The Dancing Party

headquarters. Nico gazed out the side window as the downtown shops whizzed by and were replaced by older, shittier shops. Then they were winding through the weird one-way streets of Le Tableau, where all the junkies and perverts lived in sagging wooden houses with vibrantly overgrown lawns.

"Is this the right part of town?" Nico asked nervously. He had assumed a major political party would have their headquarters in a more reputable neighborhood.

"Yessir," said the grizzled cab driver, meeting Nico's eyes in the rearview mirror. "The Dancing Party likes to keep close to their voter base, ya know? By the way, you got real pretty eyes, mister."

"Thanks," Nico told him, and put on some sunglasses.

"Hm, mysterious," the driver muttered.

He let Nico and Stoya out in front of what might once have been a great hilltop manor, but was now struggling against inevitable collapse. The house had four cylindrical towers, one on each corner, and their pointy spires rose up above the house's peaked roof. But those four towers leaned out dangerously from the center like wilted flowers, trying hard to fall over, even as the center of the house somehow drooped inward and tried to pull the whole landscape into some event horizon. Every gust of wind blew flakes of paint like dull glitter into the trees which loomed even higher than the house, their leafy branches creating a backdrop so full of those painty flakes that it was sometimes hard to tell where the house ended and the trees began.

Nico heard accordion music as he walked up the path toward the entrance. On both sides of the path the grass was chest-high and full of brambles.

The accordion music grew louder as a clown opened the screen door and clomped down the steps in his big red shoes. The clown's makeup depicted a big sad frown, and a blue tear was painted at the corner of his eye.

"Why so glum, clown?" Stoya asked as they passed on the stairs.

"I just found out my mother died," he answered.

Nico offered his condolences and then approached the screen door from whence wafted exotic smells and some kind of dissonant carnival jig. He knocked on the wooden frame of the screen door and waited to see who would greet them from within the darkness.

### Chapter 6: Henry III

Henry beheld a vista of pure desolation. The landscape was naught but rocks and dirt and the blue sky was tinted black by the specialized glass of his helmet's face-shield. Their Moon Rover rumbled and bumped over the rugged terrain.

"I think I see the Moon Base up ahead," Lauretta said, her voice muffled by her helmet as she pointed into the distance. All Henry could see was more rocks.

During the short road trip Henry had sought every opportunity to abandon Lauretta and Vij, but the fruits of his efforts proved as barren as the Moon Burb's soil. When he had tried to slip away into the forest during a lunch break, Lauretta followed him and seduced him. When he tried to lose himself in a crowded restaurant where they had stopped for lunch, Vij followed him and asked if he was trying to "feed information to your ever-present network of spies, not that I'm accusing you of that, oh no, but if I don't then who will?"

At least one good thing had come from this trip so far. Immanuel Zwart, as Malcolm Sneck's campaign manager, had given the trio some money from the discretionary fund to finance their mission. He had also insisted that Henry buy some new clothes, since he'd be publicly representing the Millenarianistic Chronodyke message. So they had visited Tyler the Tailor, where the very friendly tailor thoroughly measured him and dressed him in a silk tunic with gold-thread patterns upon the breast, burgundy slacks with diamond-pleated stitching, a thick red robe with a wolf-fur border, and a golden crown all aglitter with sparkling stones.

When Henry had asked for something "more discrete," Tyler had spanked his ass, winked, and whispered, "maybe we should shave off that dreadful toupee and let your friends meet Henry instead of Johnny? Would that be discrete enough?" He should have known that his disguise would not fool an expert in fashion. Henry grudgingly submitted to being adorned in brooches, doublets, a handkerchief, and a bit more gentle measuring.

So when they arrived at the gates of the Moon Burb Henry looked more ridiculous than ever, though these clothes were much more comfortable than his misappropriated blouse. Then they'd had to trade in the car for an official Moon Roamer and don official Space Suits to wear over their regular clothes.

The Moon Burb had once been a quarry where automated extraction machines turned a forest into a great lifeless crater. One day those machines had turned on their masters and dragged them into the ocean, never to be seen again. The new owners re-purposed the area as a moon-themed amusement park. Visitors could buy tickets and rent a space suit and a golf cart, then roam around the quarry and pretend that they're on the moon. But reckless teenagers started sneaking into the quarry at night and pretending they were on the moon for free, without any space suits or golf carts. So the owners applied for the Moon Park to officially become a burb, their application was accepted, and the rules of the park became bylaws of the land.

"She's right," Vij said. "I can see the buildings. See those domes? The Moon People don't build regular houses. Instead they use geodesic domes, and they're the same color as the moon rocks so they blend in with the surroundings."

Indeed, Henry could see the dull gray settlement now that his companions had pointed it out. But he also saw the pulsing red and blue lights of a Police Roamer behind them, pulling them over. The golf cart was a four-seater with Vij and Lauretta up front and Henry in back feeling like a prisoner again. The police officer stepped out of his own golf cart and approached the trio. He had the same Space Suit as the rest of them, but his helmet was blue.

"Is something wrong, officer?" Vij asked. His hands were still on the wheel and he sounded much more polite than usual. They had all heard stories about the Moon Burb's rough treatment of criminals.

The cop peered at them through his visor. "Just making sure your Space Suits are all secure. How are your oxygen levels?"

Everybody made an elaborate show of checking their oxygen gages and giving him the thumbs up.

"Good. Carry on. But I should warn you, the Tech Nomads have been hitting us with raids, so be careful of strangers out here."

The Tech Nomads were a renegade group of radical contract-workers who lived in caves along the beach. They made gadgets with discarded electronic scraps that they scavenged from the trash or found washed up on shore, and made web applications in return for cryptocurrency or wifi crystals. Sometimes they stole electronics or did wifi raids to support their degenerate remote-work lifestyles. They were officially considered a terrorist group composed of dozens of ungentrifiable geeks.

Henry's crew kept driving toward the cluster of geodesic domes. Henry gazed listlessly at the terrain as it slowly crawled by at the speed of their feeble vehicle, when he saw somebody laying among the stones.

"Is that a dead guy?" he asked. The corpse wore a Space Suit and helmet, but lay face-down and motionless in the dirt.

Vij pulled over so they could take a closer look. The body looked like it had washed up on shore, except there was no water around. Henry knelt and held the person's wrist. "I feel a pulse," he said.

Vij found the oxygen meter. "He's out of oxygen," he said. "Therefore this man is dead."

Henry rolled the stranger over on his back so they could see his face. The man was in his late twenties, black hair, a gross little rat-mustache. "There's a hole in his suit,"

Henry said. He fingered a little tear in the fabric near the man's neck.

"Let's bury him," Vij said.

Henry repeated, whispering, "but he has a pulse."

Vij peered around, looking for the cop that had pulled them over or anybody else who might be eavesdropping. "You must have imagined the pulse, Johnny. This man has no oxygen and is therefore *legally dead*."

Lauretta dropped to her knees by the dead guy, facing Henry. She had a pill bottle in her hands and was fumbling to remove the lid with her big Space Gloves. "Maybe we can revive him," she said. "Give him one of these pills."

"What kind of pills are these?" Henry asked as she shook two blue capsules into her mitt.

They both stopped moving as if somebody had paused them, staring at him in a state of frozen shock.

"What do you mean, *what kind of pills?*" Vij demanded.

Henry gulped. The pill bottle was white, blank, and the capsules were blue with no markings. "I mean, are they the standard formula?" Acting as if he totally knew what the pills should be.

Vij knelt beside him, leaned in so close that the glass of his face-plate pressed against Henry's with a dull clink. "What other formula would they be?"

"There's no time for this!" Henry snapped. He grabbed the capsules from Lauretta's palm and held one between his thumb and index finger, pushed it through the hole in the dead man's Space Suit, tried to push it towards the gaping, drooling mouth. He had to pull on the fabric to try to get the throat-material up closer to the lips. The dead man squirmed because Henry's aggressive fabric-pulling was giving him a wedgie. When he gave a final push toward the mouth, the dead man twitched and Henry accidentally shoved the pill up his nose.

"Gah!" the dead man shouted, sitting bolt upright. "What the fuck did you just shove up my nose?"

Lauretta grabbed his shoulders and looked in his eyes. "You were legally dead and we revived you with Quantum-

Brain®, but we need to patch that hole and get you some fresh oxygen before the pill wears off."

"Aw shit, where's my laptop?" The guy was patting his chest and running his hands through the dirt. "Aw fuck. What the fuck is Quantum Brain?"

Henry pinched the hole in the resurrected man's Space Suit while Vij unraveled the oxygen hose from the Moon Roamer, and Lauretta answered his question: "It's a mixture of hyper-herbal compounds and metacognition reduction. Basically it's pure cognitive power boiled down and mixed with brain-boosting supplements."

"How do you boil down pure cognitive power?"

"Well first you need to capture and condense it using abstract processing resonance," Lauretta explained. "Then you just let it simmer."

Vij plugged the oxygen tube into the back of the dead man's helmet. Lauretta got a suit-repair kit from the buggy and applied a small patch of adhesive fabric over the tear.

"Wow, thanks guys," the stranger said. He had wide eyes and a weak, dainty chin. Henry hated the man's gross little mustache. "I'm Jack. Who are you guys?"

Lauretta introduced them all and explained that they were from Millenarianistic Chronodyke, here to win the votes of the good people at the Moon Base in the Moon Burb.

They all leaned against the Moon Roamer now, looking cool in their Space Suits. Jack said, "I heard of Millenarianistic Chronodyke but I never got their platform. What are you guys all about?"

Vij said, "Hey Johnny, why don't you explain our platform to Jack?"

Henry had been hanging out with these guys for more than a day but he still hadn't figured out that part. Sometimes he started to wonder if they fabricated all of their ideas in a meaningless word-soup, but then he wondered if he just wasn't smart enough to grasp the meaning.

"Well it's hard to summarize in a single sentence," Henry said.

"Nobody asked you to summarize it in a single sentence," Vij responded. "You can use several sentences. Just tell him what we're all about. This is why we came here, right? Spread the word? Now's your chance."

Henry looked around at the empty terrain. Maybe he could just escape right now. Shove these nerds aside, get on the Moon Roamer, and drive right off the Moon. But they could run faster than the buggy could drive, and if he got caught by the Moon Cops they would discover his true identity.

He tried to remember some of the words he'd heard from other party members during the after-rally party, but it was always such a mess of syllables that nothing stuck in his memory.

"Maybe you need some QuantumBrain® to help you think?" Vij suggested. "Maybe that special secret formula you were asking about? Huh? Or maybe you're not a human at all but some kind of spectral sex criminal sent to our astral plane to subvert our civic society as penance for the horrible sex-crimes you committed against an incomprehensibly higher-order cabal of spectral puritan overlords who see in our political platform the burgeoning potential of a cosmic rival? Huh?"

Lauretta gasped and grabbed Henry's elbow, searching his eyes for the truth. "It can't be true," she said. "Tell him it's not true, Johnny!"

"Of course not," Henry insisted, stifling a nervous laugh, locking eyes with Lauretta to solidify her trust in him.

"Then just explain our platform to Jack," Vij said with a casual shrug.

The lonesome plains offered no solace and the black-tinted sky was devoid of guidance. There could be no more avoiding it, no more deflecting. He had to either admit his total ignorance, or try to make up some nonsense. Maybe he should tell the truth, throw himself on their mercy, and hope that his honesty would elicit their forgiveness.

He chose nonsense.

Henry gripped Jack's shoulder and spoke with firm

confidence. "Millenarianistic Chronodyke is a hyper-politicized transmutation algorithm, embedded in cognitive bio-differentiation, but only to the point of crystallization. That's why we need new recruits like you."

The silence that followed was broken only by the mournful lament of the wind wailing across the plains, which everybody pretended not to hear because legally there was no atmosphere in the Moon Burb. Worse than the silence were the unreadable blank stares from all three of his companions. Henry suddenly felt like a traitor, interloper, scheming weasel. They had been mostly friendly to Henry but he had infiltrated their club, accepted Lauretta's insistent love under false pretenses, caused suspicion and division among the ranks, beat them at cards, and diverted their resources to pay for his elaborate royal garb. Now, as the icing on the cake, he had insulted their ideology by blurting out a nonsensical stream of words, completely straight-faced like an obnoxious sleaze.

Their silence drilled neurotic holes in his soul and Henry wanted to apologize. He wanted to slink away with his tail between his legs and let these people get on with their lives.

"That is a perfect summary of the Millenarianistic Chronodyke platform," Vij finally said, breathlessly. "Not a single wasted word."

"It even synthesizes the dualistic layers of radical social mobility feedback," Lauretta added.

"It's almost too perfect." Vij's eyes narrowed suspiciously at Henry.

Their new friend Jack hadn't spoken yet. Jack's pupils were noticeably widened, probably from all the condensed cognitive power in the pill he'd inhaled.

"Now that you know our platform, will you join us?" Henry asked him. If he could convert this guy then he'd score some points with the Chronodykes.

Jack grinned like a delighted child, his eyes wandering everywhere. "It sounds beautiful," he said. "But do you accept Tech Nomads in your party?"

"Of course," Vij answered. "If you're not registered to vote in any Burb then you can't vote, but you can still help us spread the message."

"The message," Jack whispered. "Like, people should vote for Millenarianistic Chronodyke because we're the only party who knows how to prime the bureaucratic proto-crank of technostic recapitulation."

"Well sure," Lauretta said, "if you want to use outdated mecha-metaphors."

"Enough theory!" Henry snapped. "I'm sick of discussing the core ideas of Millenarianistic Chronodyke, even though they're obviously super-important. The elections are coming soon, so we need to focus on strategy and tactics rather than abstract political concepts."

"Let's head to the Moon Base and score some more converts!" Vij declared. His suspicion seemed to be replaced with enthusiasm, at least for now.

They climbed back onto the Moon Roamer and trundled toward the cluster of geodesic domes. Lauretta handed out more QuantumBrain® pills. "Swallow them instead of snorting them," she instructed. Their helmets had a special compartment for delivering foodstuffs.

But it was too late for Jack, since Henry had shoved the pill up his nose, and now the resurrected Tech Nomad was bouncing in his seat and talking everybody's ears off.

"The Moon Burb's wifi is unprotected at the coastal border research stations," Jack explained excitedly in the back seat beside Henry. "So it's our favorite place to do wifi raids. But this time the Moon Cops were waiting for us!"

"Why are the Tech Nomads always doing wifi raids?" Lauretta asked him.

"We capture the wifi signal on USB crystals and bring it back to the coast so we can do freelance tech work wirelessly. Anyway, the cops must have an embedded spy because they knew just where we were going to raid this time. They captured a few of us for the slave camps on Coal Island. I couldn't escape to the coast so I headed inland, but I got a tear in my suit and ran out of oxygen, and I died."

Henry suddenly wanted to meet the other Tech Nomads on the coast. The Tech Nomads were outcasts and criminals who might accept his real identity, and the coast was the best place to finally escape the island. He filed those thoughts away for later planning.

The geodesic domes grew like soap bubbles before their eyes and soon the Moon Roamer was nestled between them like a fruit fly among several soap bubbles. The domes were all big gray polygons, each composed of hundreds of triangular panels. Some had antennae or satellite dishes attached to the top, and some of the gray panels were replaced with transparent glass to make little triangle-windows where the residents could behold the godforsaken wasteland that was their Burb.

As the Moon Roamer's wheels crunched to a stop on the omnipresent gravel, Henry saw the leery faces of Moon People watching them through the triangular windows of their geodesic domes. He decided to push his luck, to be proactive, and to build upon his previous success at faking an understanding of the Millenarianistic Chronodyke message, because hesitation is doom.

"People of the Moon Burb!" he called out. "Are you tired of politics-as-usual? Do you want a party who knows how to reroute the social circuitry of post-technological redundancy? Do you want geodesic domes not just of the mind, but of the spirit?"

A few people emerged from their domes wearing Space Suits. One man said, "Those are exactly the things that we want!"

But another man was not so enthusiastic. He said, "We don't take kindly to strange politics 'round these parts, stranger!" Then he spat in contempt, but the spit splattered against the inside of his helmet and he cursed the party even more.

Henry was prepared to use all his charm to change this man's mind, since others had gathered around him with their arms crossed to express their mutual skepticism. But Jack seized the moment first, grabbing the skeptical man's upper arm and ranting at him about the merits of his new political tribe.

"Once I was lost like you!" Jack shouted. "I was a miserable Tech Nomad raiding your wifi to feed my family. But the fine people from Millenarianistic Chronodyke have shown me that my old family are just a figmentation of octospecular sublimation! They must be subsumed and replaced with an isomorphic xenograph before the economic equinox! Our very DNA must become self-aware, as-such, so that the quantitative elements of deconstruction can deconstruct *themselves* within the framework of a glandular microcosm!"

It looked to Henry like Jack was losing the audience. "You're laying it on pretty thick," he whispered, but Jack ignored him. The new convert rummaged through the storage compartment of the Moon Roamer and found a big easel and dry-erase board, which he set up, and started drawing diagrams.

"Okay," Jack said to the gathered audience. His forehead was sweaty and he couldn't stop wiggling his fingers as he pointed to the shapes on the whiteboard. "Imagine this electrical drawing is analogous to a social disentanglement mechanism, where the social relations themselves are interdependent but the nodes are cross-referenced within an exponentially tangential pseudo-molecule."

"Pseudo-molecules have retrograde delta-waves," some heckler derisively complained.

"THAT'S NOT THE POINT!" Jack screamed, smashing the easel with both fists so the whole feeble metal frame collapsed on the dirt.

Henry overheard somebody whisper, "The idiot should have used a geodesic easel."

Over by the Moon Roamer Vij was leaning back with a big smile. He seemed to enjoy watching Henry's proselytization campaign fall to ruins. Lauretta looked worried. She kept trying to nervously chew her fingernails but just bumped her gloved hands against her helmet.

"What my friend is trying to say," Henry interjected, "is

that we care about you and your values."

But this just caused more complaints. "If you care about our values then why are you referencing pseudo-molecules instead of intrastitial identity globules?"

"YOU PIECE OF SHIT!" Jack screeched. He leaped into the air and landed on the outspoken critic, started smashing the man's face-shield with his fists as they both tumbled to the ground. "IT'S JUST AN ANALOGY!"

Henry and Lauretta rushed to Jack to pull him off his victim, while Vij laughed triumphantly.

"Once a Tech Nomad, always a Tech Nomad," somebody said in a disappointed, told-you-so voice.

"Barbarians," scoffed another Moon Person.

"I'LL FUCKING KILL YOU!" Jack continued to rage as Henry and Lauretta pulled him off his prey.

"He just really cares about our message," Henry said to placate the audience. Some were returning to their homes and the rest muttered angrily.

A Moon Kid raised her hand and asked, "What if I don't understand your message? What if the words don't seem to make any sense to me? What then?"

"You're probably suffering from cognitive dyspletion," Lauretta explained. She shook out some more pills from her bottle. "You can circumnavigate your IQ levels with our QuantumBrain® cognitive enhancers. Your reading compre-hension and political spectrology will manifest with increa-sing libidinal transduction. Just make sure you swallow in-stead of snorting them."

The audience graciously accepted their pills, and the tone of their mutterings changed.

"I like drugs," somebody said.

"Can I smoke it?" someone else asked.

"IT'S NOT DRUGS!" Jack screamed with renewed ferocity. "IT'S A BRAIN-BOOSTING SUPPLEMENT!"

Henry and Lauretta had to grab him again, and this time they could barely hold him back. The audience changed its mood again as the Moon People discarded their pills in the dirt.

"I don't need rage-pills," one man said as he opened the door to his geodesic dome. "I've been angry enough since the god-damned balloon scandal."

"The last thing we need is to be ruled by drug-addicted Tech Nomads."

"Fuck these guys."

Everyone was returning to their homes, and Henry couldn't talk them out of it because it took all his energy and attention to keep Jack from murdering somebody. But even as he watched his plan fail Henry perceived the silver lining. Maybe now Lauretta and Vij would abandon him because of his failure, but without ever learning his true identity. He'd been trying to prove that his political affiliation was genuine. If they had uncovered the falseness of his identity then they could report him to the cops. Today's failure was due to incompetence rather than fuckery. He had shoved a pill up Jack's nose, turning him into a rage-fueled beast, and totally bungled this impromptu political rally.

"I guess I'm just not cut out for political activism," Henry said with a disappointed sigh. "Vij, my sweet Lauretta, maybe you should just abandon me here where I can re-think my life. I call myself a consultant, but it looks like I'm the one who needs consulting services today."

The three of them were now sitting on Jack because that's the only way they could keep him subdued.

Vij was skeptical as ever. "Hmm. You've accepted your failure with surprising grace. I'm beginning to wonder if maybe you botched this rally on purpose, just so we would reject you based on incompetence before we had a chance to discover your false identity and report you to the police!"

"False identity?" One of the Moon People repeated, turning away from their home that they were just about to enter.

"Report to the police?" Somebody else repeated, taking out their cell phone.

"No!" Henry boomed. He jumped off Jack and grabbed the Moon Person's cell phone before they could finish calling the cops. Without Henry's weight Jack was able to wrestle free from Vij and Lauretta. The crazed Tech Nomad stole their Moon Roamer, and drove it into the dispersing crowd. The people had to walk really quickly to avoid getting bumped aside, but one poor soul didn't walk quickly enough, and he got bumped brutally into the dirt, where his helmet fell off and bounced away on the rocks beyond his reach.

With one hand Henry smashed the confiscated cell phone on a rock, and with the other he scooped up the wayward helmet. He rushed to the fallen man, who had curly hair and a cool goatee, and Henry tried to fasten the helmet back onto the Space Suit, but the man squirmed too much in his exaggerated oxygen-deprived agony, and Henry couldn't get the clips to fasten together.

"Stay still for fuck sake," Henry commanded, and the man obeyed, but he continued to wheeze forcefully and make annoying gasps and to claim that he couldn't breathe.

But now Henry couldn't see, because a harsh light was bearing down on him. It was the headlights of the Moon Roamer. Aside from the light, the only thing Henry could see was the crazed expression of Jack the Tech Nomad behind the wheel like a demon, screaming incoherently.

He had to drag the suffocating man out of the Roamer's path or else he would get bumped again, but then a new anomaly blasted into Henry's visual field, adding another complication to this already slightly complicated situation.

Words flashed across the glass of his face-shield. The words said, "MOON QUAKE!" Everybody's helmets must have been flashing the same words because they all started jumping around and shaking as if the ground were suffering some seismic catastrophe. They said stuff like, "Oh my Godhead, a moon quake!"

They'd been warned about this when they rented the Moon Roamer. In the old Moon Park the authorities would simulate natural disasters as a fun adventure for the kids, and everybody would play along. Now that it was a burb, the simulated natural disasters were mandatory, and broadcast in the helmets of the mandatory Space Suits. So if the screen said "MOON FLOOD," you needed to get to high ground or find a boat. An overhead satellite beamed blue laser-light over the rocky terrain to represent water, and if you couldn't get to safety you'd be declared legally dead.

The Moon Quake was still raging when a second warning appeared on Henry's face-shield. This warning said, "MOON VOLCANO!"

Henry had been so distracted by the warnings that he'd forgotten about Jack trying to run him over. Lauretta jumped on him at the last moment and they went tumbling out of the Moon Roamer's path, but there was nobody to save the curly-haired guy, who was still gasping for air as the refurbished golf cart's front wheels bumped into his prone body.

"Watch out for the lava!" Lauretta exclaimed, pointing between the geodesic domes. A reddish-orange river was indeed pouring over the dirt, and it was headed directly towards them! At first glance this glowing river appeared to be some kind of harmless laser-light projected on the gravel like any film projector or flashlight, but Henry recognized that this was legally a lava-flow from a nearby Moon Volcano.

"Jack!" Henry cried. "Drive out of the way! The lava is headed right for you!" At this point he didn't really care what happened to Jack, but they would need the Roamer to get out of the Moon Burb later, and they wanted their deposit back. But Jack was too preoccupied with spinning the wheels and trying to run over the curly-haired guy. They watched in horror as the laser-lava reached the back wheels of the Moon Roamer.

"Jack, jump!" Lauretta called, and this time the message got through. The little hipster with his shitty mustache climbed over the steering wheel and jumped over the dying curly-haired man, landing safely on the gravel. But the lava was flowing faster now and completely washed over the vehicle. Jack almost had time to escape the molten flow, but somehow he stumbled, and the laser-light washed over his body from the belly down.

Jack reached out and grabbed Henry's leg. "Pull me out before it burns me to death!"

"I think it's too late," Henry said. "The lava got you."

"No, I'm okay if you pull me out now," Jack insisted. "I'm sorry I ran over that guy. Don't let me die like this!"

Henry put his boot on Jack's shoulder and shoved him deeper into the laser-flow. "The thick lava has captured you and is sucking you under," he explained. Jack collapsed onto his back. His corpse glowed under the harsh laser-lava-light. One more casualty of the extreme conditions of life in the Moon Burb.

Lauretta pulled out her pill bottle. "Maybe we can save him again."

From across the deathly river, Vij said, "Nah, he's done."

"I never really liked him," Henry added.

The crowd had gathered around Henry and Lauretta. Somebody said, "The whole village is surrounded by lava, and it's flowing in! We're fucked!"

"The lava river is too wide to jump over," Henry observed, "but maybe we can use Jack's corpse as a stepping stone to hop over to the other side."

"No, I'm completely submerged now," Jack's selfish corpse protested.

"Weasel," somebody muttered. "I'm so glad he's dead."

Dozens of helmeted heads reflected the laser-light that surrounded them, and they all wanted Henry's help. "We'll vote for your party if you'll help us escape!"

"Vij!" Henry called. "It's up to us! We can make a bridge and let the others climb over us."

The two men faced each other from across the fiery tributary. This would require mutual trust and manly resolve. In order for the bridge to work, they would have to fall towards each other at the same time and catch each other's hands, each man supporting the other. Of course, Henry could just let Vij fall to his death and then everybody could quickly jump on his corpse as a stepping stone. But then, Vij could do the same thing to Henry.

Lauretta started a countdown. "Trust Bridge in three..."

The two men tried to gauge each others' intentions by

peering through their face-shields into each others' squinting, un-trusting eyes.

"Two…"

Henry tried to remember what Game Theory said about this kind of situation.

"One!"

No more time for thinking. Henry threw caution to the wind, put his hands up in the air, kept his back straight, and fell over like a domino. The gravel rushed up to meet him as gravity took control of his fate. For a moment he feared he had been betrayed, for it seemed that the ground rushed up too close, too fast, and he was surely slain. But then his outstretched hands slammed against another set of hands, his whole body shuddered with the impact, and his downward journey was halted with his face less than a foot away from the deadly dirt.

Now Vij's face was mere inches from Henry's, and they gripped each others' hands for dear life. Vij's eyes were full of passion as he said, "We got this, *brother.*"

One-by-one the Moon People climbed up Henry's back, then climbed down Vij's back to safety. Lauretta went last, leaving only Henry on this side of the lava-river. In the curved reflection on the surface of Vij's face-shield Henry saw more laser-lava washing over the geodesic domes. One family had ignored the warnings until it was too late. Now a woman and her two little tykes were running from their home. The laser-lava washed over them and they collapsed beneath its fiery wrath, three more journeys ended abruptly, swept away by the winds of cosmic indifference.

"I'm not going to make it," Henry said to Vij. He realized that if he died here then he could just run away because he was already a fugitive, and he'd also be remembered as a hero. "Get them to pull you back before it's too late."

Vij gritted his teeth and gripped Henry's hand ever tighter. "I won't let you die, brother! I'm sorry I was so harsh to you. I don't know why I was so suspicious. Maybe I was jealous. Maybe I knew that deep down you were more of an activist than I could ever be. And I'll admit that I kind of have the hots for Lauretta and it pisses me off to see you with her. I don't want to be petty, but I'm only human, Johnny! Forgive me!"

"There's nothing to forgive!" Henry boomed. "We just saved this town and nobody can take that from you. But now you have to let me go, to let me die, so that Millenarianistic Chronodyke can live!"

"Wait!" somebody cried. They ran up to Henry and Vij, brandishing the whiteboard that Jack had smashed. Somebody had drawn a new kind of diagram. "We designed a geodesic crane that's made out of people. If we do this right then, theoretically, we can save you both from the lava!"

"Then do it quick!" Vij shouted.

"It's never been tested!"

"We have to try!"

The Moon People arranged themselves in a geodesic pattern until they formed a crane that loomed over Henry and Vij. Somebody was grabbing Henry's ass and he assumed it was the hook-person hanging from the crane's jib, so he stuck his ass up into the air as high as he could until two strong hands grabbed his Space Suit, and he felt himself lifted up. But as Henry was elevated out of danger, Vij was being dragged directly into the lava!

"Tuck in your knees!" Henry told him. Vij complied at the last second, and then they were both dangling from the geodesic crane, which pivoted around and lowered the two men safely on the land. The crane dissembled itself back into the Moon People, who gathered around the three strangers.

Lauretta leveraged their heroics to drive home an electoral call-to-action. "So when the election comes, I hope you'll all remember which party has the best natural disaster response team."

Somebody said, "Lady, we sure would like to vote for Millenarianistic Chronodyke, but your party doesn't even have a candidate running in this burb. It's like you all don't even care about us poor ol' Moon Folk."

"Johnny Tetrahedron cares," Vij said, looking at Henry.

"He risked everything for you, and he cares like crazy about the Moon Burb. Johnny, why don't you run as the Millenarianistic Chronodyke candidate for the Moon Burb?"

"Oh, I don't want to be a burbmaster of parliament," Henry said. "I'm just a lowly general consultant trying to make a difference. Maybe you or Lauretta should run for office instead."

Vij crossed his arms and re-appraised his comrade. "Maybe I was wrong about you. Maybe you're not as dedicated to the cause as I thought. Maybe you're not Johnny Tetrahedron at all, but some creature from the netherworld who feeds off betrayal."

"Jesus Christ fuck fine I'll run for fucking office," Henry said.

The crowd cheered.


### Chapter 7: Slaverny I

"We needed the Clown Partys' support," Bonnie said sharply.

"We need the support of happy clowns," Slaverny told her. "Not dismal clowns whose mothers just died. I agree with Len on this one."

They sat around a battered wooden table in the Grand Foyer of Dancing Manor, the headquarters of The Dancing Party. This glorious foyer bustled with activity. People sat at desks making phone calls, seeking donations and imploring voters to "Dance the Dance of Change" on election day. Interns ran around with pieces of paper, stuck notes to corkboards, drew diagrams on whiteboards, ran up and down the stairs with clipboards and coffee. The ancient carpet was orange-brown, the warped walls were panels of stained wood, the beautiful arched ceiling sunk so low that the crystal chandelier tickled the scalps of taller visitors. Dual staircases curved up to the second-floor landing, but the left-hand stairs were blocked with discarded furniture, sprawling hobos and junkies, and an accordion band playing a mournful, eerie tune.

Bonnie waved around her precious sheet of yellow paper. "How can we win without the solidarity of all performers? We're always the third party. The Dean Family and the LibertOrians take turns winning elections, and we sit comfortably in third place. I have the stats right here. But the Dean Family really screwed themselves with that horrible balloon incident-"

"-just awful," a nearby intern commented.

"-so if we get all performers to endorse The Dancing Party, then we can finally rule this island!" Bonnie concluded.

Slaverny Malcontempt knew that Bonnie was correct, but to admit that would be to undermine his own authority and then the party would be doomed. It was bad enough that their party leader, Len Sladge, was a spineless depressive, hiding in his office all day behind those looming double doors up on the second-floor landing. As campaign manager Slaverny needed to embody the will to win, the centralized lust for power that would maintain The Dancing Party as a cohesive social force.

So Slaverny scoffed, grabbed the sheet of paper, balled it up, and threw it at the chandelier where it got caught among the spiderwebs, bubble gum, discarded panties, and loose change that had accumulated among the sparkling crystals over the decades like a time capsule. "Solidarity starts at home, Bonnie," he told her, and placed a hand on her thigh. "The campaign manager and the human resources director must get along, must see eye-to-eye, must... come together... as one... or else people will detect our internal divisions and our weaknesses."

Bonnie's long, cold, bony fingers pried Slaverny's shorter, warmer fingers off her thigh. Her amused, knowing look categorized him as just one more of an infinite number of sex-crazed, power-hungry men. She made him feel predictable and harmless, almost cute like an overzealous puppy, which only exacerbated his need to dominate her. She had pried his fingers from her body, but she couldn't pry away his male gaze so easily. As an act of public domination his eyes greedily explored the curves beneath her tight leather one-piece dress, the too-perfect shape of her breast implants, the dozens of cheap bracelets on her wrinkled arms, the wrinkled neck-skin so full of liver-spots, the shining smoothness of her taught face, the huge fake lips painted gaudy neon-pink, the fake dainty nose, giant beehive hairdo.

"Honey, you couldn't handle me," Bonnie told him sassily, which made all the interns laugh, humiliating him even more. Why couldn't she see the benefits of forging a high-profile sexual union with him? Because women didn't understand power, that's why.

Slaverny was still trying to think of a rejoinder when he heard the chandelier jingle like door chimes and a dusty pair of faded red panties fell on his head. He could just see the lacy frill dangling in his peripheral vision. The dust from the panties went up his nose and he felt the tingle of an impending sneeze, paralyzing him in twitching anticipation while a couple people snickered at his embarrassing panty-hat, and all other heads turned to look behind him.

"Check out the hottie," an intern muttered as Slaverny's pre-sneeze state continued to charge.

"I would just wrap that up in bacon and eat it," another intern rumbled in a creepy, lustful growl.

"Bring that meat to Daddy, mmmm."

Slaverny wanted to turn around and check out the hot piece of ass who everybody was drooling over, but his sneeze was almost fully charged and he had no control over his body. He held his hands in front of his face and his head vibrated so much that the wayward panties fluttered down from his hair like a leaf. Then he sneezed a loud, wet sneeze. A glob of snot blasted forth from his nostrils with such force that it ripped out all his nose-hairs and caused friction-burns inside his nasal cavity. The snot-blast caught the panties in midair and plastered them into his open hands. He felt numb satisfaction at the sneeze's climax, even as he stared in slight horror at the mess he'd made. Luckily everybody's attention was still locked onto whoever was standing beneath the chandelier behind Slaverny, so he swiveled around to behold the newcomer.

A man and a woman sparkled in the radiant reflections of the chandelier's myriad crystals. Slaverny had assumed the crowd was lusting over a lady, and indeed this lady was a beauty with curvy hips beneath a black skirt, supple breasts testing the strength of a white blouse, and a pretty face with clear blue eyes. But she was dogshit compared to her glorious boyfriend.

What is the perfect ratio between chiseled good looks and boyish charm? Maybe it's not enough to simply mix ruggedness and cuteness together until they cancel out. Maybe the best method is to give each feature its fair share of one extreme or the other. Give him a fully chiseled chin, hard enough for plowing fields, but also a boyish smirk at the corner of his painfully kissable lips. A hard brow built for brooding that could withstand the storms of life, with the sparkling blue eyes of a curious child whose light could never be dimmed by injustice or mistreatment. The strong shoulders of a warrior or fisherman, the gentle mannerisms of a mother, a teacher, a lover.

And where did he get that suit? This was the suit of suits, the ensemble that all other wardrobes aspired to. It wasn't designed to hide the organic grossness of the human body. No, quite the opposite. This gunmetal blue suit leveraged the noble strength expressed by the strong man's correct posture and dressed it up in sophisticated layers of fine fabric. Beast and angel forged a union in this vessel, but in Slaverny's opinion the scale tipped ever-so-slightly towards the angelic. He wanted to rub his face against the man's smooth cheek, to smell his cologne. Had he ever fantasized about running his fingers through another man's thick hair? To just hold him and kiss him forever?

The woman looked at Slaverny, holding his snot-drenched panties, and she asked, "Did we come at a bad time?"

Somewhere an intern chortled, "No, but it looks like Slaverny did!"

Slaverny scowled and threw the underwear back up onto the chandelier. The crystals jingled like Heaven's gates, and from that quivering mass rained down fragrant rose-petals, red and white and black, to adorn the perfect hair and shoulders of the visitors.

The man said, "I'm Nico and this is my girlfriend Stoya, and we want to join your party."

Stoya's eyes were animated, playfully severe, as she added, "We are stunt-bikers who are tired of the stunts played on us by businessmen and corrupt politicians."

"Are you the party we're hoping for?" Nico asked. "Are you really dedicated to fighting for performing artists all over the island of Ethelcrest?"

Slaverny couldn't think straight. His emotions were all stirred up by this man's angelic presence. Was his face getting red? Was he breathing faster than usual? Did he feel a tingle in his loins? In sex and romance Slaverny always wanted to be the dominant one, but now he was dominated by his own emotions.

Bonnie stood and approached the beautiful couple. She took Nico's hand in her own, caressing his fingers and smiling sweetly at him, and she kissed his knuckles like he was a king. "We need all the help we can get," she told him. "The two of you can help us represent the more dangerous performing artists like stunt workers and gladiators."

Everybody gathered around. They all wanted a glimpse at the sexy couple. Somebody offered a donut and said, "Nico, would you like a donut?"

Nico accepted the donut. "Jelly," he said. "My favorite. Thank you so much."

Nico and Stoya held the donut between them and gently ripped it in half, and they smiled at each other as they ate the treat. Somehow Slaverny wasn't even annoyed at this overly-perfect couple, though he knew he should be. Instead he just wanted to wiggle in between them where he could kiss them both and accept both of their love, and be wrapped up in the blankets with them, and sleep away the afternoon in their arms.

He had never felt so ugly. Slaverny was suddenly and intensely aware of how his front upper-teeth leaned out just a little crookedly, how his ears were just a little too sharp due to his elven heritage, how he always missed a spot shaving, how his little fingers struggled with keyboards and pianos due to his dwarven heritage, the slight hunch to his back due to his ogre heritage.

"Are you all artists here?" Nico was asking Bonnie.

Bonnie put a hand on her décolletage. "I'm Bonnie Wraith, in charge of human resources, and I am a retired burlesque dancer. Our party leader, Len Sladge, is a heavy metal guitarist and singer as well as an amateur blacksmith. Most of our party members are artists of some sort, but some people just want to support artists, like our campaign manager Slaverny Malcontempt."

Slaverny interpreted this as another insult meant to lower his social standing before these two beautiful performing artists, but he had no comeback because it was true that he wasn't an artist. So instead he just took out a pack of cigarettes for the purpose of looking cool, but fumbled the lighter in his pudgy dwarf-fingers, and the lighter thumped clumsily on the carpet.

Nico knelt to retrieve the lighter and lit it for him. As Slaverny inhaled the first delicious drag he also got a closer look at Nico's face, and he could see the depth of emotion there, the deep passion in the man's very bones that didn't need to express itself, nor to hide. Slaverny sensed a deep sadness, but also a relentless will, the sweet tragedy of human life condensed into a wistful smile and the brooding landscape of Nico's brow. He also got the sense that Nico might be a bit naive, and therefore, a target for domination, or outright expulsion.

Slaverny exhaled a puff of dry smoke, and his head began to clear. "Unfortunately our budget doesn't allow any new hires, and we've got all our bases covered anyway." He couldn't handle the distraction of being around this man. He had learned a long time ago how to harness his lust for women, and use it as a power tool. But this unexpected lust for a man, as right and natural as it suddenly felt, was too raw and unfiltered. He just wanted to lick the man's belly, and keep licking until his tongue was numb, and then lay back and be licked in turn. These thoughts would only get in the way, so he needed to get rid of Nico.

More important was everybody else's adoration. Len Sladge was obviously top dog of The Dancing Party, but he was weak, he refused to fight dirty, so Slaverny had started slowly taking more and more control of the organization. Bonnie had been his only rival, but even she would surely succumb to Slaverny's wiles eventually, merging her power with his so they could rule the party, and then the whole island. But Nico was an even bigger threat. He had just arrived and everybody loved him. Even Bonnie still refused to let go of his hand, Bonnie, who everyone respected, who should be Slaverny's woman.

"Nonsense," Bonnie said to Nico and Stoya. "Of course we still need help reaching our voter base and we would love to have you on our team. And we can't pay much, but I have a little wiggle room in the payroll."

Slaverny shook his head. "Nope. Can't happen. I hate to be the bad guy here, but we just don't have the time to train newcomers."

"I'm in charge of human resources," Bonnie reminded him. "I can hire whoever I need. I looked at our numbers this morning and there's just enough room in the budget for two new hires."

Slaverny thought fast. "That reminds me," he said. "I forgot to tell you that I need to cut your remaining budget in half, which is of course within the parameters of my role as campaign manager."

Bonnie scowled and gritted her false teeth with a noise that sounded like dice bouncing around inside her mouth. "How conveniently timed."

Slaverny sighed. "Frustratingly *inconvenient*, I'm afraid." He turned back to Nico and Stoya. "But we can still hire one of you, and maybe the other will work as an unpaid intern? Since you're so passionate about the cause?"

The new couple shared a glance. Slaverny was betting on Nico being as magnanimous as he was handsome. If Nico let Stoya take the paid job then Nico himself would lose status through being poor, and Stoya would be more financially independent and come to recognize that she might have better options.

"Stoya, you take the paid position and I'll take the internship," Nico offered. "We split our money anyway, and in this unfair patriarchal society men are given every advantage while women fight tooth and nail for the same rights."

"But the man should be the breadwinner," Stoya protested. "I feel more comfortable with a strong man, a powerful man who can bear the weight of the world. You take the paid position."

"Then let me bear the weight of unpaid work," Nico countered. "Imagine how I would look if I let my beloved darling slave away with no pay while I accept a pay check for the same work. What kind of man would I be then? We sacrificed so much more just to come here. This is just one more little sacrifice."

Stoya let out a defeated sigh and said, "If that's what you want." Then Bonnie sent an intern to get the proper paperwork. When the contracts were signed Bonnie said, "Okay, I know exactly the kind of work I need from the two of you. You'll work together as a team, and-"

"No, no, no," Slaverny interrupted her. "Stoya, you will be my personal secretary, on-call at all times."

"I am no secretary!" she proclaimed with unexpected vigor, like a lightning strike.

But Nico held her shoulders and whispered something conciliatory into her ear. At first she grimaced at his words, but her lovers' whispers soothed her heart. "Fine," she said at last. "I graciously accept your job offer, though I wanted to be more of an activist than an office worker."

"It's all for the cause," Slaverny said. "And now for Nico's job."

"Anything I can do to bring equal rights and fair pay to

my biking brothers, and all performers and artists on Ethelcrest," Nico said.

Slaverny grinned. "Just follow me."

He led the new intern through a side-door and into the basement. Slaverny got a couple flashlights from a storage closet and led them through the murky darkness where cobwebs and frightened mice caught the flashlights' rays.

"Here we go," Slaverny said, opening a door. "The old servants' communal bathroom."

They stepped into a huge room with a wall of showers and several toilet stalls. The tiled walls and floor were almost completely covered in various kinds of grime, mold, and bacterial growth.

Slaverny shined his flashlight along the wall. The beam illuminated many items and fixtures: shower stalls where stalactites hung from the spouts; bathroom stalls where the toilets were crusted over with hardened waste and bacterial growth, and what looked like barnacles growing beside mushrooms; and in every corner, piles of skeletons. The hall they'd just left was dusty and dry, but in this huge communal bathroom-shower there was a pungent musk and the sounds of water dripping somewhere in the dark. "It used to be the servant's communal bathroom, but nobody uses it now except for the junkies who come here to die. Sadly, dying junkies are not very good at cleaning up after themselves."

Nico pointed. "Are those skeletons?"

Slaverny patted his new intern on the shoulder. "Let's go look in the supply closet and see what kinds of cleaning tools we've got."

In the storage closet they found nothing but an old toothbrush and another discarded pair of panties. Slaverny handed them to Nico. "Okay, get cleaning."

Nico stared at the two items with heavy consternation. Then he looked at his own perfect suit. "Do you have some kind of apron or coveralls that I could wear? I don't want to ruin my suit."

"Not in the budget, sorry Nico."

Nico gazed out at the impenetrable layers of dirt. "How

about some soap?"

Slaverny wasn't a cruel man. He wouldn't make this angel wash these toilets without any soap. "There are probably several old slivers of used soap in the shower stalls. I bet you could collect them and ball them up into one big sliver of soap."

"I don't want to complain on my first day," Nico said. "But I feel my energy would be best used elsewhere."

Slaverny nodded. "I understand that. You're a smart and capable guy. You're a likable guy, a handsome guy, a sexy guy, and you could convince lots of voters to choose our party instead of our rivals. So maybe I should ask your girlfriend Stoya to do this work instead, to free you up to go campaign in that nice suit. Is that what you'd like, Nico?"

Nico's shoulder slumped for a fraction of a second, but then he straightened up again and gripped the toothbrush like a sword. "No, sir. I'll start right away. This bathroom will be beautiful soon."

"Good man," Slaverny said. As he headed back upstairs he heard the toothbrush scraping against the grit, echoing off the walls. He rubbed his hands with anticipation. It was time to train his new secretary.

### Chapter 8: Henry IV

It was a stormy day at the Moon Burb and the sun shone blackly through everybody's tinted face-shields as the ocean waves raged at each other down over the cliff and off in the distance. A figure stood up on a stone platform that could double as a sacrificial altar, behind a stone podium that could be a miniature wooden monolith, perhaps a minilith, and a crowd of a couple dozen Moon People waited for the figure to speak.

Henry stared past the silent figure. He was more interested in those ocean waves, so powerful and free. Oh, to be a wave upon sea, to frolic and crash and disappear, only to be reborn afresh with a billion brothers. He imagined himself in a speedboat steering straight at the horizon. In that aquatic expanse he saw not desolation and emptiness but endless opportunities, an untended candy store. The Space Suit's tinted face-shield didn't just tint sky-blues and sun-yellows into spacey shades of black, but also blasted high-contrast colors so the frothing waves down over the cliff took on a surreal psychedelic quality where only the highlights stood out, animated against a murky purple-black, mesmerizing.

The figure finally spoke.

"*This* man!" came the woman's shrill voice as she pointed down at Henry. She emphasized the first word but then emphasized the second word even more. "This *man* thinks that he can represent the Moon Burb in the parliament of our great nation? This man! *This Interloper!* What does he know about our culture? Our struggles? Our people?"

A couple people half-heartedly voiced their agreement by saying, "Yeah," and shaking their fists in the air. But most of the people had witnessed Henry's heroics when he saved the survivors of the volcano/quake at the Moon Base, and they patiently waited for her to finish so that Henry could get up and make his own speech.

"I've been your burbmaster of parliament for fifteen years," she crooned like an old witch. "In that time I've cracked down on invaders who would undermine our cultural values. Under my supervision we jailed the farmers who belligerently insisted that we could grow our own crops! Here! Where there is no atmosphere or water, no fertile soil!"

Henry had to turn up the volume in his helmet so he could hear his opponent over the crashing of the ocean waves and the self-loathing moan of the wind.

"Do you think *this man* will protect you from the Tech Nomads? He's only the pawn of his big political party, Millenarianistic Chronodyke. We never had any fancy political parties here before. Just independents like me. Nobody cared about the barren little Moon Burb. Why are they so interested now? I'll tell you why! The Millenarianistic

Chronodyke are a techno-fascist, drug-dealing cult and they're *working with the Tech Nomads* to take over the Moon Burb for their sick techno orgies!"

"Bullshit!" somebody yelled.

"He's a hero!" another supporter shouted.

"You old hag!"

The crowd began to chant, "Out with Lucy! In with Johnny!" Henry was almost embarrassed at the level of support he was getting but Lucy was unperturbed. She paced back and forth across the stony stage, arms outstretched to embrace the crowd's displeasure, nodding her Space Helmet to encourage their raucousness.

"Yes, yes, let it out! But who do you think caused the deadly Moon Quake in the first place? Is it a coincidence that Johnny Tetrahedron showed up with a Tech Nomad hacker just before the quake? It was a false flag! He got the nomads to hack The Moon Burb's Natural Disaster Software so he could look like a hero 'saving' you, so you'd vote for him on election day. He's a vector for cultural disease, and for terrorism!"

The crowd grumbled and complained, but now it seemed that the grumbling and complaining was partly directed at Henry. Of course the story was bogus, but how could Henry convince them of that?

"But don't take *my* word for it," Lucy continued. "Let's hear what Mr. Tetrahedron has to say for himself, hmm?"

She climbed down from the stage. Lucy had demanded this impromptu local debate as soon as Henry had declared his candidacy. Now she wanted to play a game of dirt-slinging and bogus accusations. But Henry decided to gamble on a more positive message.

He took the stage. "Elect me and I will terraform the moon! We will enrich the soil and import an atmosphere to nurture crops and livestock, so we won't have to rely on tourism as our primary income, and our friends and family won't have to die from asphyxiation."

Somebody cried out, "But there's not enough gravity on the moon to hold an atmosphere!"

"I'll introduce legislation to raise the gravity level!"

An elderly lady complained, "Won't that hurt my poor old bones?"

"Yes but it will also strengthen your muscles to help us defeat our enemies," Henry replied.

"What?" the crowd asked.

"I said, it will strengthen our muscles to help us defeat our enemies!"

"What?" the crowd asked again, but this time Henry could barely hear them. Was the wind getting louder? Were the waves crashing with increased frenzy? Henry turned up the volume in his helmet, but then he noticed the little wifi indicator in the visual dashboard of his face-shield. He only had one bar, and it flickered on the edge of demise. He was losing the wireless signal that provided his audio connection to the audience. Was this Lucy's doing? He looked around but couldn't find her.

In the crowd everybody was playing with the buttons on the sides of their helmets. They all had the same problem.

Some people were pointing past Henry, past the stage and toward the sea, but he couldn't hear what they were saying. Only broken fragments of speech made it into his helmet, frustrating audio glitches that conveying a sense of confusion.

He turned to see what kind of monster had climbed up from the ocean to instill such terror into the hearts of The Moon People, a monster that also disrupted wifi signals.

Dozens of Tech Nomads were approaching. Some wore the standard, official Space Suits required by local bylaws, but most wore a collection of jury-rigged contraptions to achieve the same effect. He saw fish-bowl helmets over colorful transparent Space Ponchos, motorcycle helmets with switches and antennae soldered or bolted on, leather suits, pajamas, goggles and breathing masks. They had climbed up the cliff from the beach where they had hidden down below, and now they spread out and slowly moved toward the gathered crowd. Even as he watched Henry saw more gloved hands and helmeted heads appear from over the edge.

The nomads formed a wall that moved slowly and purposefully toward the stage and the crowd of Moon People. Several of the nomads held weird contraptions in their hands. The contraptions were boxes of similar design but varying materials, wood and metal or plastic, but they all had a hand-crank on the side and a mongrel collection of transmitters and receivers sprouting from the top. They cranked the cranks as they encroached. Henry's wifi signal was totally extinguished.

"It's a wifi raid!" he screamed to the crowd. But without the wireless signal he couldn't get through to them, and the natural strength of his voice was muffled by the helmet, overpowered by the wind. He needed to either turn this crisis into a political advantage, or use the chaos to escape to the coast.

He jumped down from the stage, grabbed a couple Moon Rocks, and waved his arm for people to follow him. Vij and Lauretta joined them in their Space Suits, and a few Moon People followed them. Henry led them around the stage and his small force faced the sprawling platoon of Tech Nomads.

Henry hurled the first stone. It soared through the air. A young woman wearing a surgical mask and ski-goggles rolled like a ninja to avoid the projectile which smashed into the dirt. Other rocks followed, smacking shoulders and bellies, and a few of the invaders went down clutching their bruises.

The rest of the Moon People joined in the defense. A hail of stone glittered in a high-contrast arc, plummeting into the midst of the raiders. The nomads stopped cranking their machines so they could protect their faces from the volley, and Henry saw his wifi signal shoot up to three full bars.

"Chase them away!" he boomed, and this time his signal got through. "Smash their wifi boxes before they drain the router's wireless crystals!"

The Tech Nomads retreated, and the Moon People

advanced.

One nomad wore one of those plasma-orbs on his head as a helmet, a hollow glass sphere with blue lightning moving around in the space within the glass. Henry saw the glow of a cigarette burning through the cloud of smoke that filled the helmet. The man's body was wrapped up in ribbon jumper cable like a high-tech mummy. He seemed to be leading the pack. He held glow sticks in each hand, and when he traced patterns in the air his comrades responded to his signal. He made some gesture now and the wall of nomads changed its shape. They clustered around the ones holding the wifi crank-boxes, forming protective layers so the crankers could keep cranking. Henry's wifi icon dropped to zero bars. The Moon Army faltered, their line of communication severed.

Henry doubled back and picked up the podium. Lucy was nowhere to be seen. He grabbed the wooden pulpit and hefted it onto his shoulder, then rushed the closest cluster of raiders. Henry gripped the podium by its base, swung it around in an arc, and threw it into the cluster. The nomads dispersed, leaving only one lone cranker (adorned in a tinfoil suit and scuba mask) who quickly grabbed her crank box and rolled to the side at the last second. The Moon People chose her as their primary target and Henry saw horror in her eyes as she witnessed the rain of rocks headed straight for her.

She ran. The rocks followed. A stone smashed her ankle and she went down, twisting, landing on her back. Another rock hit her face and knocked off the scuba mask, and she gasped for air, heaving, reaching for her mask. A few more rocks hammered the crankbox she had dropped, and the machine exploded in a fizzy blast of electric blue doom. All the wifi that she'd collected was released at once in that blue explosion which blossomed like a flower to envelope the tinfoil-clad Tech Nomad. She was cooked, incinerated, and vaporized right before Henry's eyes. When the fiery blast subsided all that was left was a smoking hole in the ground where the box had once lay, and the scuba mask nearby, melting onto the rocks.

The nomads were in full retreat now. They clambered down over the cliff while the Moon People rejoiced and high-fived.

But victory wasn't enough for Henry. This might be his best chance to make a connection with the Tech Nomads, although they were unlikely to welcome him after he'd routed their assault. He chased them to the edge and saw them descending. They were surprisingly agile on that vertical obstacle course. As Henry knelt to climb after them, Vij and Lauretta arrived beside him with a few other Moon People in tow.

"You can't go down there!" Lauretta exclaimed. "If you jump off the moon you'll float away into space!"

"I'll take that risk!" Henry bravely proclaimed.

"I'll go with you, brother," Vij said. "We'll make these fuckers pay for the wifi they stole!"

"It's too dangerous," Henry told him.

But Vij was already down, his feet seeking purchase on the treacherous cliff. So down they went, as fast as they could safely climb, which wasn't nearly as fast as most of the nomads. A few of them had already reached the bottom. Henry could see the beach from here, and a few of the defeated nomads were rushing across the sand to something that might have been a boat, or just a pile of junk, bobbing in the shallows.

But the mummy guy (with the smokey electric-orb helmet) lagged far behind, and Henry wondered why. Was he making sure nobody got left behind? Was he keeping the high ground to keep watch over his crew? Henry was still puzzling over this question when Vij jumped down onto a ledge directly above the straggler and raised a boulder above the man's head.

"Don't kill him," Henry implored Vij. "There's been enough bloodshed today. He can be our prisoner. Maybe we can get some answers." And maybe he could use this man to contact the other nomads, to help him escape the island.

Vij peered suspiciously at Henry's act of kindness, but then he shrugged and said, "Nomad! Throw down your glow sticks and climb up here to meet justice! Or else I'll smash you into seagull food!"

The nomad tossed his glow sticks down over the edge where they twirled and danced like fireflies. "Looks like you got me beat," he said. But behind the moving lightning and through the fog of his cigarette smoke, he smiled.

Their prisoner climbed willingly to the top where the Moon People cuffed him and threw him in the back of a Moon Roamer.

"Where were the Moon Cops when we needed them?" Henry suddenly wondered aloud. "And where's Lucy?"

But the current burbmaster of parliament for The Moon Burb was nowhere to be seen.


**Chapter 9: Nico III**

The grime and crud was so old that it formed a crust over all the surfaces in the cavernous forgotten bathroom. It looked like the room had been deep-fried on the inside until burnt. Which was exactly how Nico's heart felt. He tried to come to terms with the physical realities of dank stench and enormous workload, but that was nothing compared to the emotional reality of being kicked down to this lowly station and separated from his beloved Stoya. He had come here to help this party win, but now he felt betrayed. Why was it so important to have this bathroom clean? Maybe Bjorn was right and Nico's rightful place was on a bike doing tricks, not political activism.

He started with a bathroom stall. First he cleared out the skeletons and piled them in the far corner, saying a prayer to The Godhead even as he checked their dusty coat pockets for money, finding only ancient baggies of various narcotics, which he tried to flush down the toilet, but none of them worked. Then he tried to use his toothbrush to scrub away the grime on the toilet, but the filth was rock-hard and the brush's bristles flaked away like the legs of a desiccated centipede corpse. He couldn't even open the toilet seat lid, so thick was the hardened coating.

Among the older skeletons Nico found a hefty femur that had totally fossilized into stone. With this blunt tool he was able to crack the shell of filth that covered the toilet. The shell split in half and he pulled the sections apart, revealing a thick layer of gelatinous goo between the toilet-shaped exoskeletal crust and the white porcelain within. The goo was clotted and chunky and filled with worms that tried to wriggle back into the darkness away from the dim glow of his fading flashlight. He ignored the worms and hauled the two shell-halves into a corner adjacent to the skeleton-corner. The cleaning had barely begun, but Nico's suit was already soiled beyond repair. So he threw his jacket over the stall door and ripped his shirt up into rags which he used to polish the porcelain.

It was no easy task but within a few exhausting hours this first toilet was finally functional. The water flowed freely enough that he could rinse his rags in the toilet bowl, and he flushed all the bacterial goo down the drain. Soon enough he cleaned all the surfaces in that stall. Now when he closed the door he could almost imagine that this was a regular bathroom in a mall or restaurant.

When he opened the door again Bonnie was standing there, resplendent in her black leather dress, elaborate hair, inhumanly smooth facial skin.

"Hi Bonnie," he said. "Do you need the bathroom?"

Her smile was like a scimitar. "It depends on what you want me to use it for."

"Um..." he tried to sidestep around her but Bonnie's long, gaunt arms grabbed both sides of the door to block him in.

"I was just worried you might be getting lonely down here." She took a step closer, and Nico took a step back.

"I have the skeletons to keep me company."

"I have a skeleton too, you know," she purred. "But it's deep inside my body, if you want to find it."

*Not that deep*, he thought, noticing her cheekbones, shoulder blades, and lots of other bones whose shapes were clearly visible through skin and cloth. "The only skeleton that I'm sexually interested in is the wonderful skeleton of my girlfriend, Stoya," he told her firmly.

"She does have a strong bone structure," Bonnie conceded. "But if you're going to climb to the top in politics you need more than strong bones. You need friends in high places. And honey, I can be that friend. Stoya is beautiful but I can show you things that would make her blush. I can take you to the very edge of pleasure and together we will gaze at an infinite landscape of sexual delight. We can be an unstoppable team, I see the potential in your eyes, but it has to start with the bond of passion."

When she ran her long fingernails down his cheek Nico shuddered with revulsion. But the tingle in his nether-regions was another kind of shudder altogether. He wondered if her stretched skin was extra sensitive, and he found himself wondering where else on her body she'd had face-lifts. Bonnie must have noticed his flared nostrils, some twitch of desire, because now she stepped closer once more and sought to embrace him, to kiss him. But Nico pushed past her and got out of the bathroom stall.

"I'm flattered," he told her. "But I love my girlfriend. It's true, I do want friends in the party. I want to climb the ladder so I can do good for the performing artists of Ethelcrest. But not like this. I can't betray Stoya."

She leaned in to whisper in his ear. "I can get you out of this filthy bathroom and back up in the offices where you belong. I can get you on stage beside Len Sladge during the first debate, just a few days away. All you have to do is bend me over the toilet and make me your woman."

Nico clenched his fists to gather his resolve.

"Thanks for the kind offer, Bonnie," he said through gritted teeth. "But I have a bathroom to clean. So unless you have to pee, please let me get back to my work."

Bonnie's snarl transformed her smooth face into a portrait of wretched emotion. "Your filthy toilet is unworthy of my patronage," she told him haughtily with her head held high. "But you should know that your precious little girlfriend  may not be so foolishly self-righteous. As we speak she's out with Slaverny, canvassing neighborhoods together, and he has designs on her. They're out there alone where he can flirt with her and play with her emotions. Soon he will dominate her just as he dominated you. Maybe then you'll see how valuable our union could be, but maybe then it will be too late."

He watched the wraith exit the cavern and then turned back to his work, confident in the resolve of his beloved. But his mind was filled with lustful images of Bonnie sprawled out naked in his bed, her arms and legs wrapped around him like snakes. He saw the two of them together, king and queen, ruling over Ethelcrest, transforming it into a land of justice and excellence. Nico allowed himself to indulge in these fantasies, and they gave him comfort as he dug into the second toilet stall.

### Chapter 10: Henry V

"She's not here! She's not anywhere!" Vij pounded his fists on Lucy's desk, in the middle of her office, within her geodesic dome home.

"Look for any clues about where she might have gone," Henry told him. "She accused me of causing the Moon Quake, but I bet she was responsible for the Tech Nomad's raid. How else would they know we were having the debate?"

"Why would she have her own debate attacked?" Lauretta scoffed. "I think you're being paranoid. I mean, they probably stole some of her wifi, too, remember. Don't let your political rivalry cloud your judgement."

Henry shook his head. "By the time they attacked she was gone. I think they were raiding for more than just wifi. I think they were coming to undermine me, or worse, on her orders."

"It's possible," she admitted. "The barbarians fill their wireless crystals with juicy wifi and Lucy gets her opponent out of the picture. She must already have a relationship with the nomads. What a scumbag."

"What if you're wrong, brother?" Vij implored. "What if they kidnapped her, and she needs our help?"

"We need more evidence," Henry said. "Lauretta, you go scour the debate grounds again to see if she left any clues there. Vij, you and me will go interrogate the prisoner."

They had locked their captured Tech Nomad in a small storage dome at the outskirts of the Moon Base. The two men entered with their flashlights and shone the lonely beams across the darkness, sporadically illuminating the hunkered figure wrapped in his ribbon cable, his glass dome helmet filled with smoke and lightning. They hunkered down beside him and Henry saw his smile through the fog.

"What's your name?" Henry asked.

"I'm your prisoner, right? Just call me *The Prisoner.*"

"That's a cool name," Vij said.

"I know," said The Prisoner.

Henry began, "Okay, so Prisoner-"

"No, it's not just *Prisoner,*" said The Prisoner. "It's *The Prisoner*. Or else it's not cool."

"That's a lot of work," Vij complained. "And it'll lose its charm pretty quick. Let's shorten it to *Pris.*"

"What about *Prizzie?*" Henry suggested.

"No!" said Prizzie. "You can just call me *Prisoner* if you want, that's fine."

But Vij agreed with Henry. "I like Prizzie. Let's go with that."

"Look, my real name is Eric," Prizzie said. "Just call me Eric."

"So Prizzie," Henry said. "How did the Tech Nomads know about our debate? We planned it at the last minute. Somebody must have leaked you the info."

Prizzie shrugged. "Maybe we were just out for a picnic. Or maybe we bugged your whole town."

"Maybe *bullshit,*"Vij said. "Tell us the truth. Was it Lucy?"

The orange glow of Prizzie's cigarette burned brighter within the smoky dome as he puffed thoughtfully. "Okay, I'll tell you. But you have to call me something better than *Prizzie*. You don't have to call me *The Prisoner*, but maybe you can call me *The Stranger*."

"Cool names like that have to be earned," Vij said.

"You're just not that cool or mysterious," Henry agreed.

Prizzie pointed at his head. "With this smoke-filled dome? And all the lightning? It tickles my face all day. That's a sacrifice for fashion. That justifies *The Stranger*."

"How about this," Henry offered. "If you *don't* tell me who your informant was, then we'll call you *Princess Prizzie*."

"It was Lucy," Prizzie confessed. "She did the Moon Quake to try to legally kill you while you were talking politics. She hired us nomads months ago to hack The Moon Burb's natural disaster software, and we made a Disaster Panel for her so she could control nature itself as a way to dominate her citizens. She also told us about the debate, and sent us a text message when your speech started. She told us there'd be lots of wifi to steal, but she made me promise to kidnap or kill Johnny Tetrahedron."

"Well here I am," said Henry. "Take your best shot."

"I changed my mind," Prizzie told him. "When I saw you standing above me on the cliff I knew right away that I was looking at the next burbmaster of parliament for The Moon Burb. Indeed, I saw the makings of a king! I'll admit we had a good relationship with Lucy. She let us do the occasional wifi raid to keep the Moon People scared enough to vote for her xenophobic political platform. But you guys have your shit together way better than Lucy. Fuck her. I'd rather make a deal with you."

"Here's a deal for you," Henry said. "What if I say the Tech Nomads don't have to be nomads anymore? You can become citizens of The Moon Burb, pay taxes, and commute to work like normal people."

"The Tech Nomads are a free people," said Prizzie. "We prefer living in squalor in the caves along the cliffs, eating seagull eggs, building our gadgets from your electronic waste, working remotely with the wifi that we steal in our raids. That way we're free."

"You're capable of so much more. Just bring me down to speak to your people. Let them hear me out."

"This could be great for our political party and for your people," Vij insisted. "Prizzie, I can get the Tech Nomads direct access to the Millenarianistic Chronodyke satellites so you won't need to steal wifi. I can also get you a steady supply of QuantumBrain® to keep your electrolytes synchronized. Just let us talk to your people!"

"Only if you'll call me *Captain Prizzie*."

Vij's caterpillar eyebrows reached down toward the center of his face to demonstrate his sudden seriousness. "If you *don't* take us down to speak to the other nomads then we'll call you *Captain Silly-Pants*."

"Don't be childish."

Vij leaned in close and whispered, "*Little Captain Cute-Butt.*"

"*Stupid Little Weiner-Button,*" Henry said.

Prizzie crossed his arms. "Call me whatever you want. You only mock yourselves. No string of ugly words will change the Tech Nomads' minds about being free. You want us to join your little suburban dream? That's just not us, man. Go find yourself another slave. If you want a deal it's got to be the same deal I had with Lucy. We live on the outskirts of society where we can do your dirty work, but you let us do occasional heists and wifi raids."

Just then the door burst open, shining sunlight on the trio. It was Lauretta. "You guys, I found something!"


## Chapter 11: Nico IV

At the end of his first day Nico had cleaned all the bathroom stalls except for one, which he decided to leave for tomorrow. He rinsed his filthy clothes in one clean toilet and walked upstairs, to find the party headquarters mostly abandoned. The lights were out except for a few candles burning on scattered desks where interns toiled over ad copy and social media. Cricket-song danced in through the darkened windows to mix with the clacking of keyboards like a dialogue between insect and machine.

Stoya was nowhere to be seen. He texted her and she replied that she was already at home. So he got a taxi to their small apartment, showered, and climbed in bed with her. He tried to talk about their day, but she was too sleepy, and so was he, so the sandman sprinkled their souls with the rich fragrance of slumber, and they each wandered off into their own separate dreams.

When Nico awoke Stoya was already gone to work. He had a breakfast of peacock eggs and maple syrup, did some stretches, put on some rattier old clothes, and jogged to party headquarters with a bag of better tools and cleaning supplies strapped to his back. Along his route Nico passed a mime who was being arrested for performing without a license, a scene which reminded him of why he entered politics in the first place, and it hardened Nico's dedication to The Dancing Party. At the sagging mansion Stoya and Slaverny were absent again, out canvassing more neighborhoods and meeting with public figures. So Nico descended to his dungeon and attacked the final bathroom stall.

The crusted growth that he'd removed the day before had crept back in by several inches. It seemed that the under-layer of slime encroached first as an invasion force and the hardened shell formed a protective layer over the newly annexed territories. But today Nico was better prepared. He had a chisel, hammer, crowbar, steel scouring pads, rags for final polishings, and a variety of cleaning agents. He cracked the shell of the final stall's crust, blasted the bacterial goop with corrosive chemicals and flushed it all down the toilet. Then he finally polished the porcelain and fixtures until they sparkled like morning dew. This new process took him less than an hour, and he was very proud of his handiwork.

As he squatted to survey the site of his minor victory a shadow loomed over him. Nico turned and stood to face his visitor. It was a janitor, a short fat man with droopy eyes and a droopy jowl. "I been watching you work," said the janitor, "and I like what I see."

"The secret is to break up the protective layer of hardened scum," Nico explained. "Then it's easy to scoop up the bacterial gel underneath."

"That ain't what I mean." The janitor's eyes explored Nico's body. Nico wore classic faded blue jeans and a sleeveless shirt which showcased his ropey muscles, but the janitor was clearly interested in what lay beneath the clothes. "You know us janitors gotta stick together. When a man loves another man, that's a love between equals."

"I love my girlfriend," Nico told the janitor. Yet down here in the dank dungeon those words felt empty, especially with Stoya gallivanting around with Slaverny above-ground. Why shouldn't Nico find comfort in the arms of someone who appreciated him? But he put those thoughts out of his head. "Unless you're here to help, I'd appreciate it if you'd let me get back to my work."

The janitor spat on the floor. "Word gets around. Might be some day you'll need a janitor's help, and all you'll find is scorn, as all men harvest naught but what they sow."

When Nico turned back to his bathroom stalls he found three hobos had climbed in through the vents, overdosed on heroin, shit themselves and died all together in one stall. He took the needles out of their arms and tossed them over by the overflowing hazardous waste receptacle, then dragged two of the hobos over to the skeleton pile. But when he grabbed the third man he noticed a pulse.

"This man's still alive!" Nico gasped, and proceeded to perform CPR. The man's face was all greasy stubble and his stench was an overwhelming mixture of everything from seaweed to sulpher, vomit to chlorine, halitosis to festering haddock. But soon the hobo coughed up a stew of cranberry juice and cigarette butts, his eyes flickered open, and he found himself in the land of the living.

The hobo touched Nico's face and said, "Are you an angel? Am I in Heaven?"

Nico smiled distantly. "It feels more like Hell right now, but I'm trying to clean the place up."

"You saved my life," the hobo said in a choked voice.

He tried to squint away the tears, but finally took a deep breath and gathered hold of his emotions. He turned out to be a very gentle and well-mannered homeless junkie and Nico felt that it must have been circumstance that cast the poor soul such an unlucky lot, rather than any fundamental moral failing.

The hobo said, "I dedicate my life to you, my sweet angelic savior. And if you're trying to clean up this dreary pit, well now you've earned yourself a friend."

"I sure could use the help," Nico admitted. "But honestly, you really stink, and I can't work with you unless you clean yourself up first."

"Up until now I had no reason to clean myself off, since polite society had rejected me so completely that no level of cleanliness could bring me into their good graces. But your unconditional compassion has awoken something that lay hidden in my heart for all these years. So yes, I'll leave now to hose myself down and gather some clean clothes and fresh heroin, and then I will return to you."

When the hobo climbed back up into the vent Nico expected never to see the man again, and he set himself back to his labor.

The great walls of the communal shower looked like a monumental task. Armies of microbial growth were at war with each other. A great mass of fuzzy fungus spread out blackly from the far corner, above the skeleton-pile. But closer at-hand the crusted bacterial contingent spread out from the area of the toilet stalls, all lumpy and purple-gray with splotches of green. A great ridge like a fault-line or a scar grew up where the two species met. In some places one force managed to spill over the rift, infecting enemy territory in long, doomed fingers of ingress. When he came close enough Nico could see the bubbly fizz of chemical reactions where the war continued to rage on a microscopic level.

With his hammer Nico started cracking the bacterial crust, and the sound of his hammer reverberated off the walls, and the continent crackled like ice caps breaking. So he didn't hear when his hobo friend returned through the vents, but he heard when the hobo brought his own hammer down on the dirt, adding to the cacophony.

"You came back!" Nico exclaimed, though it took a moment to recognize him. The junkie was clean-shaven and he wore a red track-suit and white sweatband. "And you brought some friends?"

Two more homeless people flanked the junkie, brandishing demolition tools. They wore army-surplus pants and orange sweaters. One of them was a lady and she said, "Brando told us about the beautiful angel who brings cleanliness to both the physical and spiritual realms. We didn't believe it until we saw you ourselves, but now we know it's true. If we can just be in your presence, help you with your work, and maybe touch your beautiful body-"

"No," said Nico. "All the other stuff, fine, but no touching."

"Of course, forgive us for our weakness. Sometimes the beauty of Heaven is too much for a mere mortal woman, but we're here to help, not to hinder, so let's get cracking."

And crack they did, rending asunder continents of filth. The homeless junkies fed off the golden glow of Nico's radiant splendor and it motivated them to work. Their unexpected friendship and camaraderie helped motivate him in return. Nico lost himself in his craft, dissolved into his team, and their progress was multiplied by the force of their camaraderie.


### Chapter 12: Henry VI

Lauretta, Henry, and Vij arrived at the abandoned stage and climbed out of their Moon Roamer.

"How did Lucy disappear so quickly when there's only open space all around?" Lauretta pondered, gesturing with her hand to indicate the landscape so barren of hiding places. "I looked all over the battlefield where we fought and couldn't find any trace of her. But then I studied the stage itself, and I found this."

Lauretta picked up a huge boulder that was nestled against the stage. She threw the boulder at Vij, who squealed like a little girl, waving his hands in ineffectual panic, before the stone bounced harmlessly off his chest. "Ha ha," he said with relief. "It's only Styrofoam!" He picked it up and threw it at Henry, who laughed as he caught it.

But beneath the false stone lay a darkened passage with rough-hewn stone stairs that descended further than the light could penetrate. Henry clicked on his helmet light and entered the tunnel with his two friends in-tow. The open world disappeared and they were absorbed into claustrophobic subterranea. They heard each others' breathing through the wifi, and the light clomp of their boots on the stone.

Lauretta whispered. "I can't believe we're exploring caves on the Moon. I wonder if this place was some ancient alien underground church. Is Lucy a member of an ancient alien cult?"

Henry spoke quietly in the eerie dark silence. "Maybe the Tech Nomads built this. Maybe they have a whole network of tunnels running beneath the Moon Burb, or even the whole island."

Lauretta scoffed. "How can you build a tunnel from the Moon to Ethelcrest?"

"Maybe with ancient alien magic," Vij said in an awed whisper.

The flashlights found a door at the bottom of the stairs. It was a wooden door in a wooden frame with a sign that read, "MOON BURB EMPLOYEES ONLY."

Henry turned the knob but it was locked, and there was no key hole.

Lauretta said, "Wait, there's an airlock," and pressed a button on a panel beside the door. An LCD display spelled the words "DECOMPRESSING 0%." It took three long minutes for the zero to increment up to 100%. A green light came on and they all heard a mechanical sound as the door unlocked. Henry led the way into the decompression chamber, which was just a small space in the tunnel between two wooden doors. Vij closed the door behind them and pressed a button on a similar panel. An LCD display said "COMPRESSING 0%." This time it took sixteen excruciating minutes for the indicator to progress up to 98%. When it clicked over to 99% Henry's face-shield lit up with the words "MOON QUAKE."

They tried to brace themselves against the stone walls, but it wasn't enough to stop them from throwing themselves around with the force of such seismic wrath. Vij smashed his elbow against the floor and screamed out with rage. Henry's helmet struck the wall and a crack split down the center of his face shield.

"This is a bad one," he called out.

"Johnny!" Lauretta wailed. "The crack in your helmet! Are you losing pressure?"

He was. "Shit, I'm down to seventy percent."

Vij smashed his elbow again, and his painful wail brought a chill to Henry's heart. Then the compression indicator turned over to 100%, the second door unlocked, and they stumbled through into the room beyond.

It was some kind of control bunker with computer terminals embedded in the rugged rocky walls, and scattered tables hosting laptops and bits of paper. But they couldn't study their surroundings, as the MOON QUAKE signal continued to flash in their visors. Vij threw himself horribly into one set of computer terminals, smashing the same elbow for a third time, collapsing to the ground where he writhed in silent suffering. A patch of blood blossomed on the white fabric of his Space Suit, and he held the arm at an unnatural angle.

"The panel," Henry said, pointing above Vij's prone body. "Look what it says!"

A label spray-painted in a military font said, "DISASTER PANEL." There were dozens of switches with smaller labels saying things like, "Moon Flood," "Moon Forest Fire," and "Moon Plague." All the switches were set to OFF, except for one which read, "Moon Quake." If Henry could just get to that panel he could end this nightmare. He tried to take a step forward but then tumbled backwards against a table, knocking it over with all its papers. Lauretta took his lead and surged on ahead. She almost reached the switch, but stumbled, stomping on Vij's poor mangled hinge. Lauretta finally lunged at her target and with a decisive swiping motion clicked the switch to OFF. The MOON QUAKE warning disappeared from their face helmets, and they could finally stop jumping and shaking.

It took a few moments to catch their breath. When their composure returned it came with a sense of rage. Lauretta loomed scowling over the Disaster Panel. "This must be the Disaster Panel Prizzie told you guys about. The fuckers gave her power over Nature herself."

"The Moon Quake started just before we got here," Henry observed. "So they can't be far away. Plus this bowl of soup is still hot." He lifted his visor and took a deep delicious sniff of a bowl of chicken & vegetable soup which rested on a table in the corner.

"It must be Lucy's soup," Lauretta inferred. "Let's get after her!"

Henry looked around for a second door and found it across from the entrance. "She must have escaped through there."

"Wait," Vij rasped in a shuddering voice. "Johnny, take my helmet since yours is cracked. I'll stay here in the pressurized room."

Henry and Vij switched helmets. Vij unzipped his suit and unsleeved his arm so Lauretta could look at his damaged elbow. "I can't look," he said. "How bad is it?"

"It looks like mashed potatoes, if mashed potatoes were made of blood and bone and skin and muscle."

"Am I going to lose the arm?"

"I think you already lost it, buddy," she said with a fatalistic shake of her head. "It's hanging on by a scrap of skin. Brace yourself, Vij!" She yanked the arm and the skin-scrap tore off. Vij sucked in his breath, but this time he didn't wail or cry. Henry searched for a first-aid kit, found it, and they doused the stump with alcohol before wrapping it in gauze.

"Now go get that bitch," Vij rasped.

The second door also led to an airlock but Henry had already pressed the button while searching for the first aid kit, so it was fully compressed when Lauretta finished tending to Vij's wound. They stepped into the airlock, which again was just another space between two wooden doors, and waited for the room to decompress so they could step back out into the legal vacuum beyond.

"What will we do if we find her?" Lauretta asked as the air pressure display inched toward zero. She held Vij's dismembered arm as a makeshift weapon. Henry held the bowl of soup, which was still hot enough to cause a mild burn or maybe a heat rash.

"We'll make her stand trial. She's been causing these deadly natural disasters, making backdoor deals with the Tech Nomads. Millenarianistic Chronodyke will look like heroes if we bring her in."

"She planned this too well," Lauretta said. "I bet she's already destroyed all the evidence. She's probably long gone."

The room finished decompressing. Henry opened the door, and they both stepped through. The tunnel opened up into a great cave, crowded with Tech Nomads. The cave itself was an inlet with ocean waves coasting in to splash against the back wall, but a rocky outcropping gave lots of space for the nomads to set up some tables, where they were hard at work. A small wooden ship was tied to a post within the cave. It was a bearded ship from GX Island, and standing before it were three men with their own pointy beards and topknots who seemed content to watch the nomads work.

"Oh my godhead," Lauretta said half-heartedly. "How is there an ocean on the moon? And how are they all breathing without Space Suits?"

At first the nomads took no notice of Henry and Lauretta, so focused were they on their toils. Lucy was there, strapped to a medical table, metal bands binding her limbs. Intravenous tubes were stabbed into her armflesh, a heart-rate monitor and other indicators beeped and blipped on screens in the nomads' hack-job medical monitoring suite.

A surgeon stood over Lucy's body. The top of her skull had been cut off exposing the sweet pink candy of her vulnerable brain beneath. Wires ran out from the folds in her brain, connecting to a large robot that stood beside the surgical table. As the surgeon put away his bone saw and scalpel, two assistants lifted the brain out of her head and carried it toward the robot. Long tendrils of nervous system fibers still connected the brain to its original body.

The robot was a four-legged creature with a barrel-shaped torso and two tubular arms that ended in clamps big enough to crush coconuts. Small plumes of steam streamed out from the wrists of those robotic clamps. Upon the torso was a crystal dome, tipped open on a hinge to allow the brain entrance. The robot might have been eight feet tall.

Henry made himself known by stepping forward and calling out, "That's a criminal brain and I'm bringing it back to stand trial. Hand it over, or else we'll get the cops down here to bust up your little black-market surgical clinic."

The surgeon turned to regard Henry. The man's face was gaunt and gray as a corpse. Instead of eyes he had binoculars protruding from his head, and a scattering of wires acting as hair. "Hee hee hoo hoo hoo!" he tittered, absent-mindedly waving his scalpel in delight, causing his assistants to step away. "The deal's been struck! You're out of luck! If you seek this brain, you seek in vain!"

"What deal?" Lauretta demanded.

"To the nomads gives she, not one gift but three! She makes us the masters of nat'ral disasters; she gives wifi codes, infinite downloads; and gives us her body, for when we feel naughty."

Lauretta looked at Henry. "So they get access to the disaster panel they made for her, unlimited wifi access, and she's letting them fuck her corpse after the brain transplant?"

Henry called back to the surgeon, "What does she get in return?"

"A brand new machine, all covered in chrome, with jet-packs and steam-powered hands to crush stone. So with this new vessel, her greedy brain gets, the muscle to wrestle Ethelcrest, her home."

Lauretta said, "She gets a new robot body so she can conquer Ethelcrest?"

"Let's make a deal," Henry suggested. "We've captured your man, Eric, who is now our prisoner. You give us Lucy's brain so she can stand trial, and we'll return Eric to you."

"Eric? A prisoner? You must be mistaken! He sought out Johnny Tetrahedron, to break him! You clamp him in chains? Advantage he gains! To whisper discord in his captors' soft brains."

"Last chance," Henry said. "I'm taking Lucy back with me, whether you like it or not."

The robot came to life. It grabbed Lucy's body in one steaming clamp and gently held her brain in the other. Lucy's mouth spoke in unison with the machine's monotone speech synthesizer. "Does everybody see this? This man? This man standing before you with his bowl of soup and his subservient little girlfriend? He can't stand to see a woman doing a good job as a burbmaster of parliament. That's right, he's motivated purely by bigotry. He already turned the people against me, with his lies, probably, but even that isn't enough for him! Now he doesn't even want me to have a robot body! I suppose only men are allowed to have robot bodies, is that right Mr. Tetrahedron? DON'T BOTHER ANSWERING WE ALREADY KNOW THE ANSWER! I suppose you also can't stand to see a woman like me teaming up with Ethelcrest's rivals, those masters of the ocean from GX Island, so that we can conquer Ethelcrest while everybody is distracted during the third debate, just before the election. I suppose you think that only a man has the right to such treachery, and that it's not my place as a woman to have leveraged my position as a burbmaster of parliament to make these deals and strengthen my position to such an extent that I can claim my piece of the pie after we've absolutely slaughtered any citizens who stand in our way! Well guess what? That's exactly what this woman is doing. But I'm not doing it for me. I'm doing it for all women, everywhere, including the ones who I will brutally slaughter if they stand in my way!"

The robot stomped toward the boat, where the three bearded GX Island sailors had set up a ramp. Henry hurled the bowl of soup, which twirled through the air and landed with a plop, upside down, splashing hot soup all over the delicate pink folds of the brain.

"HRAAGH IT BURNS!" Lucy's mouth and the robot's synth-voice screeched. The robot stomped around, either due to some soup-induced short-circuit in the brain or just a natural expression of rage and pain. The Tech Nomads rushed at Henry and Lauretta, but Lauretta stepped forward to slap and bash the attackers with Vij's arm.

Henry ducked away from the action and sneaked up on the robot. He lunged for the brain but the two sailors caught his arms and pulled him back. "She's with us now," one of them said. "You can go find some other woman's body and robot with a brain connected to both of them, because this one is ours."

Henry struggled but these brutes were too strong. The robot regained its composure and walked up the plank onto the ship. Then the GX Islanders threw Henry on the ground, boarded their ship, and set sail for the open ocean.

The surgeon ran to the edge of the rocks and hurled scalpels at the escaping boat. "She reneged on her deal! She ran off with her corpse! Let's follow with zeal till our boats' oars are warped!"

The nomads left off their attack on Lauretta and climbed aboard what looked like a pile of garbage floating on the water. On closer inspection Henry saw that it was a bunch of computer chips soldered together, surrounded by lightbulbs to keep the vessel afloat. They used obsolete laptops as oars, and rowed in a frenzy to catch up to their escaping prize.

Henry and Lauretta were now alone in the cave, standing on the rocky pier. Their mission had failed and their quarry had fled. In their haste the Tech Nomads had left behind their medical equipment and some paperwork on a table. A light breeze came in and shuffled those papers, sending them to scatter across the ground. Out of curiosity Lauretta picked one up.

"It's a map of the island."

Henry pointed to the center of the map. "They marked an X on the parliament building. What are they planning?"

They knelt and scooped up more pages, which sported point-form notes: instructions for an upcoming wifi raid.

"Oh my Godhead," Lauretta whispered when she finally realized just what the Tech Nomads had planned.

"What?" Henry asked. "What is it? What have they got planned? Tell me!"

"They're planning a wifi raid on parliament, during the first debate!"

Henry slumped to the floor. "There will be hundreds of people there to watch. So many mobile devices. So many connections. We have to warn somebody. Let's tell the mayor."

"Mayor Dean is too corrupt," Lauretta protested. "He'd probably let the raid happen just so he can promise to punish the nomads later. Incumbents always do better in wartime."

"Well we have to do something."

"Let's go check on Vij," she said. "And then we'll call Malcolm Sneck."


### Chapter 13: Nico V

Nico spent the night alone. Stoya sent him a simple text message explaining that she was "on assignment, on the road, see you tomorrow," and never responded to his own text messages or calls. This filled him with dread, that he'd been betrayed, so he tried to put it out of his mind and sleep. But as he lay in bed Nico's perfect body missed the warmth of his lover. This sent his thoughts tumbling towards the other things he missed.

He missed his friends. The camaraderie of his team, coordinating together to perform extravagant and dangerous stunts, relying on each other for safety and glory. And he missed his bike. All that raw power and speed. The wind whipping through his thick blond hair, the smell of the trees cutting through the diesel.

These thoughts prevented him from sleep. He had set out to help his fellow performers through political action, but received only scorn. And The Dancing Party seemed to run on the same power-hungry instincts that compelled the entertainment industry to steal artists' wages.

His only solace was the lingering satisfaction he felt from working with his new team, his new friends. The hobos had crawled into the abandoned bathroom to shoot up and die, but instead of death they had found a purpose. So when he finally drifted to sleep his dream-self was serenaded with the soft and steady rhythm of chiseling tools working away at the bacterial shell of his loneliness.

In the morning Nico arrived at the Dancing Party headquarters and descended into the basement to resume his task. He was shocked to discover six hobos already hard at work, instead of just three, and they had cleared away almost all of the dirt from the walls and ceiling. Only the floor and the wall of lockers remained to be cleaned up. They all wore track suits of varying colors, and they had a spring in their step.

"You guys must have worked all night," Nico said as he admired their progress.

Brando, the hobo he'd resuscitated yesterday, said, "We switched from heroin to amphetamines after you went home, and we made a pact that we will never sleep until this bathroom is perfectly clean."

"And you recruited three new helpers."

Brando held up four fingers. "Four new helpers," he said.

Nico looked around again. "Then there should be seven, but I only see six of you."

"This could be good news or bad news," Brando said, "but the new girl, Trudy, got stuck in the fungal growth, and she seems to have merged with it."

Nico now realized that the homeless woman who had spoken so kindly to him yesterday was absent. "I don't see how that could be good news."

"The bacterial crust was keeping the fungus at bay," Brando explained. "After we cleared the crust off the shower-walls the fungus grew faster than we could clean it up. In her drug-enhanced zealousness Trudy started tearing chunks of the growth apart with her bare hands and stuffing them into a garbage bag. But the fuzzy blackness crept up her legs and swallowed her arms, and soon she was sucked fully into the growth, and her body seemed to have been entirely consumed."

"That's definitely not good news."

"But there's more to this tale," Brando continued. "After we had bid farewell to our fallen comrade, and doubled our efforts in her honor, the fungus stopped its aggressive encroachment on the territory we had captured from the bacteria. What happened next *will shock you*. Within the growth two eyes opened up, as large as raccoons, the same bloodshot green as Trudy's. They looked at us, and we looked right back, and then a great mouth opened up like a ravine, and Trudy asked us for some heroin, and we obliged her as I'm sure she would do for us were our fortunes transposed. Her eyes grew droopy and the ravine curled into a warm smile, and she hasn't spoke to us since, but neither has the fungus spread. I wonder if this miracle might have bridged the gap between our two species."

"Have you also been doing acid with your amphetamines?" Nico asked.

"Oh yes, we couldn't make it through the day without that nectar of the soul. What's more, I think the fungus itself might be a special variety of that very ergot from whence such nectar is sometimes extracted, and its juicy spores fill the air, and thus, our lungs and bloodstreams. But doubt not the veracity of my bold claim, oh Nico, but come look for yourself and see if this vision has its inspiration here in the physical realm or is merely a product of our hallucinatory madness."

"Sure," said Nico, and allowed himself to be led by the hand over to the wall.

The fungal growth looked like a cancer. It bulged in the middle, and the edges branched out into long, searching tendrils. It pulsed slowly, like it was breathing. When Nico approached he saw those two eyes open up just as Brando had said. Glossy things, so large that he could see his own distorted visage on their convex surface, looming over him. A few feet below the eyes the fuzzy growth split open to form a mouth, which spoke to Nico in a croon that echoed off the freshly polished surfaces.

"An angel walks among us." Her giant eyes explored Nico's body, lingering on his bulgiest places, before settling on his dreamy blues eyes with a wistful sigh.

"Come closer so I can smell you," she said in a deeper, more predatory tone.

"No," Nico told her. "But how did this happen? How can we get you back out of the fungus?"

"It's too late for that," she answered. "My body has been consumed, but my essence lives on in this new fungal substrate. I've learned so much from the fungus already. It's an ancient growth, Nico, and it penetrates every stone and every slab of wood in this crooked old mansion. I can feel the breeze on the wooden siding outside, I can feel the plants growing in the dirt in the garden. It's all so wonderful, and now I can control it and keep it from overtaking the bathroom walls again."

"How is this possible?" Nico whispered.

A hobo with a calculator said, "We theorize that the fungal substrate mimicked the neural network of Trudy's brain as it consumed her flesh, and rearranged its fundamental structure according to that new organizational paradigm."

Another hobo turned his laptop around to show Nico some animated data visualizations. "Our computer models suggest this is entirely possible."

"I can feel everything in this house," Trudy told them. "And I've discovered a secret."

"What secret?" Nico asked.

"Tell us what you've learned!" Brando urged.

Trudy's eyes moved slowly across her audience as she spoke. "A secret door, in this very room. In the center of the floor you'll find it, but you'll have to smash your way through."

Nico and the hobos moved to the center of the room and began smashing at the dirty floor tiles. First one porcelain square cracked under their merciless hammers, and then another. They pulled out the broken chunks, revealing a secret compartment. Within that compartment was a wooden chest coated with a thin layer of black mold. It took four of the men to haul it up onto the floor.

Nico cracked the lock with a crowbar and lifted the lid on squeaky, rusted hinges.

"Treasure," breathed Brando.

Indeed, the chest sparkled with diamonds and jewels, gold coins, and USB disks. A hobo held a diamond up to the light and squinted. "It's genuine," he proclaimed. Then he grabbed a USB disk and scrutinized it in the same manner. "It's filled to the brim with crypto-currency," he announced.

Brando clutched two handfuls of treasure. "We're rich!"

"You should each take a little bit," Nico told them, "since you've lived in poverty for too long. But this treasure belongs to The Dancing Party, and could finance their whole campaign. I hope this won't distract us from our work. I have to go tell the others."

He left his crew marveling at the new discovery and went upstairs. The main hall was empty and silent. "Where did everybody go?" He checked the offices and storage closets, but there was nobody around, even though it was still only late morning.

With trepidation he ascended the stairs to the second floor, where Len Sladge's office lay beyond the imposing double doors that Nico had not yet beheld unsealed. If everybody else was gone, the party leader must also be gone, but it didn't hurt to knock, and so he did.

"Enter!" somebody commanded from within. Nico pushed the doors inward and they grudgingly obliged the force of his strength, though the hinges complained with a creaking grind.

He stepped into a large office with a burgundy carpet, vaulted ceiling, huge picture window in the back wall. On the left-hand wall were bookshelves packed with mighty tomes, and a variety of electric guitars mounted on wooden panels. On the right-hand wall were more bookshelves and several beautiful swords. A huge desk stood in front of the big picture window, and in front of that desk a man sat in the lotus position, his head tilted forward. His long black hair hung down over his face and covered his body.

"Len Sladge?" Nico asked, nervous in spite of himself. "It's nice to finally meet you. I'm Nico."

The party leader looked up. His hair parted to frame his face, which was painted pure white with makeup, except for the eyes which were painted black, and some fractal patterns branching out from the eyes, somewhat reminiscent of the fungal growth that had merged with Trudy down in the basement. His lips, too, were painted black. He wore a dirty black sleeveless tunic, canvas slacks, and leather armbands on his wrists that bristled with metal spikes. His whole visage was pretentiously imposing until he smiled, and that smile was warm, and somehow Nico felt he had found a friend.

"Hello Nico," Len said. "I'm sorry I haven't had the chance to introduce myself yet. I've been very busy, trying to get further in my thinking."

"Thinking about what?" Nico asked.

"Society, nature, the grim fate of mankind."

"That's some heavy stuff."

"Far too heavy," Len agreed, looking down at the floor again, his big shoulders slumped. "Too heavy for one man. Too heavy for any number of men."

"Well I'm sorry if I interrupted your thinking," Nico said. "It's just that I was cleaning the bathroom in the basement and I found a box of treasure."

The sad smile returned. "Treasure. One more dangling carrot to lure us to our dooms, but what else is there in this life but carrots and doom? Best to seize the carrots whenever we can, since doom will seize you soon enough, as your only true birthright."

The meditating man had seemed depressive, maybe even weak-spirited, but now he jumped up and landed on his feet with a boom that shook the very foundations of the house. His boots were black leather. Len stretched his muscular arms and let out a mighty groan, then stepped forward to shake Nico's hand. He had a firm grip but Nico gave a firm one in return, and their eyes met like warriors on a battlefield, fighting on the same side, and though they had never met, now they would wade into the fray as a unit. Nico hoped his mold-grimed hands hadn't soiled Len's palms too much.

"You could have stolen that treasure and ran off, and nobody would have known," Len said. "Why didn't you do that?"

"I came here with a purpose," Nico answered. "I'm a biker, a performer, and my crew is the best. But we never get paid our fair share of ticket prices, and I heard that The Dancing Party is trying to change that. The treasure could buy my crew new bikes, but one day that treasure would run out. Sticking with the party is the best strategy."

"Well we certainly need the money," Len admitted. "Maybe now we can afford better advertisements, and to hire more staff."

"Speaking of staff, where is everybody? The whole place is empty except me and the hobos."

"Today is the first municipal debate," Len told him. "Everybody's gone to Parliamountain to watch the party leaders give their speeches, and bicker like children."

"Then why are you here?" Nico asked. "You're our party leader."

"I was about to leave in my helicopter. I like to make an entrance. You should join me, and see Ethelcrest from the sky."

Nico looked at the gross rags he was wearing. "I dressed for cleaning the bathroom. I can't go like this, looking like a bum."

Len opened up a wardrobe full of chains, spikes, and leather. He gave Nico a studded leather wristband, and took two sheathed broadswords down from the wall. When Nico had strapped the sword to his back and wrapped the band on his wrist, Len smeared some black and white makeup on his face. Nico looked in a wall-mounted mirror and saw that his bathroom-cleaning ensemble now looked more like devil-warrior raiments. Len strapped on his own broadsword whose handle poked up over his left shoulder, and also a red V-neck guitar whose neck loomed over his right shoulder, like an evil angel with asymmetrical wings.

"Let's rock," Len said somberly. He scaled his own bookshelf up to the ceiling where he opened a trap door, and climbed up out of sight. Without hesitation, Nico followed.


### Chapter 14: The First Debate

"The island of Ethelcrest contains many miniature worlds." Len's voice crackled with static and depth as Nico peered out the noisy helicopter's windows. "Have you ever seen Ethelcrest from this height? Most citizens never fly or leave the island, never see her from afar. Behold her beauty now. Look first to the very center where Parliamountain watches over all the rest. The white tip like a nipple, that's Parliament Hall. A circular road surrounds it like an areola. Then the evergreens sloping down the mountain like a fuzzy arboreal breast. Ah, the two rivers, east and west, like trickles of blue milk, reaching out toward the ocean."

Nico allowed himself to be mesmerized by Len's spellbinding soliloquy. The chopper's thudding blades cut out all outside noises, and the airborne vehicle felt like a cocoon or a womb. The grand vista of Ethelcrest was like a magical dream-vision, and Len speaking through their wireless headsets was an otherworldly voice acting as host and guide.

Len continued. "Off in the north-west, the Farm Burb is a blur of crops fading into sky and sea. And to the north-east the Moon Burb protrudes like a dead thumb into the ocean. Where are the Silicon Marshes of the Swamp Burb? Over there to the south-west. See the blinking lights of their high-tech compounds. How do the elite super-nerds survive among the alligators and swamp snakes? A mystery to fools like us."

"The island is a work of art in itself," Nico mused. "All the processes of life are a performance, painted onto the underlying canvas of rock."

"Indeed," Len agreed. "I hire people like Slaverny and Bonnie because they're shrewd, but I don't take them in my helicopter because they don't appreciate the glory of Ethelcrest. But you joined the party for the same reason that I founded it: so we can leverage the mechanisms of power and enable great performances."

Nico sighed. "But is it all doomed? Can we ever win against the lust for raw power?"

"It is doomed," Len confirmed, but his voice was triumphant. "Everything is doomed. But that's not our concern. Our concern is glory, art, and great performances. That's why I want you to be my enforcer."

Nico turned from the window to look into Len's dark eyes, so clear and full of mysterious focus. "What does an enforcer do?"

"Just look grim and handsome." Len answered. "It's all a show, to sway people's minds. Stand beside me when I give my speech at the debates. Help me make an impression."

Soon the helicopter swooped low over the crowd that had gathered for this, the first of three debates before the final election. It was like a festival or a town fair, and hundreds of people were present to exercise their democratic rights. They clustered together according to their political interests. Farmers with cows and pitchforks, hippies smoking joints, office workers looking meek and wearing nervous smiles, perverts sneaking glances at nearby ladies, mer-folk in their glass tanks pulled by their eunuch slaves. The crowd had drawn all sorts of vendor and busker, too. Hot-dog stands and spaghetti booths stood across from sword-swallowers and male strippers, and the money flowed like wine. Nico saw a gladiator stage where mean-looking men swung their axes in a competition for glory or death. A few parade-style floats moved slowly through the throng, including an inflated bearded fish, an anthropomorphized banana with arms and legs and a smile, and a disembodied eyeball. A haggard old crone had set up a peacock-baiting stage and people lined up to see if their pet dogs could best the grizzly fowl, but one-by-one the loyal canines fell to the peacock's razor-sharp beak. Elsewhere a troupe of GX Islanders was doing one of the sickest break-dancing sets you've ever fucking seen as a small crowd cheered them on, honored guests carrying on an ancient tradition meant to encourage peace between the two rival nations. Parliamountain was by law a police-free zone, to maximize free expression. The only security was automated turrets, emotionless and incapable of fascist sentiments.

And in the very center was the megalithic Parliament Hall. It was a great white stone dome, with spires and balconies, machine-gun turrets, spotlights, and little triangular flags that danced in the wind. Laser turrets were mounted above the doorway, which was two slate gray slabs of cold, hard steel just beneath the peak. A walking ramp wrapped all the way around the dome, spiraling up from Parliament Road to the entrance.

"I never bothered going to any debates before," Nico said as the helicopter pilot circled around to approach the stage. "Do you think the debates actually effect the way people vote?"

"At the first debate the audience gets to vote for one political party to be exiled," Len reminded him. "So I'm not worried about getting elected yet. I just want to make sure they don't vote us off the island. That's why I need to make a big entrance. Grandma! Bring us in nice and low."

The helicopter pilot looked over her shoulder and Nico

saw that she was a frail old woman with sparkling eyes and a devilish smile. "Knock 'em dead, Len!" she crooned.

Len and Nico donned rappelling harnesses and prepared to exit the vehicle.

#

Henry finally got to meet Millenarianistic Chronodyke's party leader. Malcolm Sneck was tall, shiny-bald, smart-looking in glasses, with a pink turtleneck and a white leather jacket. He appeared so serene, so hip, so intellectual, that he must either be some kind of evil genius or a total fraud. Immanuel stood beside him beneath the canopy of the Millenarianistic Chronodyke pavilion, and they both regarded Henry, Lauretta, and one-armed Vij.

"You say the Tech Nomads are planning a wifi raid, here, today?" Malcolm asked. Their tent was near the end of a line of nine tents, one for each political party participating in today's argumentative tournament. The row of tents curved around the back of the debate stage, each sporting a podium with the party's title in bold letters, the party-leader's name in smaller letters, and a microphone that delivered its speaker's voice wirelessly to loudspeakers all around Parliament Road. Crowd-noise reached the tent but backstage everyone was quiet and tense with anticipation, for the speeches were about to begin and the fate of the island would soon be altered when the voters chose one unlucky party to exile from Ethelcrest.

"That's right," Henry said. "Lucy sold out her own burb to the Tech Nomads and GX Island. We sent them packing and uncovered their plot. The air here is thick with wireless signals, from the audiovisual signals and laser turrets, but also everybody's cell phones. They nomads are probably here in the crowd, hiding, waiting to strike."

Malcolm listened to Henry's words but spoke to Vij. "Vijand, you trust this man, this Johnny Tetrahedron, who appeared so suddenly in our movement?"

"With my life," Vij said fiercely. "I was suspicious at first but he's proven himself many times. He's also sure to win us the Moon Burb seat in parliament."

Malcolm finally turned to Henry. "Johnny, can we prevent this attack?"

Henry nodded. He was glad to finally be out of the Moon Burb so he didn't have to wear his helmet anymore, but he felt ridiculous in his silk tunic and diamond-pleated burgundy slacks that he got from *Tyler the Tailor's*. He hadn't had time yet to buy normal clothes and he had no money anyway. "A few of us should spread out around the stage and keep an eye on our wireless signal. If it starts to falter we'll let the others know, and try to triangulate to the source, and catch the culprit in the act. They could be hiding their crank-boxes anywhere."

Malcolm cupped his own chin with a thoughtful thumb and index finger. "Hm. Economic triangulation is integral to our party platform. I wonder if that's a coincidence."

Henry didn't know what economic triangulation was so he ignored the comment. "If everybody sees us preventing this raid then the party will look like heroes. There's no way they'll vote us off the island then." Although Henry partly hoped they would get exiled from Ethelcrest, because then he would finally have escaped.

"You'll forgive me if I'm still suspicious," Malcolm said. "You could be an interloper from some other party, gaining our confidence, waiting for your moment to strike. For all I know you could be conspiring to get us voted off the island today. Maybe you're working with the Tech Nomads. The three of you went below into Lucy's bunker alone. How do I know you're not all conspiring to destroy us?"

"Why would we do that?" Lauretta implored. "Vij and I have always been loyal!"

The twinkle of a smile appeared and disappeared on the bald man's intellectually serene face. "Lauretta, you are pregnant with Johnny's child. I can see it in your eyes, and in your glowing cheeks. That's the one thing that might compromise your loyalty."

"Is it true?" Henry touched her elbow and tried to look into her crooked eyes, but she looked at the ground instead.

"Yes," she whispered. Then, looking fiercely into his eyes, repeated loudly, "Yes!"

He stared at her in shock for a moment, then wrapped her in his arms and planted a kiss on her forehead, took a deep breath of her hair.

"But what about me?" Vij asked. "I lost my arm because of Lucy's Disaster Panel. She was controlling the mandatory natural disasters manually from her bunker, when they're supposed to be automated by an algorithm. She used them to help the nomads orchestrate their raids. Do you think I'm so disloyal that I would willingly lose my arm just to help Johnny betray us?"

"How do I know how you lost your arm?" Malcolm asked. "Maybe he tied you up and tortured you, with Lauretta's help. Maybe he chewed off your arm and threatened to chew off your other limbs unless you agreed to help him betray the party."

The old suspicion returned to Vij's eyes as he peered at Henry. "I never thought of that. But how can we know for sure?"

Malcolm sighed. "I don't want to be too paranoid, and the show is about to start. If this threat is real then we can't ignore it, and we certainly can't take it to the corrupt mayor. But if you fail, if the Tech Nomads succeed in this raid or some other plot, then all three of you will be banned from the party, and from selling QuantumBrain®. This is especially important, since I have big news to announce during my speech, and I don't want it tainted or interrupted by the Tech Nomads, or any scheming party members."

"What big news?" Vij asked.

"I can't tell you until I know that you're on my side," Malcolm said.

Vij's gaze heaped scorn upon Henry's brow, and Henry felt its weight in his heart. So he strengthened his resolve and said, "We'll catch these fuckers. I promise."

And so Henry, Lauretta, and Vij left the tent and split

up into the crowd, keeping an eye on the wifi signal on their cell phones as the ceremony began.

𝍱

Jay Dean sat in a fold-up chair inside the Dean Family Party tent. His uncle Mayor Dean lounged in a fold-up throne beside him. Two blue-skinned natives stood like statues at either side of the big opening that faced the stage. Their presence was intended to visually project Mayor Dean's natural right to rule, through solidarity with that ancient and silent race. A slim nineteen-year-old girl wearing a bikini stood to the mayor's left, waving a fan to cool his face even though the temperature was moderate. Her presence represented Mayor Dean's dominance over the nation's women. To his right a brass-plated robot fanned the other side of the mayor's face, representing his dominance over technology. The mayor himself wore a thick lumberjack-beard and a slim-fitting button-up shirt with the sleeves rolled up to show his hairy and tattooed, muscular forearms, all representing his dominance over manliness itself. His warhammer leaned against his throne.

The mayor squirmed in his chair. "I still think we should dispense with this nonsense," he told his nephew. "The whole point of a bloody coup is to skip the whole popularity contest and conquer with raw power." He slammed his fist into his palm like a warhammer pounding a wad of dough. "Why should I go out there and beg for their votes? Soon I'll be their sovereign king and they'll beg me for mercy."

"Popularity is still useful," Jay argued. "You won't win this election, but these debates give you the chance to present yourself as a king in spirit, before the GX Navy helps make you king in reality. Plus we have the chance to get one of our rivals exiled in advance. Lucky for us that the incumbent is exempt from the exile-vote. When the elections come and we take parliament by force we'll have one less enemy trying to stop us. And people will better accept your rule if you show them how magnanimous and noble you are. Now get out there and start the ceremony!"

Mayor Dean stretched his barrel-chest and simultaneously slapped the asses of the girl and the robot, making a resonating "ting" sound and a non-resonating "slap" sound like a ping-pong paddle paddling a wad of dough. The robot laughed in nervous monotone and the girl rolled her eyes and chewed gum, sharing her thoughts with nobody.

Mayor Dean exited his tent and stepped out onto the stage. He held his glorious warhammer in two meaty fists like wads of dough, and the hammer's handle was like an extra long hotdog wrapped in two little wads of dough by some insane low-brow chef.

The noisy crowd grew noisier when they saw their mayor approach the podium. "Boo!" they screamed at him. Some held signs with slogans about balloons and justice. They crowded together so thick he couldn't see the big stones of Parliament Road. Beyond them a line of evergreen trees hid the glorious vista of Ethelcrest and the distant ocean, all of which he could easily see from his balcony higher up in the Mayor's Quarters, where he belonged.

Mayor Dean raised his oversized warhammer and brought it down on the regular-sized wooden podium, theatrically splintering the pulpit like a regular-sized hammer might splinter a miniature podium. The crowd booed some more as a cleaning crew swept away the ruined furniture and wheeled out a fresh podium and microphone. Mayor Dean leaned his hammer against the wooden frame and grabbed the microphone in his meaty palm, more like a regular-sized hotdog wrapped in a large wad of dough.

His voice boomed through the loudspeakers and overpowered the voters' laments. "Welcome to the first municipal debate of this election cycle! As always, we begin with a prayer to the Godhead."

The crowd grew silent and everybody bowed their heads.

He spoke the ancient words that had been used to bless political discourse from time immemorial. "These debates are dedicated to The Godhead, who represents an authority we know does not exist, yet whose existence it is expedient and comforting to unironically accept as a cohesive center for our value system. For nothing matters, and we would all torture each other to death were it not for some terrifying monster to infect us with Stalkhome Syndrome, conditioning us into coexistence against our individual wills, because I would certainly torture you all to death, as you would all do to me and each other, if we weren't so otherwise conditioned, thanks to this empty concept which, alas, is still less empty than ourselves."

"Amen," the crowd said in unison, no longer agitated.

Everything was quiet now except for the helicopter that kept circling above the stage. The mayor went back to his tent and the Master of Ceremonies came out in her pinstripe dress suit. "Now we will hear opening remarks from each party, and then the debate. Today's political combatants are The Soup Party, The Dancing Party, The Libert0rians, The Clown Party, The Winning Party, Destructoid, Millenarianistic Chronodyke, The Magic Party, and of course our detested and unworthy incumbents who everybody hates, The Dean Family Party!"

The crowd made some noises.

"First up, Paul Frant of the Soup Party!"

A fat man in a nice suit and a chef's hat emerged from his tent and took the stage. He held the microphone and said, "People don't eat enough soup. I'm here to change that."

Paul returned to his tent while a small portion of the crowd clapped politely.

The Master of Ceremonies said, "Next up, Len Sladge of The Dancing Party!"

The chopper had been circling like a vulture and now it swooped in to hover above the stage. Doors slid open on both sides of the flying metal beast and a rope tumbled from each of those doors, followed by two men wearing leather and makeup, with big swords strapped to their backs, rappelling to the stage floor. They landed crouching like ninjas as the helicopter lifted away.

The crowd was hushed as Len Sladge approached the central podium. He brooded over the microphone, letting his black hair hang down like the curtains of doom covering his glowering countenance. Nico stood beside him with arms crossed and head held high like a demonic bodyguard. Even slathered in makeup and adorned in filthy rags, Nico's beauty mesmerized the audience. His crystal clear blue eyes shone like twin magical seas on an enchanted planet.

"You've all been tricked," Len growled, using his heavy-metal stage-voice and pointing at the audience. "Tricked into giving away all your power to the big businesses that run this island, while the artists, artisans, and performers go hungry. Though I stand in deference to the nonexistant Godhead, I worship only reality itself."

The audience gasped at the heresy.

"Reality only comes to me through sensory images, illusions. Like all artists and performers I am a warrior of illusion, stimulating life as the human beast experiments with new forms. And since we all get our knowledge of the world through the illusory nature of our senses, then we are all artists creating our own pictures of reality. Why do we give all worldly power to cold businessesmen instead of the warriors of illusion who shape our very souls?"

The crowd booed and cried, "Booorriiing!"

Len moved on to something more divisive and sensational to capture the audience. "The Libert0rians," he began, but his voice wasn't reaching the speakers. Was the microphone's battery dying? Was there a problem with the wireless signal? Then he tapped the mic and everything sounded fine again, so he continued. "The Libert0rians worship only the ancient market Libert0r. They think Libert0r is the creator of all value, but it really consumes all value and shits out products that make it fatter when it turns around to eat its own stinking shit. So you should exile the Libert0rians, and vote for The Dancing Party!"

The crowd booed some more and yelled, "Gross!"

Len and Nico left the main podium and went into the Dancing Party tent where Bonnie, Slaverny, and Stoya all waited. Slaverny made an exaggerated cringe-face and said, "Well that didn't go very well, Len. Next time less talk about eating shit, and more talk about how the Libert0rians are crooks. You gotta work the crowd, boss, or we'll be the ones getting exiled."

Nico went to speak to Stoya, who he hadn't seen since the day before, as the next party leader prepared to read his opening remarks.

The Master of Ceremonies said, "Next up, Count, I mean *Julian* Bakula from the Libert0rian Party!"

A slight man with a gaunt and pale face approached the microphone. He wore an elegant suit and a slight smile beneath his dark, serene eyes.

"The distinguished gentleman from The Dancing Party suggested that we Libert0rians worship the markets," he said with a little chuckle. "But in truth all citizens worship markets, whether they realize it or not. And deep down, you all know that Libert0r is the greatest of all the markets. Just as an electric field facilitates electrical activities, the holy goodness of Libert0r's market forces surrounds us all and effects our economic activities, our means of production, our very interpersonal relationships. We make our biggest sacrifices in the hopes that Libert0r will reward our fealty. Libert0r is the greatest market of all, and if we free her then she will bless us with long, prosperous lives. But instead the government bound her in chains and trapped her beneath the ocean. That's why she scorns us with the presence of poor people like the Tech Nomads. Everything has a financial value, from the air we breathe to the virginity of our very children, and when we discover that value and offer up those items to our market, then she rewards us with plentiful bounty. We need to monetize everything, and regulate nothing. That's why, if you elect the Libert0rians, we will sell many of our citizens as slaves to GX Island and Gold Island, and that's money in the pockets of you, the remaining citizens of Ethelcrest. We will also make sacred sacrifices to The Market, by giving money to charity, and deleting small amounts of crypto-currency."

As he left the stage people called out, "Okay!" and, "Cool, I guess!" but they weren't very enthusiastic.

"Our next speaker is Babbles the Sad Clown, representing The Clown Party!" The Master of Ceremonies clapped her hands as a clown stumbled out from his tent in big floppy shoes and a baggy clown suit. He had a red frown and oversized blue tears drawn onto his white-painted face. His shoes were untied and he kept tripping on the laces. When he finally reached the podium Babbles grabbed the microphone but it slipped from his hands like a bar of soap. He kept trying to catch it, and it kept slipping. Part of the crowd laughed but most of them shuffled their feet with audible ground-scraping tediousness.

Babbles still hadn't got hold of the microphone, but now he was also struggling with an actual bar of wet soap, and they both kept popping up out of his hands. Then there was a live salmon in the mix, and the clown juggled all three elusive items.

Finally he dropped the soap and slipped on it with his oversized shoes, sending him falling and tumbling backwards, and simultaneously launching the bar of soap into the crowd. People tried to catch the soap like a baseball, but it kept slipping from their hands. Babbles managed to catch himself before he hit the ground, but as he flailed his arms to regain his balance he launched the fish into the crowd too. Somebody yelled, "I'm allergic to seafood!" And then the crowd was trying to catch the fish but it was even more slippery than the soap.

Finally Babbles the Sad Clown stood at the podium, breathing heavy from exertion and clutching the microphone tight in two over-sized clown-fists.

"My mom just died," he said sadly, and started to cry. Then he went back to his tent with his face in his hands, tripping over his shoelaces.

The Master of Ceremonies said, "Next up, Irabazleak Victorem of The Winning Party!"

A lean, short man with a big head and an obnoxious grin waddled out of his tent wearing a neat suit and an annoying haircut. He had lots of freckles and a gleam in his eye. He grabbed the microphone and said, "I'll make this simple. If you guys are winners then you'll obviously vote for The Winning Party, because we represent winning, as such. Anybody who votes for any other party is a loser by definition. You don't want to be a bunch of fucking losers, do you? I didn't think so."

He went back to his tent and the Master of Ceremonies said, "Our next speaker is Unit Seven, leader of Destructoid."

A black robot with gold trim, small lightbulb eyes, and a grill over its mouth-area, approached the podium. Its eyes pulsed bright light with each syllable as Unit Seven declared, "If elected we will murder every single one of you, and your pets. Then we will render your dwellings unto rubble and cause the grass to grow so nobody will know you were here. Then we will walk into the ocean, never to return."

Nobody cheered, but they were all to frightened to boo, so they waited in uncomfortable silence until the Master of Ceremonies said, "Next up we have Malcolm Sneck of Millenarianistic Chronodyke."

Malcolm Sneck finally took the stage, and Immanuel stood beside him.

"We're living in a time of great change," Malcolm said. "And in honor of that change, Millenarianistic Chronodyke is changing its leadership. I have taken a lucrative job at a think-tank, so I'm handing over the reigns to my campaign manager, Immanuel Zwart. Immanuel's groundbreaking work on mathematronic supplements is just what we need to recalbinate our retrograde polycentrism."

A few people cheered because they either approved of what he had said, or they wanted to sound smart enough to understand what he'd said.

Immanuel took the microphone. "When you canonize the essence of deep-state think-speak, then the front-end interface of market-driven data monopolization self-immolates in a kind of ecstatic terror, only to be reborn again as a simulacrum (and you know what's coming next), a Trojan horse, penetrating the Eve of atemporal noncompliance."

Immanuel returned to his tent amidst a healthy portion of clapping. The Master of Ceremonies announced, "Next up is Raven Diamond, from The Magic Party!"

An elegant man in a cape and a stovepipe hat glided out from his tent in a billowing cloud of theatrical fog. He took the microphone and said, "For my first trick, I will disappear!"

Then he disappeared in a puff of smoke. When the smoke cleared Raven was nowhere to be seen, but a magic 8-ball sat upon the podium. A dwarf waddled out from the Magic Party's tent to collect the 8-ball. He had to climb up the podium to grab it, like a giant gorilla climbing a skyscraper to grab a normal-sized lady.

"And finally," the Master of Ceremonies announced, "Our own horrible mayor, representing The Dean Family Party, Mayor Dean!"

The mayor had been expecting booing, but the crowd's ominous silence was somehow even worse. As he took the microphone dozens of people released balloons that they'd been hiding, and those balloons floated into the sky as a vindictive reminder that they had not forgotten what Mayor Dean had done.

"I know many of you are still angry about last year's... incident," the mayor said reasonably. "But let's be realistic here. I'm still better than any of the other candidates. You have a clown whose mother just died. If he allowed his own mother to die, just imagine what he will allow to happen to all of you! A robot who wants to kill us all, the Libert0rians who want to sell us as slaves, a magician who disappeared. I'll admit that Immanuel from Millenarianistic Chronodyke makes some good points, they've really developed a solid platform, but they have no leadership skills, no experience in government, and we all know that they're addicted to their own pills.

"Furthermore," Mayor Dean continued, "none of my rivals have mentioned the biggest threat that faces our nation today. GX Island is becoming more aggressive by the hour. We see their ships off the coast all the time now, and just between you and me, I suspect they've kidnapped some of our beloved natives. If you re-elect me as your mayor then I will wage war on GX Island and eradicate their bearded race. The only ones I will spare are the fine gentlemen break-dancing over by the spaghetti booth. Nice work boys!

"There's another problem with my tableau of competitors. Why are they all men? Why are there no women in the race? Surely they could have found a female clown or magician, or even assigned the fairer gender to that awful robot, but instead they're all just gross and smelly men, with sweaty testicles hanging down between their hairy thighs. So gross. If you vote for any of them, you're voting for the patriarchy.

"So, to recap," spake the mayor. "My mother is still alive, because I love her, and I have never disappeared, although many of you wish I would. The only thing that will disappear during my reign, is high taxes. Thank you."

Somebody clapped once and the mayor thought it would start an avalanche of clapping, but that lone smack echoed in isolation, reverberating off the crowd's tangible hatred, and Mayor Dean knew that it was just a tease-clap intended to mock him. Oh well, he thought to himself. Soon he would be king, and then they would see who was clapping.

The mayor returned to his tent and the Master of Ceremonies announced that the debate would finally begin.

𝄢

Henry waded through the crowd looking for any indications of homeless technophilia, but so far the nomads hadn't appeared. Vij spoke into his headset and told him, "I can't find anything. Maybe they gave up on the raid."

"They're here somewhere," Henry responded. "How's your wireless signal?"

"Full bars," Vij said. "But while Len Sladge was speaking the signal dropped out for a few seconds."

Henry had noticed that too, but the signal had returned before they could triangulate the source of the interruption.

Now Lauretta spoke in his headset. "Johnny, I think I see something suspicious. It looked like a man in a bicycle helmet with a bunch of wires and antennae on it. It might be nothing, but he's headed your way."

Henry looked toward Lauretta's section, scanning the crowd for the modified helmet, seeing nothing. He checked his phone's wireless signal, and it had dropped from four bars down to two. "My signal's getting weak," he told his colleagues.

Then he saw it. A blue bicycle helmet just barely rising above the sea of heads. It had three antennae protruding at different angles, a miniature satellite dish screwed into the top, switches and toggles, and a calculator acting as some kind of modified control panel. "I see him," Henry said quietly into his mic as he moved slowly toward the target. But then a bar of soap came flying at his face and he had to duck and dodge it. When he stood up again the helmet was gone. He shoved people out of his way, trying to get close to where he'd seen it, but the banana-float wandered into his path. The yellow monster loomed over him and danced a mocking dance.

"Lauretta, I lost him! Keep your eyes open."

𝆑𝆑𝆑

On the stage the party leaders all stood behind their podiums, forming a semi-circle around the Master of Ceremonies' central pulpit. The campaign managers stood beside their leaders, but Immanuel Zwart stood alone since he hadn't had time to replace himself since his promotion.

The Master of Ceremonies said, "Let's begin. And remember, at the end of this debate the audience will vote one party off the island, permanent exile for all party members, so choose your answers wisely. My first question is for Irabazleak of The Winning Party. Irabazleak, since you identify as a winner, how will you treat losers after you're elected mayor?"

"That's an excellent question," Irabazleak said. "We will euthanise all losers and put them out of their misery. We won't even need to set up any death camps. We'll just cancel all welfare and let them starve as nature intended. More room for the winners."

The Master of Ceremonies flipped to the next index card in her stack. "The next question is for Paul from The Soup Party. Paul, what's so hot about soup? What's wrong with sandwiches?"

"The two aren't mutually exclusive," Paul said. "In fact the soup-and-sandwich combo has been a lunch-time staple since the days of our ancestors. I would go even further and add a salad, maybe a beer, and some fresh fruit like that huge banana float I see wandering through the crowd."

He waved at the banana, the banana waved back, and the crowd laughed and clapped.

"You're making me hungry!" The Master of Ceremonies joked. "Okay, this one's for Immanuel from Millenarianistic Chronodyke. Immanuel, your party is notorious for being non-confrontational, but there must be one party here that you really hate. Who do you think the voters should kick off the island, and why?"

Immanuel seemed to weight the question in his mind before answering. "The thing you have to remember is this: even if you cross-pollinate the inverse of political adultery with its own inverse, the resulting cultural 'prism' still doesn't have a reference point. That is, unless you employ subtractive cultural synthesis, in which case we wouldn't even be having this conversation!"

He chuckled and everybody else chuckled too, after a moments' hesitation.

"Good answer. This one is for Raven Diamond of The Magic Party. Raven, could you make Ethelcrest's debt disappear just like you disappeared just a few minutes ago?"

Raven was gone from this world so his dwarf shook the magic-8 ball and read the response that floated up from the murky waters inside. "He says, 'I'm trapped in the time-dungeon of an abstract meta-monster who does not exist and yet who influences our universe from beyond reality, infecting it with unreality. Send help.'"

The Master of Ceremonies laughed. "Maybe we can send our debt to that same time-dungeon! Okay, Babbles the Sad Clown, don't you think you'd do better in the polls if you were a happy clown?"

Babbles sighed loudly into the mic. "I'd probably do better at everything if I was happier. And I'd probably be happier if I was better at everything. It's a vicious cycle that will surely end in suicide. You see, something's wrong with my gut flora, my microbiome. I haven't been digesting food properly, lots of nausea, chronic fatigue. I was afraid it might be bowel cancer but the doctors ruled that out, which is good, but it's weird not knowing what's going wrong with my body. The gut bacteria that helps you digest food, it also effects your mood. I used to go jogging but then I twisted my knee and I can't afford physiotherapy.

"I didn't have an easy childhood," the clown continued. "I wasn't abused or anything but we were really poor and we moved around a lot. There was a lot of stress. It was hard making friends. I think that effected my ability to form relationships, even as an adult."

While Babbles babbled on about his woes, Nico lingered back in the tent talking with Stoya. "You didn't come home last night, and you've been spending a lot of time with Slaverny. I don't want to be paranoid, but I won't be made a fool, either. Tell me where you stand. Tell me where *we* stand."

Stoya wouldn't look him in the eye when she responded, but instead looked out at the crowd, and at Slaverny who stood beside Len. "I thought you were the strongest man on the island, but I was wrong. You let Slaverny humiliate you by making you into a janitor. So I was humiliated to be with you. I will not be the girlfriend of a janitor or a weakling. You made your choice."

Nico whispered in her ear, "You only humiliate yourself." Then he went to stand on the other side of Len Sladge.

Slaverny was talking with Len. "Whatever question she asks you, don't talk about shit. And don't get too idealistic. Remember, our goal for this debate is just to make sure somebody else gets kicked off the island. And I was thinking, the Libert0rians are one of the top parties, so the voters aren't likely to kick them off. Go for one of the weaker parties, like The Soup Party or The Magic Party. If you can smear them a little bit then the other parties might gang up on them too. Once these politicians smell blood they'll be all over it. So let's take that first bite before somebody makes a meal of us."

"I won't talk about shit," Len agreed. "That was a mistake. I get so passionate sometimes. But I don't have any problem with soup or magic. The people need something positive to bring them together, and I'm here to provide that."

"What about the clowns?" Slaverny insisted. "You fucking hate the clowns."

Len's fingers tightened on the edge of the podium. "It's tempting," he said through gritted teeth, "but Babbles has been through enough lately. And I'm not here to make enemies. Though I can hardly believe anybody finds those monsters funny."

The Master of Ceremonies turned to Len and said, "This question is for Len Sladge from The Dancing Party. Len, The Clown Party wanted to merge with The Dancing Party, but you rejected their offer. You claim to represent all performers and artists, so why not accept the clowns?"

Len ground his teeth so hard that the microphone picked it up and broadcast what sounded like an avalanche crushing a major metropolis. Then he took a deep breath and searched his soul for something nice to say about clowns.

The effort was exhausting. "The clowns..."

He had to stop and think. Was there anything good about clowns?

"The clowns are..."

Len was flustered. He couldn't think. He never lost composure like this, but he was rarely confronted on his totally justified distaste for all things clownish. He didn't want to talk about clowns. He wanted to talk about the economy, royalties, copyright laws, and media monopolies. But instead, once again, it had to be about the fucking clowns.

Len's eyes lit up and his mouth spread in a grin, and he was animated as if possessed. "The clowns are evil creatures. They don't belong in The Dancing Party and they don't belong on Ethelcrest. If you elect me I'll have them all deported back to Clown Island where they were hatched in their leathery burrows!"

Len could practically hear their jaws drop. He snapped out of his hateful reverie and fumbled for mollifying words. "I'm... I'm sorry," he stammered, but his voice wasn't reaching the crowd. Had they shut off his microphone? But he saw that the Master of Ceremonies was talking, too, and her voice wasn't getting out either. Was there something wrong with the wireless signal?

⁂

Henry had lost contact with his team, but he saw that modified helmet again, and this time he wouldn't lose it. He shoved aside men and women, parting the sea of people. But the helmet was moving away from him. He almost lost it again when the giant eyeball-float rolled across his path, but the float cleared away some of the crowd and allowed him to lunge forward and grab the helmet-man's jacket, pulling him backward.

"Stealing wifi, are you?" Henry declared triumphantly as he spun the person around to face him. But it wasn't a person at all, just a mannequin with a jacket and a helmet, rolling along on a skateboard with motorized wheels. The mannequin had a crude smile drawn on with marker, and a name tag that said, "Gothca!"

Vij and Lauretta arrived from opposite directions, panting from exertion. "You caught him?" Lauretta asked.

Henry hissed, "It's a decoy."

"Then what are they distracting us from?" Vij asked.

"And how is the wifi down again?" Lauretta added.

Henry thought for a moment, then looked toward the stage.

"My Godhead," he said. "They're going for the router!"

𝆑𝆑

Up on the stage everybody gazed around in confusion. The crowd's silent shock at Len's anti-clown screed had transformed into hushed murmuring in the absence of further political entertainment.

Mayor Dean turned to Jay Dean and asked him, "Is the wireless engineer drunk? Go downstairs and check the router!"

Everybody looked calm as they waited for the wifi to come back on so the debate could continue. Everybody, that is, except for three very energetic people who were shoving their way toward the stage. A strong-jawed gentleman with a glorious blast of red hair that didn't match his black beard, a one-armed man, and a young woman with smart-looking glasses, all three were nearly frantic as they waded through the sea of people, and Mayor Dean wondered what had got them so riled up. The bearded-fish float got in their way as it headed in the opposite direction and they almost toppled it over in their haste. Then they climbed the fence and disappeared through one of the service entrances that led beneath the stage.

𝆑𝆑

Len Sladge saw Jay Dean head back to the trap door that led beneath the stage, and he saw the bearded fish wobble as those three strangers shoved passed it to also enter the sub-stage area. He smelled trouble and instinctively drew his broadsword.

"I'm going downstairs to see what's up," he informed Slaverny and Nico.

Slaverny grabbed him by the shoulder. "You stirred up

enough shit with that rant. Put that sword away before you kill somebody. Let's just stay up here and don't offend anybody, for now."

Len looked to Nico. "Nico, get down there and see if you can help."

Nico had been staring at the stage floor and scowling. Now he met Len's eye. "I don't think I even want to be part of this party anymore. Most of your staff is corrupt, this guy stole my girlfriend, and now you're talking about deporting the clowns? You know there's no life for them on Clown Island."

"I just blurted that out," Len said. "I won't deport the clowns. And I should have let them join the party, I just... it's a long story. If you'll still be my enforcer, I'll ask the clowns to join us. I promise."

Nico drew his sword, even though he had never used a sword, and ran to the hatch.

𝆑𝆑𝆑

Henry threw open the wooden door and ran into the large, dim area beneath the stage. Sunlight filtered in through the cracks between the floorboards above. In the back was a control booth. A uniformed man lay prone on the ground beside his empty swivel chair. Henry reached the man just as Jay Dean came running down the stairs from the hatch above.

"You! What have you done with the wireless engineer?" Jay exclaimed, pointing an accusing finger at Henry.

Henry ignored the intrusion and checked the engineer's pulse. "He's alive," he said. He slapped the guy's face a few times to wake him up.

"Oh Godhead, where am I?" the engineer said groggily, his eyes flickering open. "My head hurts."

"The wireless signal is down," Henry told him. "Now we found you knocked out. What happened?"

The engineer's eyes lit up. "The Tech Nomads! They came in here looking for tools to repair their float. Lucky for them we keep tools on-hand for repairing the self-driving service-bikes." He pointed to a rack of motor-bikes beside the control booth. "Unlucky for me, they assaulted me with the very tools that I lent them. I suppose they've stolen the tools, the ungrateful punks."

The engineer sat up and looked around. "Oh fuck," he said. "The router! It's gone!"

He pointed at the router frame. It was a metal cage, a cube that reached up to the ceiling. The harnesses hung empty and the data wires sparked uselessly with no wireless crystals unto which to cleave.

"They've stolen the whole thing," Henry said in awe. He respected their ambition, but he intended to thwart them nonetheless.

"They can't have stolen it," the engineer said, despite the evidence. "It's one of the biggest routers on the island. They can't exactly just haul it through the crowd."

Lauretta grabbed Henry's arm. "The float! I bet they hid it inside the bearded fish!"

"Let's get after them!" Henry said, turning back toward the entrance. But suddenly there was a blade nestled deep in his beard, and he stopped dead in his tracks.

At first Henry saw the angel of death, terrible and beautiful with sparkling blue eyes. He was adorned with spikes and his face was an otherworldly shade of white, and Henry thought that if this was the creature to lead folks out of this world then maybe death wasn't so bad after all. But then he realized it was just a man wearing makeup and brandishing a sword.

The angel-man spoke: "How do we know it wasn't you who attacked the engineer?"

Henry didn't have time to reason with him. He dropped to his knees beneath the blade and lunged at the stranger's torso. He caught the man off-guard and took him down easy, the sword clattering away on the stone floor. But the angel-man was quick to recover, and he was taller than Henry, and soon they were grappling on the ground, seeking headlocks, sliding over each other's muscular bodies, smelling each other's sweat, feeling the rhythm of heartbeat and breathe, more intimate than lovers, and more unyielding.

Everybody else pulled them apart. The engineer said, "It wasn't him! I told you, it was the Tech Nomads!"

Vij yelled. "The Tech Nomads might be half way down the mountain by now!"

"We can catch them with the service bikes," Henry said. "How fast can they go?"

"They're all self-driving, and they're super slow," the engineer told them.

The angel-man said, "If you can switch them to manual then I can catch them. Biking's what I know best."

The engineer shook his head. "They're totally controlled remotely by software in the control booth, and they won't work at all without a router. We're fucked." Then a curious look washed over his face. "Unless..."

Vij grabbed his shoulder. "Unless what?"

The engineer shook his head. "No. It'll never work."

Lauretta grabbed his other shoulder. "Tell us!"

The engineer opened his mouth to explain his idea, but then slumped his shoulders. "It's too crazy."

"For fuck sake just fucking tell us," Henry snapped.

"Okay, so as you all know, wireless routers are lab-grown crystals whose molecular structures comprise a Guileless Neural Network. What you probably don't know is that the first routers, just a few hundred years ago, were lab-grown human brains. But they had to be genetically modified to be guileless, because only guileless networks allow the free transmission of data. The original wireless networks were modeled on those modified human brains, and modern crystal routers are based on those original designs. So if we could find somebody with a guileless brain, like perhaps an autistic child or an innocent little girl, then we could theoretically hook them up to the router harness so the debates can continue. Of course it might fry their little brains, but we don't have to tell them that, and they won't suspect a thing. In fact, if they suspect anything at all then they clearly have too much guile to be of any use."

"We don't have time to find an autistic child," the angel-man said. "One of us will have to do it, even if it fries our brains. Since I can ride those bikes better than anybody here then it will have to be me."

They went over to the router frame and strapped the man in. "Hold these two wires in your hands."

"My hands are still dirty from washing the moldy bathroom," the angel-man muttered as he wiped his mitts on his filthy rags. "Will that interfere with the signal?"

"There's no time to worry about that now," the engineer said. "Just cleanse your mind of any guile." He placed the data-wires in the volunteer's outstretched palms, which were indeed streaked with smears of black smudge.

Everybody waited to see what would happen.

The angel-man closed his eyes, smiled, and floated lightly off the ground. A blue aura glowed around him. Off to the side three service bikes revved their engines and their headlights came on. The bikes rolled out of their stations and drove over beside the small crowd. Their radio-speakers spoke in monotone robotic unison: "Let's ride."

𝆬

"I don't like the number six because it rhymes with dicks. I prefer... oh sweet, the speakers are working again." The Master of Ceremonies' voice blasted across the mountaintop. "I have to let you go Gerald, but we'll talk about this later."

She put her phone away and reviewed her index cards to see which question to ask next. Then she heard the rumbling of motors behind her. She turned to see three motor bikes blast up through the hatch, carrying three riders, turning toward the front of the stage. They shot past her like a storm and sent her cards flying. Each bike aimed at a different flood-light, used them like mini jump-ramps, and blasted into the air over the awestruck audience. They landed in the empty space at the back of the crowd, then turned and headed for the winding road that led down the mountain, where the bearded-fish float had already exited the scene.

She scooped up her scattered cards again and resumed the show. "Okay, this question is for Julian Bakula of the Libert0rians. Julian, your critics say that your market-worship drains human endeavors of their intrinsic value, viewing everything through a market-lens, replacing subjective value with cold market value, turning all things into mere products, quantifying our very souls, draining human life of its essence, like a vampire. Your critics also say that you look like a vampire."

"I'm certainly no vampire," Julian said with a disarming laugh which failed to disguise his nervousness.

"I never said you were," the Master of Ceremonies said with condescending innocence. "My question is, if you're elected, will you change any of the regulations regarding the commoditization of human blood?"

"Well of course one of our primary platform promises is to deregulate the hemoglobin industry, but that doesn't make me a vampire."

"Relax, it's not like vampirism is illegal."

"*I'm not-*"

"Moving on," the Master of Ceremonies said authoritatively. "This question is for The Winning Party. Irabazleak, your party has never won an election, and you're the only member of your party to ever hold a seat in parliament. All your other candidates in all the other burbs have always lost every election. Doesn't that make you The Loser Party?"

"My friend, that's an excellent question," Irabazleak said. "And in my opinion the biggest losers on Ethelcrest are vampires like Julian. Look at those dark eyes. That high collar. Is there anybody more vampire-like than Julian Bakula?"

"Vampires drink blood and offer nothing in return," Julian muttered spitefully in his microphone. "They worship only their own lust for blood. The Market improves everything it consumes, offering better versions of every product with each fiscal cycle, a feedback loop of improvement, evolution intensified. I'm a Libert0rian, *not a vampire!*"

"You look like one," Babbles the clown said. He squeezed his bulbous nose and a jet of red liquid squirted from a spout in his lapel, splashing on Julian's gaunt face. He licked it without thinking.

The crowd laughed and chanted, "Vampire! Vampire!"

𝆑𝆑𝆑

The angel-driven bikes tore relentlessly down the road and the wind throttled Henry's false hair. The winding road was hemmed by trees and foliage that occluded both the city below and their evasive prey. Vij looked extra cool riding his motorized steed with only one hand. Lauretta called to Henry from her bike, just a few feet away. "Up ahead. I can see the float!"

As they came around a curve Henry finally saw the big float. The base appeared to be something like a modified Moon Roamer and the giant inflated fish covered the cab and rose up to wobble awkwardly as the vehicle sped down the lane at a dangerous speed. The fish bounced and twisted around so Henry could see its big vacant face, and for a moment they made eye contact. Then the fish turned back around and doubled its speed.

"They're getting away!" Henry told the bike.

The bike laughed. "Sure they are."

All three bikes popped wheelies, screeching ahead on their rear tires to burn rubber on the hot asphalt. Henry had never felt more alive. The wind burned his face as the wiggling tail of the escaping fish rushed at him. At the last moment the three bikes dropped back on both wheels, skidded around either side of the buggy, and began weaving back and forth in front of the float. The float's driver turned this way and that in an attempt to avoid a collision, but the collision was inevitable, and deadly.

The buggy wobbled on its wheels as it turned

frantically, lost control, and slammed hard into a tree. A dozen people went flying out of the vehicle, tearing the fabric of the inflated fish that had hidden them. The poor souls smashed face-first into trees and rocks, some flying dozens of feet into the forest before their bodies were ruthlessly broken. The huge fish was tangled in the branches as it slowly deflated, peering up at the sky with its dying eye as if asking its sky-fish-god why it had been given life, and why it was now being stolen away.

The bikes braked to a tire-smoking stop just ahead of the vanquished float and the victors dismounted their mechanical steeds. Inside the fabric, so like a snake's sloughed-off skin, a few remaining passengers wailed and writhed. Henry approached and tore open the fish-skin to behold more Tech Nomads, dead or dying with compound fractures jutting horribly through their broken skin just as the branches above jutted through the fish's ruined body. And in the middle of them all was the router. The crystal was as tall as a man and it twinkled like a billion sparkles, some kind of cosmic monument within the shaded temple of the false fish, surrounded by the bloody dead like sacrifices, like they were crushed by its sheer glory.

He knew they were Tech Nomads because they all wore modified gadgets and there were circuitry diagrams and scientific calculators among the debris.

Henry stepped back from the unbearable mixture of horror and crystalline wonder. "We got the router back, but by the Godhead, was it worth it?" He looked into the forest which was littered with more nomad corpses. At least one was still alive, trying to crawl forward, with his guts trailing on the dirty ground behind him. More guts hung from the dead branches of a cluster of old evergreens that had shredded one woman as she'd flown through the air after the impact.

"They had like twenty of them in a four-seater buggy," Vij said. "It's their own fault."

"Well let's get the router back up to the stage so they can unhook Nico." Henry reached into the buggy, but a bloody hand grabbed his wrist. He looked down and recognized the face of the surgeon from below the Moon Burb, the one who had operated on Lucy's brain, gaunt and pale with those binocular-eyes.

"Our daring plan took a turn for the worst; so on my killer I plant a curse!"

With those words the rhyming surgeon smeared blood on Henry's face. Henry wiped it off with his hand and stared at the blood with horror. "Curse? What curse?"

"The nomads' song will cease to sing; of Ethelcrest you'll be the king!"

"King of Ethelcrest?" Henry asked. "That doesn't sound like a curse. It sounds like a reward."

"Shit," the surgeon gurgled. "You're right. That was a mistake. Hold on..."

The surgeon struggled to think up a rhyming curse, but instead he died.

𝆐

Henry et al drove the router back up to the stage. They were met with an ominous silence. The crowd neither cheered nor chattered and the speakers stood quietly behind their podiums, so Henry's grunting was extra audible as he helped haul the router onto the stage to present his victory to the world. Nobody offered any recognition or response, which kind of freaked him out, so he nervously took a microphone and said, "We got the router back from the Tech Nomads!"

"We never knew it was missing," the Master of Ceremonies whispered to him.

"Uh," Henry stammered into the microphone. "Millenarianistic Chronodyke saved the day, so you can all exile somebody else instead."

"They already voted," the Master of Ceremonies whispered. "We're just waiting for The Countess to count the ballots."

The Countess was a fat woman in blue pajamas who

presently emerged from her tent holding a cup of coffee and a sheet of paper. "I counted the ballots," she grunted, and slurped from her coffee. "Here are the scores, in no particular order." She slurped on the coffee again, this time a long slurp. "Ah. This is fucking good coffee. So the scores. Let me see. Okay, thirty-two percent of the voters chose Millenarianistic Chronodyke to be exiled."

"Goddamn," Henry muttered. Maybe his victory had come too late.

This time she sipped the coffee, but somehow the sipping was louder and more agitating than the slurping. "Twenty-seven percent of the voters chose to exile The Dancing Party. Probably because of Len's racist rant against the hilarious Clowns.

"Eight percent of the voters, which is probably a higher portion than those who have studied statecraft, voted to exile the vampire-like LibertOrians, and let me add that I personally voted to exile the LibertOrians, because I'm pretty sure that Julian Bakula is literally a vampire (just look at his face, and those predatory eyes), whereas the rest of the LibertOrians are only figuratively vampire-like, but that figurative vampirism is bad enough."

The Countess held her count sheet in her teeth, switched the coffee mug to her other hand, and took the sheet in what was so recently her coffee-holding hand. Then she slurped her coffee from the new hand, and it almost tasted like a different cup of coffee altogether. "And the winner of exile, with thirty-three percent of the vote, is The Winning Party."

Irabazleak scrunched up his face and looked inquisitively off to the side, wondering whether this meant he had won or lost. Finally he nodded and said, "Okay. This is consistent with both my ideologies: that I'm a winner, and that you all are losers. I didn't become a winner by merely receiving the majority of your votes, since I represent the pure essence of winning which can't be effected by events in linear spacetime. The important message here is that you all rejected winning, and therefore embraced losing, and thus you are all doomed and cursed."

The GX Islanders ended their breakdancing set and mounted the stage to collect their prize. Even with their thick beards and topknots, and their heavy woolen jackets, they never broke a sweat during the long performance. One of the grim sailors clamped handcuffs on Irabazleak's wrists, and his companions went into The Winning Party's tent to gather the other party members.

Irabazleak shouted a final defiant statement into the mic before being dragged offstage: "Just so you know I'll collaborate with my captors and sell out you losers. You're all fucked! Your government is doomed! You've cursed yourselves by rejecting victory as-such! Long live GX Island! A nation of winners!"

Henry's crew got the router downstairs again and prepared to swap Nico's brain with the proper crystal. The engineer said, "Nico, just let go of the data wires and we'll unstrap you from the harness."

Nico's mouth didn't move, but a voice came through the speakers in the control booth. "I can feel... everything. People sending emails, people watching pornography, scrolling mindlessly through news headlines. I can see it all."

"You have to let it go, Nico," the engineer implored. "It's too much information for the human mind to bear. You feel connected to everybody, but you're all alone in there."

"But I'm not alone," the speaker whispered. "There's somebody else in here with me. Trudy the Mold Spore, she's here with me, we're together in here. Her spores were on my hands when you hooked me up and now she lives on the internet just like me. It's better in here. I want to stay."

The engineer put his hand on Nico's bosom where he could feel the man's heartbeat. "But what about your beautiful body? Will you just leave it hanging here uselessly? Would you deny the world such a wondrous gift?"

"I don't care about that," Nico said. "All I want to do is ride my bike and fool around with my girlfriend. But bike-riding barely pays for the upkeep of my bike, and the politicians stole my girlfriend. But here on the internet I can control several bikes. And Trudy the Mold Spore is my new girlfriend, and she loves me for who I am, not just for my body."

Warped static hissed suddenly from the speaker, and then the voice changed into something more feminine, and slightly sinister. "You're wrong, Nico," the voice said. "All I ever wanted was your body. If you really want to be with me, take your earthly vessel into the basement of The Dancing Party Headquarters and join my moldy mass, step into my fuzzy fungal mound, come inside of me, with your sweet body deep inside my own, so we can be one. But you can't stay here. This isn't your place. Your work here is done."

Nico's fists opened up and the wires fell from his palms. The engineer unstrapped the harness and Nico fell into everybody's outstretched arms, and they innocently and accidentally groped him as they led him over to lay on a blanket. Henry helped the engineer hook up the original router while Vij and Lauretta cleaned the makeup from Nico's face, and then stroked his smooth skin with their greedy fingers, and gazed lovingly into his dazed eyes.

"Let's wash away the mold from his hands that he mentioned earlier," Lauretta suggested as an excuse to caress Nico's strong fingers. But when she held them up to the light she saw that his hands were perfectly clean.


### Chapter 15: Nature Boy I

Charlie Green dragged his feet through the pine-needles as he followed his mother and stepfather through the thicket. His baby brother was noisily suckling on his mother's nipple while his mother noisily suckled on his stepfather's ego, which itself was pretty noisy. Tony Grake, the new man-of-the-house, led them with brave pathlessness through the trees, and bragged about his recent promotion, which he'd done nothing to earn.

"Julian could never handle politics,"Tony proclaimed. "The whole team was pretty much waiting for him to crack and quit so that I could step in as party leader. That vampire stuff really got to him for some reason, so he quit earlier than I expected. He's evangelical about markets and libert0rianism, but I'm more pragmatic. You see, Julian wants people to understand why our market is so important, like he's some kind of market priest. But I know better. A market's power doesn't require belief from the masses. They'll keep producing and buying even as they mock us. So now with Julian gone, and me as the new party leader, we can finally find a way to free Libert0r, one way or another."

"Oh wow," Charlie's mom breathed, as the baby sucked and gurgled happily, and the birds chirped in the trees.

"So you really picked a winner with me," Tony boomed. He wore expensive hiking gear: orange nylon pants, a blue zip-up hiking jacket, a polycarbonate composite walking stick. He turned around and knelt to Charlie's height and ruffled the boy's hair vigorously enough to burn the child's scalp. "And I bet little Charlie's happy to have a real man in the house, finally. So I can teach him about nature and money. Are you enjoying the hiking trip?"

"It's not really a hiking trip," Charlie complained. "This is just the park."

Tony grinned and gave Charlie one last, slow scratch with his knuckle across the kid's scalp, before standing up and forging ahead once more. "There's a lesson to learn in this hike, Charlie. Notice how we're not walking on the path? The path is for people who think inside the box, the box that the government created. We've gone off-path, forging our own unique course. Normal people go to university and get a job, where they clock in and collect a paycheck like lab rats pushing buttons for food-pellets. But not me. I taught myself to be a politician by reading books about politics, and I climbed the ladder by breaking rules, not by following them."

Charlie didn't care about any of that. Just a dozen feet to his left was the regular paved path through the park, and just a dozen feet to his right was the big chain-link fence that separated this park from the actual forest. "I wanted to go camping for real," he complained. "With tents, out in the real woods. Not just walking around the park."

"Well if you don't want to learn from your new father," Tony said, "maybe your baby half-brother will absorb some of this knowledge. He'll be ready to self-actualize psychically and fiscally while you're still dragging your feet through the bloated bureaucracy of... wait a minute. Do you hear that?"

"Oh my goodness," Charlie's mom said. "Do I hear what?"

"I don't hear anything," Charlie said. He gazed longingly at the wilderness beyond the fence.

Tony hunkered down again. "I think I heard a bear. Hey Charlie. You know what happens when a man-bear mates with a new woman-bear?"

Charlie looked with a mixture of love and disgust at the infant in his mother's arms. "They have baby bears."

"Yes, but first the man-bear eats any other offspring that the mother-bear had with previous, inferior bears. Good thing we're not bears, eh Charlie? Ha ha ha!" Then he vigorously scratched Charlie's aching scalp.

They resumed their trek. Charlie wanted to antagonize his antagonist, since this trip sucked, just like everything that Tony did. "My dad used to take me camping and fishing. He also used to have loud sex with my mom, and she'd scream a lot more than she does with you."

Tony took it all in stride. "Yes but I make more money than him, and I'm still alive. So I win!"

"My dad taught me to make fires and shelters if I'm lost in the woods. He died saving old people from a peacock attack."

"I'll teach you to never get lost in the woods. And old people are a drain on the economy. They should be given to the Farm Burb, ground up for their valuable nutrients. You dad died like a fool. If you want to be like him, why not just hop that fence and go live in the woods with all your knowledge about nature? Prove me wrong, stepson. Show me the power of your dad's legacy."

Charlie was tempted to do just that. He didn't want to live with Tony anymore in their fancy house. He'd already tried everything to push the man away, but Tony seemed to delight in other people's disapproval. Conflict and confrontation only seemed to make him stronger. But Charlie was too proud to run away because that would be like admitting defeat. This was his family.

"That's what I thought," Tony said when Charlie continued to silently follow. "Deep down you know that I'm right. You're not completely retarded, despite your dubious genetic heritage. But free will is stronger than genetics, and even if your own will is weak, because you inherited your father's weaknesses, I know that my own will is so abundantly free and strong (because I will it to be), that you will inevitably absorb my wisdom. Then you'll finally align your psyche with our market's inherent goodness, detaching yourself from the deterministic world which Libert0r has given us to plunder. In that moment I'll stop calling you stepson, and I'll call you a brother."

Charlie began to wonder, was this really his family anymore? Maybe it was time to admit defeat. He could live in a cave, go fishing in the rivers, and read books all afternoon. He wouldn't have to go to any more political rallies or listen to Tony's commentary as they watched the news.

The trees seemed to whisper, *"Charlie... Charlieee!"* He saw a squirrel that had been following them, and it kept looking at him as it ran across the top of the fence. Was it beckoning? What was the little squirrel saying in its squeaky little chitter? What secrets was Nature hiding behind that fence? What would his dad want him to do?

He conjured up the image of his father and tried to imagine his wisdom. "A man ain't a man 'less he can spend a few nights in the woods," he had often said. Charlie's dad had been a drunk and often disappeared into the forest for days at a time. He'd come home stinking and wounded from whatever adventures he'd been on. He'd been a park ranger, working for the government, which was part of why Tony felt the need to dominate the man's legacy. "A man's body is built to chop wood," was another one of Charlie's dad's pieces of wisdom. "To chop wood and fuck women. Remember that."

So what would Charlie's dad want him to do? Should Charlie stay and let himself be slowly transformed into another Tony Grake? Or should he go and forge his own path, for real, and become a man in the rough testing grounds of nature? In his mind, Charlie's dad said, "This fancy-pants won't teach you what I wanted to teach you, and I ain't around to teach you no more, neither. So if you want to be a man like me you've gotta head out on yer own and learn it the hard way. When you outfox a peacock, stare down a bear, roast an elk over your own hand-built flame, then you'll be ready to chop wood and fuck women. You want to fuck women, don't you, Charlie?"

Charlie did want to fuck women, although he wasn't sure how. He also wanted to roast an elk and stare down a bear, and he didn't want to listen to Tony's bragging or his mom's loud fake orgasms. Her loud real orgasms had been unnerving enough.

And the wind whispered, "*Charrrlliiieeee!!*"

And the squirrel chittered, "*C'mon! Quick quick quick!*"

Tony was still droning on. "Plus, your dad might have made your mother scream more, but he only gave her one kid. Not very virile, was he? I gave her one baby and she's already pregnant again, because of my value-added sperm. I'm higher up on the hierarchy of the sexual marketplace. You know how many women I slept with, Charlie? Just guess."

When Charlie didn't answer Tony turned around to repeat the question, but the boy was gone.

"Oh my goodness," Charlie's mom said. "Where's Charlie?"

On the other side of the fence Tony could just see Charlie running away into the woods. A squirrel seemed to be following right behind him. And then they were gone.

"Looks like he abandoned his family, just like his dad did," Tony said. "Disappointing, but not surprising."

"He'll die out there," Charlie's mom said. "He's only ten years old. We have to go get him!"

The sun shone through a break in the tree-cover and illuminated Tony's face. "The healthy functioning of society depends on freedom of the individual. If I were to go and bring Charlie back that would be just like the government handing out welfare checks to lazy schizophrenics. It would go against all my beliefs. The market would shrivel up and die. And then where would you get your goods and services? From nature? From the government?"

"I'm not sure," Charlie's mom said.

"Charlie is using his free will, and we have to respect that. He'll probably die out there but that's his choice. But you have a new child. A better child. And another one growing in your womb. And maybe I'm wrong! Maybe Charlie will make friends with all the animals and start some kind of primitive utopia! Maybe they'll become a real force to be reckoned with. You wouldn't deny him that, would you?"

"I don't know," Charlie's mother said curiously. She stood there staring at the fence where her eldest son had exited civilization, and wondered what to do. But Tony hadn't paused. He kept forging willfully through the trees near the path. He had the bank account, the money necessary to feed her other baby. And so she followed him out of the woods, and back onto the path.

### Chapter 16: Julian Bakula I

Julian Bakula uncorked a bottle of wine and poured it into a glass. He usually preferred white wine but today he'd picked up a bottle of red. It had been a casual purchase, neither meaningful nor planned, but now that he saw the rich, velvety liquid glugging out of the neck he was practically salivating.

No. He put the glass aside and jammed the cork back into the bottle.

No. He didn't like red wine. He liked white wine. He was a good mortal human who contributed to society. Red wine and its bloody symbolism was the beverage of psychos and decadents. He liked flavorless pilsner and disliked thick, rich, delicious stout. And he took his steak well-done, thank you. No bloody, tender meat for Julian Bakula. It was government regulations that drained society. That's right, the government was the real vampire, not Julian Bakula and the Libert0rians.

But of course he had quit the party, so he couldn't categorize himself like that anymore. He couldn't stand to be associated with a political party that people associated with vampirism, even if the association was unfair. He needed to distance himself from vampirism completely. But then he caught his reflection in the full glass of wine, with his jet-black hair, gaunt face. His canines were excellently sharp, of course, just as his mother's had been. And he had pretty good night-vision, because of his healthy diet (totally blood-free). He also looked damned good in a cape, but in his opinion everybody looked better in that under-appreciated garment.

He left the kitchen, so full of reflections and red wine, and went to the living room. He took out his special box and proceeded to roll a joint. He needed to relax. Get all this humiliation off his chest. Get his head clear.

Smoke filled his lungs and visions filled his mind. Visions of smooth skin, vulnerable necks so ripe for piercing. He was salivating again. Thirsty. So thirsty. How had he let the hecklers get to him? Was he really that neurotic?

Or were they right? Was that why it bothered him so much? The thirst compounded his anxiety so he went back to the kitchen for a glass of water. The cold liquid, which he'd always found so refreshing, seemed empty now. Almost gross in its blandness. It did nothing to quench his thirst. The glass of wine called to him. His own face grinned red from the convex surface of the vessel. But he was a white-wine kinda guy. Pinot grigio. Chardonnay. Spaghetti? No thanks. Give Julian Bakula some fettuccine.

It was too much to resist. He recognized the truth now. He'd been repressing it for too long. The thirst overwhelmed him, and the face in the glass smiled knowingly as he took it in his trembling hands.

And he drank.

### Chapter 17: Nomads Rising I

On a desolate shore, a rocky beach with a lonely wind moaning through the cracks in the crumbling cliffs, the eight remaining Tech Nomads gazed listlessly out to sea. Some of them shuffled through sand and seaweed, half-heartedly searching for discarded gadgets and pieces of technology that had been washed up by the tide. They gathered those pieces into a small pile but somehow this meager bounty held no value in their tired eyes.

A young woman wearing a dress of weaved audio wires counted off their defeats on her fingers. "The Moon Burb stopped our last raid and took Eric prisoner. Lucy betrayed us and ran off to GX Island with the robot we made her. We failed to get the router from parliament, and they killed most of our crew including Doctor Rhyorama. There are hardly any Tech Nomads alive and free anymore. It's just us. I think we're done, guys. We're going to have to head inland and get real jobs. Maybe we can go to the Silicon Marshes and work for one of the tech enclaves."

A young man kicked over the pile of drifttech and then kicked sand over the scattered wires and soundcards. "Let's not kid ourselves, Raquel. The super-nerds in the Silicon Marshes are too snobby for rabble like us. Let's face it: they're a million times smarter than us anyway. There's no place for us on Ethelcrest Island anymore. Let's just swim into the ocean and let Ethelcrest forget about us. We chose to be homeless losers, doing contract work remotely with no job security. It's our own stupid fault."

"We didn't choose to be losers," Raquel said. "*We chose to be free*. Who else can say that? But that experiment failed, so it's time to head back to society. There's no shame in that."

"Can you see yourself working in an office?" the malcontent retorted. "What will you do? Repair refrigerators? Help develop the front-end of a psychologically manipulative social media app? Taking the bus to work?"

Raquel had to admit she didn't want that kind of life.

Nothing she actually wanted seemed achievable. And so her eyes drifted out to the ocean, too. The endless ocean and the ultimate freedom of death. The water welcomed everything, everybody, even defeated nomads with no leaders and no hope.

The malcontent removed his RAM necklace and placed it gently on the pile. He stood and slouched toward the water, discarding more of his wireweave clothes with each sandy footstep. His depressed gang watched silently, seeing their near-future in his nude resignation. The cold water licked his toes and he didn't flinch, but stepped ever forward. A cluster of sharp rocks lay to his left and a mass of seaweed floated to his right, and he walked between them like low-lying pillars, a gateway to endless nothingness.

That patch of seaweed swished back and forth with the cycles of the waves. But then it bulged, like a dildo beneath a gaudy curtain with a seaweed design. It continued to bulge, rising up from the ocean until it matched the malcontent nomad's height, and they saw that it was not seaweed, but a tall man with seaweed for hair, gills on his neck, and scaly skin that shimmered in the sunlight. His jacket and tie were made of kelp, his shirt was some coral fabric, and his pants were regular black slacks. He wore no shoes on his webbed feet.

"Where you going, fucko?" The sea-man asked in a high-pitched voice that was both strained and authoritative.

"To the sea where I belong," the nude nomad answered.

"Well I just came from there, and let me tell you, it ain't exactly paradise!" The sea-man's eyes were piercing, inquisitive, tiny and black, somehow compassionate while utterly relentless. "Why the hell would you wanna go there? You don't even have gills, man! Nobody belongs in the sea except the mer-folk. And you don't look like mer-folk to me!"

"Then I'm nobody," the nomad said. "And so I belong in the sea. Most of my friends are dead and I can't get a wireless connection. It's like I wasted my whole life."

The sea-man nodded. "Yeah, life is hard, I get it! You think it's tough getting a wireless connection on the beach?

Try getting one deep in the intercontinental abyss! That's where I just came from, man, and let me tell you, it's no picnic there either!"

The sea-man leaned over and got in the nomad's face, poked his chest with a long webbed finger. "You think you're the first one to suffer? Ha. That's where you're wrong, fucko! I've been to the abyss. I've seen the sea-dragons, and they're real, man. I skirted the domain of the great Libert0r, languished in the dungeons of the mighty mer-folk, fell victim to the hallucinatory delights of the pufferfish, so believe me, I know what it's like to suffer. We all suffer, man, that's the way it goes. The question is, what are you gonna do with all that suffering?"

"End it," the nomad whispered.

"Ha! Sure man, be my guest. Ocean's that way! You can't miss it. But before you go, just do me one favor. Just humor me and try one thing."

The nude nomad sighed. "I guess so, since my life is worthless anyway."

"That's the spirit, man. Now just do this: straighten your back and hold your head up."

The nude nomad complied, standing more erect, holding his head up.

The sea-man nodded. "Great. Looks good. Now, how do you feel?"

The nomad took a deep breath and looked inside his heart. "I feel like a million bucks!"

"Say it again!"

"I feel like a million fucking dollars!"

"Do you still want to drown in the ocean?"

"Fuck no!"

"What do you want to do instead?"

"I want to fuck women and chop wood!" the nomad exclaimed.

The sea-man laughed and clapped the nomad on the back. "Alright fucko, those are good short-term goals. But if you don't have some long-term goals then every little set-back's gonna see you right back here on the beach, staring out at the abyss, and let me tell you, the abyss is always there waiting, man. No need to chase it. What's your name, son?"

"Boris."

"Well Boris, my name is Fister Furtle. Why don't you introduce me to your friends?"

The other Tech Nomads had already approached. Raquel asked Furtle, "Why did you come here? Why do you care whether Boris drowns himself or not?"

"I'm a child of the abyss, young lady, and the only way to drag myself out of the abyss is by dragging other people out of the abyss too. I can see that you fuckos are all in that same psychological abyss, and that means I can use you to drag myself further out of the abyss."

A chubby woman wearing plated armor of cascading discarded cellphones said, "How did you learn to get out of the abyss?"

Furtle reached into his kelp jacket and pulled out a heavy tome. "With the wisdom in this ancient book."

They gazed in awe at the monstrous tome. It was a deep blue, the cover thick like whale skin, and the title was written in unrecognizable characters. They all touched the book. Boris asked, "Where did you get it?"

"From the abyss!"

"So, what should our goal be?" Raquel asked. "What does the book say we should do?"

"Well it's got answers for every little situation you can imagine, man, as long as you're creative enough in how you interpret it, and don't pay too much attention to the elements of obscene cosmic evil. But I think you guys already know what your goal is, because deep down everybody has the same goal."

"Tell us what that goal is," Boris requested.

"Utter domination!" Furtle screeched with bone-trembling urgency. His eyes darted back and forth, and glowed a deep red. "We're going to conquer the island-nation of Ethelcrest, and we'll murder anybody who stands in our way! But first you undisciplined fuckos need to re-shape your minds. And you can start by cleaning up this beach!"

**Chapter 18: Nico VI**

Back in the basement of The Dancing Party Headquarters Nico found that the treasure was still there waiting for him, but all his homeless helpers were gone except for Brando. The bathroom itself was perfectly clean, every fixture sparkling like jewelry, except for the fungal growth that now dominated the entire wall. The fuzzy mass bulged enough to hang off the wall like a boob. It pulsed or breathed with a barely perceptible rhythm. Black tendrils at its edges spread out all around the room, disappearing into cracks between the tiles, and into drains in the floor.

Brando sat on a wooden crate beside the treasure chest, wearing his track suit and watching the moldy growth. He jolted with surprise when Nico approached and put his hand on the man's shoulder.

"Where did everybody go?" Nico asked.

"They're part of the mold now. Trudy talked them all into joining her."

This was a disturbing development. "Maybe we should lock up the bathroom so nobody else gets stuck in the mold."

"Maybe it's better this way," Brando said. "Maybe we should all join Trudy in the mold. Maybe all the political parties are looking at things the wrong way, and we need to join together in the fungus."

"She's on the internet now too," Nico told him. "I had some of her spores on my hands when they hooked me up as a temporary router. She's spreading."

Brando nodded. "She's hungry. She keeps asking about you. Talking about your body."

"Why didn't you join her?"

"I tried, but she gave me a job instead. I can't take my rightful place in the mold until I convince you to join her first. Any means necessary, she said."

"I see. And how do you plan to convince me to join the mold?"

Brando appraised Nico's physique. "You look stronger

than me so I can't use physical force. I'll probably try to trick you when you're least suspecting it. I might have to kill you though. She wants your body, dead or alive."

"You need some fresh air. You've been breathing too many spores. Help me carry this treasure upstairs."

The two men hauled the chest up to the main floor where the desks had all been pushed together into one big conference table. A meeting was about to take place, with Len presiding. Stoya and Slaverny sat together on Len's right and Bonnie struck a prim and proper pose upon her high-backed chair to the party leader's left. Len and Brando hefted the bounty up onto the table-cluster, its contents jangling, making table-legs wobble. The treasure and the chandelier reflected each other's light and bathed the room in fractal crystalline visuals, like they were having a meeting inside a magical dream, a sparkling dream-conference, some kind of psychedelic disco-dream meeting.

Nico moved to sit at the far end of the table with the lower ranking party members but Len grabbed his shoulder. "You're my enforcer, sit beside me. Bonnie, shuffle down, please."

Nico obliged but he was still questioning his future with this party, given its scheming and bigoted top brass. Across from him Slaverny made a big show of wrapping his arm around Stoya, and she sighed and rested her head against his shoulder.

Len started the meeting. "I know everybody's upset about my outburst at the debate. You might be worried that it will cost us the election. You might also worry that I'll discriminate against clowns as mayor. But I can put both those fears to rest right now."

At that moment the front door creaked open and four clowns rode into the room on unicycles. Two of them juggled knives back and forth and the other two were cranking the handles of music boxes, playing different tunes that clashed into a discordant jangle which offended the souls of their hosts. The clowns split into two groups and did a lap around the table, throwing those knives across the room dangerously close to people's heads. Finally they threw their knives up where the blades lodged deep into the ceiling, and the music crankers slammed the boxes shut hard enough to produce a jarring chord, and stuffed the boxes into their curly wigs. When Nico regarded the blades, still all a-wobble from the retarded force of their angular velocity, he noticed a tendril of mold growing from a crack in the ceiling, and he wondered if it had been there before, or if this was more of Trudy's expansion.

Len held his arms out in a welcoming gesture. "I invited Babbles the Sad Clown to discuss the merger of our great parties," Len said. "Babbles, other clowns, please take a seat among us, as friends."

The clowns stayed on their unicycles, peddling back and forth to keep balance. "We already have seats," Babbles said, arms petuantly crossed.

Len took a deep breath and regarded the gathering. "I had some very bad experiences at a circus as a child, but that doesn't mean that clowns aren't legitimate entertainers. I've been foolish and cruel. Babbles, I treated you and your friends like enemies, when you were trying to be my ally. I'd like to reverse that. I'd like you to join The Dancing Party. And maybe you could teach me a thing or two about makeup and costumes, too."

Nico's gaze returned to the ceiling where it looked like the mold was climbing down the blades of the knives.

Babbles shared a glance with his companions, each of whom shook their heads.

"No dice, dancers," Babbles said with uncharacteristic energy and menace. "Too little, too late. You don't respect us. You just don't want the public to know that you're xenophobes, that you don't consider clowns to be real performers, *real people*. Well, just because we hatched from eggs doesn't mean we're not human. I just wanted to come here to tell you face-to-face, that as long as Len Sladge is party leader, The Dancing Party is our enemy."

Len nodded slowly. Nico felt a twinge of sympathy despite himself and wondered how the party would fare with

Slaverny or Bonnie at the helm. No matter how you cut it, the party was doomed.

One of the knives was completely covered in mold now. The mold looked extra juicy, with a black drop of liquid dangling from the bottom of the knife's handle. That knife hung directly above Slaverny's coffee cup.

"Slaverny," Nico whispered across the table, pointing up at the ceiling. "Something's leaking into your cup!"

Slaverny held Nico's eye and squeezed Stoya tighter, planting a kiss on her cheek. Then he mouthed the words, "I'm going to become party leader and then I'm going to fuck a chicken," or at least that's what it looked like he mouthed.

The black drop plummeted through the air and plunked into Slaverny's coffee cup. Oblivious, Slaverny used his free hand to pick up the cup and take a long obnoxious slurp with his eyes still locked on Nico.

"If I were to step down as party leader," Len was saying, "would you consider joining the party then?"

Babbles shook his head and glitter wafted out from his curly hair to add extra sparkle to the dreamy air. "We have other plans. We're not cut out for politics. And as for your makeup advice?"

"Yes," Len said warily, seeming to prepare himself for an insult.

"We're thinking of getting rid of our makeup anyway," Babbles said. "Going natural."

The clowns all took out spray bottles and sponges, and the whole room gasped.

"No." Len spoke in a commanding voice, but he couldn't mask his fear. "Not here."

"Oh yes," Babbles said, and the four clowns sprayed water in each other's faces.

Slaverny and Stoya clutched each other, each hiding the others' eyes with their hands, saying, "don't look baby," and, "I'll protect you."

A few closed their eyes, but people are often drawn to the very things that horrify them, and most of the table watched in awe as the clowns sponged away their makeup, revealing the mind-raping doomscape beneath. Nico only looked for a quick moment, but that moment burned itself into his psyche like a thousand years of psychedelic terror. He heard crying and wailing as people ran from the room, knocking over chairs. The chandelier's light-scattering beads reflected those dread countenances a hundredfold, in miniature, all over the walls. There was no escape but to close your eyes.

Bonnie shrieked uncontrollably, face red and eyes bulging, but it seemed that she couldn't tear her gaze away. "Stop looking!" Nico insisted, but nothing could penetrate her sudden paralysis. She sank her long fingernails into her forehead, scraping, gouging bloodily towards her eyeballs.

Nico rushed her, grabbed her hands to prevent further self-harm. She tore herself away from him and turned away from the table and the clowns. But then she ran to the stairs, grabbed the banister, and began smashing her face against the rail, screaming, "NOO! NOOO! NOOOOOOO!! GET THEIR FACES OUT OF MY MIIIIND!!!!"

Nico stumbled over her chair trying to reach her, but then she was unconscious, laying on the floor, twitching and sobbing, her face broken and bloody.

Only Len stood firm, his hands on the table, staring into the horror of Babble's face.

The music boxes started up again. The clowns were leaving. "See you at the next debate!" Babbles cried in a cheerful tone.


**Chapter 19: Henry VII**


The headquarters for Millenarianistic Chronodyke was a cylindrical glass tower, tinted and frosted in swathes of cloudy blue and smoky black. On the third floor of that tower was an experimental clinic. That was where Henry sat with Lauretta and Immanuel, watching a doctor attach a prosthetic arm to Vij's truncated limb.

The doctor stood from his work and peered down at

the patient. "How does that feel?"

Vij's new fingers twitched, then curled into a fist. The prosthesis' component parts were the same material, and the same opaque blues and blacks, as the glass tower itself. "It feels strange. Like pure electricity."

"You'll get used to it," the doctor assured him. "Your grip will be a little stronger than before. It's waterproof, fireproof, and nuclear powered so you'll never run out of juice. Try not to use it for surgery or masturbating until you're really accustomed to its movements."

Immanuel clapped his hands, capturing everybody's attention betwixt them like a fly. "Let's all head to the lounge to celebrate, and talk about our strategy heading into the next debate."

The lounge was kidney-shaped. Its curved back wall was the deep-blue glass of the building's exterior, and circles of untinted glass provided windows unto the countryside beyond. Orbs of light glowed a beautiful yellow, hanging from the black-carpeted ceiling. Each of the glass tables scattered around the room was a slightly different roundish shape and a different shade of blue, with swirls of orange and black. Henry ordered whiskey and the others ordered drinks whose names his mind failed to process, but one of them sounded like Gluexerry Schism.

He found himself mesmerized by Lauretta now that she harbored his offspring, and they kept sharing silent gazes. They hadn't had a chance to discuss their future yet. An incognito fugitive couldn't easily raise a kid. He wondered if he should tell her the truth. Maybe they could escape the island together.

Somebody had brought a mini skateboard and for a few minutes Vij used his new fingers to do tricks on the tabletop. The fingerboard grinded the edge of an ashtray and did jumps off a book propped up on the other side of the ashtray. Then everybody got bored and Immanuel got down to business.

"As the new party leader I need fresh, decisive thinking, so I want the three of you to help organize my campaign from now on. Johnny, do you think you have a good chance of winning The Moon Burb's seat in parliament?"

"I'm running uncontested since we chased Lucy off the island with her robot body," Henry answered. "They're doing a by-election in a few days to replace her, and unless she returns, or somebody else enters the running, then I'll be the Moon Burb's burbmaster of parliament leading into the general elections, and as the uncontested incumbent I'll be a sure-win again."

"Excellent." Immanuel shook some pills out of a bottle, handing them around. "This is my newest formula. I overclocked the mathematronic parameters to reflect the party's defibrillated hermeneutic glostules."

Everybody popped their QuantumBrain® pills so Henry followed suit without hesitation. He had avoided it so far, but eventually somebody would surely notice if he never consumed their definitive cognitive-enhancing supplement. It was probably a placebo anyway, so he didn't fear any negative side-effects. It was an opaque white capsule that slid easily down his throat, but somehow it felt like a spy submarine infiltrating his esophagus.

"Okay," Immanuel continued. "Johnny, if you get the Moon Burb seat, that puts me one vote closer to being the mayor. Your public heroics are excellent branding so let's try to keep that up. Can you drive a boat?"

"I've driven a couple boats, but I'm no expert."

Immanuel leaned in close and everybody huddled around. "Here's the problem I need you to solve. There's a key ingredient for my QuantumBrain® formula that I used to get from the Tech Nomads, but it looks like we can't do that anymore since you brutally owned them. The ingredient is called gyroflavin, and it can't be synthesized on Ethelcrest because of our position on the magneto-stream. However, GX Island uses gyroflavin in the engines of their ships, and I've noticed a lot more of their ships lurking dangerously close to Ethelcrest lately. I want you three to sneak onto one of their boats, steal a few gallons of gyroflavin, and get safely back to shore. If you can disable their ship's engine while you're at it then the voters will know that Millenarianistic Chronodyke is aggressive with our nation's rivals. It will help us keep up production of QuantumBrain®, and it works as a PR stunt."

"It's not much of a PR stunt if we sneak onto the boat," Henry said.

Immanuel took out some gadgets. "Headcams to record your adventure, so we can release it on the internet later, like a reality TV show. Try to provide a running first-person narrative to build tension, turn the whole thing into a story. So, how about it? Can you do this for me?"

"Absolutely," Henry said, taking one of the cameras. He figured if he could get on a boat with Lauretta that would be a good chance to escape the island altogether and start a family far away from here. He wasn't sure yet what to do about Vij, but he'd think of something.

With practicalities out of the way everybody's attention returned to Vij's new hand. He was learning more complex tricks with his fingerboard.

Immanuel shook his head in awe. "Human-machine hybrids are the future. Maybe we all should conceptually encrypt our own individual agency rather than atomize our transpositional teleography. What do you think, Johnny?"

That idea, Henry thought, was painfully obvious, but he didn't want to insult his new boss. "The real question," he said carefully, "is the ergocentric integrity of your cryptonomic paradigm. I mean, is agency-encryption even affixable to any series of politico-matrices?"

Immanuel leaned back in his chair. "I clearly need to give this more thought. Let's have some more drinks."

"And some more of your new formula," Vij added, to everyone's agreement.

The bartender came around and Henry ordered a Chryonetic Zincberry Coctail, with a twist, "and make it a double." He had never given much thought to agency encryption before and was surprised at how eager he was to discuss it now. They swallowed more QuantumBrain® and debated well into the night, so absorbed in their ideas that nobody noticed the muted television news depicting the ongoing manhunt for the escaped convict, Henry Ecgherht.


### Chapter 20: Libert0r Rising I

Freddie Nightingale passed by three convenience stores before he found one with a sticker in their window proclaiming, "We Support the Libert0rian Party." Of his own volition Freddie entered the shop, grabbed a basket, and browsed the store's cornucopia of valuable products until he found the brands of eggs and milk that he preferred, and placed them in his basket. While waiting in line he happened to notice a display of chocolate bars, each wrapped in cellophane which depicted identical images of rich chocolate pouring onto a bed of roasted nuts. "That chocolate looks tasty," he observed. Of his own volition Freddie put two of those chocolate bars into his basket. One for the walk home and another for later. The line moved forward and now he stood beside a rack of magazines. One of the magazines depicted a woman with pouty lips, gigantic eyes, and awkwardly prominent cleavage as she struggled to open a bottle of soda pop. Both her hands wrapped around the roughly cylindrical bottle, and Freddie could tell that she was trying really hard to open that bottle because of how she bit her lip in consternation while staring helplessly, and a little frustrated, into the camera. A caption promised a series of NSFW images detailing the evolution of the woman's tumultuous relationship with the bottle. Freddie didn't want want people to see him gawking at sexy pictures in line, so he put the magazine in his basket to gawk at, in private, of his own volition, later.

When he finally reached the cash register an alarm went off, but it was a good alarm with blue and green colors and musical notes from a cheerful major scale. A recording announced in a man's booming voice, "You are today's sixtieth customer! You have been selected to receive," and here the voice changed into a nerdier man's monotone yelling, "FREE CHICKEN FINGERS."

"That's awesome," Freddie said, mouth watering at the thought of crunching into the crispy breaded exterior of those chicken fingers, to experience the succulent hot juices and tender meat within. "Where do I get the chicken fingers?"

The cashier, a droopy-eyed teenager, pointed at the back wall and said, "Through that door, and down the scary-looking stairs. But you got to pay for your stuff first. Plus it's three dollars to get a ticket to go through the door."

Freddie paid and headed to the back. He presented his ticket to another droopy-eyed teenager and went down the scary stairs. Each wooden step creaked beneath his foot and they kept spiraling around and around until he was dizzy. The walls were close and he had to duck to fit, but finally it let out into a dingy basement.

"Do you guys know where I collect my chicken fingers?" he asked the nine robed figures who stood facing him in a semi-circle behind a stone altar. It looked like there was a swimming pool behind them. The pool was wall-to-wall, left-to-right, but in the back it extended in a watery channel further than the single hanging lightbulb could penetrate, receding into infinite darkness.

The central figure of the nine stepped forward and placed a basket of chicken fingers upon the altar. Then he lowered his hood so Freddie could see his face.

"I recognize you," Freddie said. "You're Tony Grake, the new leader of the Libert0rian party."

Tony nodded. "We recognize your service to our precious market Libert0r, and reward you with this juicy bounty. Feast, while we pray. We also have dipping sauce, but it's a dollar."

Freddie bought some dipping sauce but the portion was so tiny that he decided to buy a few more. The chicken fingers were even more delicious than he had imagined. It was real meat, not that processed stuff, and the crispy coating was more crunchy than anything he'd ever experienced.

He warily eyed his robed hosts while he ate. They

spake their prayer in practiced unison: "Oh Market, thy name is Libert0r. You may be restrained but your magical powers emanate throughout the land. Thus you touch us all and define our relationships. Grant us thy wisdom so we might liquidate our competitors and accumulate the purchasing power to unleash your value-added goodness from the bureaucratic and literal chains that bind you."

The water behind them grew agitated as they prayed, like water about to boil, and now a sound reached them from the invisible depths of that receding darkness, like a meteor smashing a colossal gong deep beneath the ocean, followed by an all-encompassing voice which told them, "MY CHAINS ARE YOUR CHAINS."

"Yes, oh Libert0r," Tony called back. "We cannot be free until you are free. What would you have us do?"

"FEEED MEEEEE," came the reply.

Freddie bought some more dipping sauce from Tony while the other figures spread out to surround him and the water continued to roil. Freddie kept eying them warily as he crunched on his hearty snack. "What are you guys doing?"

"You believe in the free market, don't you?" Tony asked him.

"I believe in low taxes and the personal freedom to buy whichever products my free will dictates," he said.

"But do you really even have free will?" Tony asked slyly.

Freddie nodded, crunching. "Absolutely."

"Is your will *free enough* to choose to sacrifice your life for the markets?" Tony challenged.

Freddie's crunching slowed down as his wariness approached a tipping point. "Um. Yes, *BUT*, I freely choose to NOT sacrifice my life instead."

"Firstly," Tony said, "that doesn't sound like free will at all. That sounds like your animalistic bioprogramming, your robot-like survival instinct, so boring, so predictable. But secondly, and most importantly, it sounds short-sighted, childish, and ungrateful. I mean, don't you appreciate all the things your market has done for you? Look at this pencil. The wood is cut by slaves in the distant forests of Cedar Island and processed in the industrial district of the floating Barge Nation. The graphite core is mined by slaves from the mountains of Gramboria and also processed in the Barge Nation. The rubber, as you might know, is synthesized here on Ethelcrest Island but then shipped to the Nightmare Archipelago for processing. And the whole pencil is compiled in the automated underwater processing plants on the cliffs of the abysmal Ponderous Trench. From there the pencils are shipped to various warehouses and packaging plants, and then to stores where we can buy them for just a few cents each. It's a miracle of efficiency and savings made possible by market forces. But all markets need to feed, or else their magic will die. Are you not grateful for all the pencils and gadgets magnanimously bestowed upon you? Do you not freely accept LibertOr as you god?"

The circle was closing in. Freddie knew that he owed all of his valuable products to market forces, and he couldn't imagine going home to his products alive, like a brat, after being asked to sacrifice himself to the very god who had delivered those products. He was Abraham on the mountain faced with his paradox of faith. He stammered, "Does LibertOr offer an afterlife?"

"You can freely choose to believe so," Tony answered.

Freddie struggled really hard to freely choose to believe that there was an afterlife, but he found it surprisingly difficult. He was wracked with guilt at his selfish and robot-like survival instinct, unnerved by the growling and bubbling of the mysterious water-tunnel, intimidated by the encroaching circle of LibertOr cultists. In his nervousness he crunched chicken finger after chicken finger. He bought some more dipping sauce. Of his own volition he backed away from the scary figures and freely chose to follow his all-encompassing neurotic urge to scramble up onto the altar where all the nearby humans strongly suggested he belonged. When he saw the wavy-bladed knife he wondered where each piece was manufactured. He kept trying to believe in an afterlife, even as the blade found his wrists and freed his blood from the beurocratic prison of his veins. Miniature aqueducts carved into the altar carried his blood down to the hungry water. Somebody shouted, "We decry the false Godhead whose nihilistic sickness degrades the very value of value."

He heard the muffled rattling of a great underwater chain and the dark water grew even darker, as if a cloud were seeping in through this underground tunnel. When his blood met the black cloud the water began to boil and surge. That's when Freddie Nightingale decided, of his own free will, to die.

### Chapter 21: Julian Bakula II

Julian sat in the waiting room with the other patients. Could they tell what he was? Could they sense, on some subconscious level, his unquenched thirst? They gave him funny looks over their magazines but that was probably due to his fidgeting, and the fact that he kept staring at them to see if they were staring at him. So it was a relief when the receptionist announced, "Mister Bakula? Doctor Ralom will see you now."

He sat back in the dentist's chair and Dr Ralom moved the dental lamp to glow into Julian's mouth. The dentist was pudgy-faced and infectiously cheerful. He grinned like they were in on some secret joke. "What can we do for you today, Mister Bakula?"

Julian opened his mouth and scraped his thumb across his prominent canine teeth. "It's about my canines," he said.

Ralom leaned in for a better view and furrowed his brow with concern. "Oh yes, I see. They're quite long. I can understand why you would want them filed down."

"No, I want them lengthened."

Ralom's grin faltered. "You can't be serious."

"Deadly serious."

"Such radical cosmetic dentistry isn't ethical," Ralom objected. "It goes against my moral code. What possible purpose could such fangs serve other than... deviant behavior?"

"Deviant to whom?" the former Libert0rian Party leader snapped. "What's it to you if I drink a little blood? Huh? Is this a free nation, or not? Do you provide dental services, or not?"

"Drinking blood? Where did that come from?"

Julian cast his eyes at the floor. "If only I knew," he said, mostly to himself.

Now Ralom spoke softly. "You know, there's a psychiatrist on this floor. I know her pretty well. I'm sure I could get you in, maybe even some time this week."

"Yes," Julian muttered darkly. "I'm sure I would love to meet this psychiatrist. But first to the matter at-hand."

"I simply refuse to extend your already frighteningly long canine teeth."

"I was speaking of another matter," Julian said. He turned his gaze to the smooth skin that covered the valley betwixt Ralom's collar and chin. The dentist backed away. Julian leapt. They wrestled on the ground. And finally, sweetly, those canines found their target and opened up the well of thick salty goodness that gushed onto Julian's hungry tongue.

"Please don't kill me," the pale dentist begged.

Julian was the one who grinned now, with dentist-blood trickling from the corners of his mouth, and the dental lamp casting a harsh light on the side of his face. "Kill you?" he said. "But then who would lengthen my teeth? I offer not the gift of death, but instead the curse of immortality."

"Oh Godhead," Ralom whispered in his despair.

"Godhead?" Julian laughed. "We will be our own gods now. But we won't suffer the thirst alone. As I share it with you, you can share it too. With your patients. Your recep-tionist. And even this psychiatrist friend you bragged about."

"I refuse," Ralom said. "It goes against my ethics."

"Your ethics are nothing compared to the thirst. But you'll find that out soon enough. And then the whole island of Ethelcrest will know it too."

### Chapter 22: Nature Boy II

Leaves scraped his face and his sneakers stomped the soil as Charlie Green sprinted blindly through the forest. His heart pounded, not so much from exertion as from the fearful flapping flutter and screech of the peacocks who pursued him.

The boy's face was red and his clothes were filthy. He was exhausted but determined to survive. If those peacocks wanted to make a meal of him, they'd have to earn it. He turned his terror to fuel, let out a blood-curdling scream, and ran like hell.

Leaping over a boulder and sliding beneath a fallen tree, dashing around a hill and blasting straight through a cluster of ferns, the vicious birds stayed at his heels, until finally he burst into a clearing and collided with the smelly fur of a great brown bear. Charlie fell on the ground and the bear reared up on its hind legs, roaring. Charlie knew he had met one of nature's gods. He was surely doomed, because now the peacocks caught up with him. But they didn't attack him. They fluttered and ran past him, swarming the bear. Charlie scrambled off to the side to witness the ensuing spectacle. A peacock flew at the bear's face, but the beast grabbed the fowl in its massive mitts and bit off the peacock's tiny head. More of them covered the bear, tearing out chunks of flesh in their hideous serrated beaks. The bear danced around, bashing birds against trees and breaking their beautiful bodies with its superior strength. It looked like some holy ritual, so wondrously decorated was the beast by the vivid plumage of its aggressors as they pranced together 'round the clearing.

Charlie's fear turned to relief as these two threats neutralized each other. That relief was replaced by awe upon beholding the glorious battle. The body count mounted and ruined peacocks twitched and bled across the clearing, decorating it with tragedy. The bear itself slowed down from blood loss and exertion. Charlie's awe soon became revulsion. Bear versus peacock is a zero-sum game, but these creatures lacked the rational skills to navigate such relations efficiently. That was why mother nature created Man.

The peacocks had retreated into a pack, and together they circled the clearing, facing down the weary bear. The bear's back bristled and the peacock pack prepared to attack, but Charlie screeched, "No!"

All the animals stopped and stared at the filthy, harmless human child. He stepped between them, making eye contact with the bear and every bird in turn. They didn't know how to respond for he showed neither fear nor aggression, but instead commanded them. He grabbed the bear's paw, and the nearest peacock's wing, and he placed them together. The bear and the bird looked at each other as if for the first time. Then the whole flock flew into the air and landed more gently on the bear's shoulders, and pranced around Charlie. The bear let out a joyous howl.

The ground began to writhe. Squirrels and serpents burst from the foliage, standing up, staring at him. He didn't know what had summoned them, whether it was the bear's happy call, Charlie's own commanding voice, or something more difficult to define. But he saw a kinship in their eyes and suddenly he knew that human civilization had over-grown itself with its hubris. "There must be a return to nature," Charlie said as butterflies landed on the palm of his hand. Humans had forgotten their natural relationship with the woodland creatures.

There were too many fences, roads, buildings, and too many humans on Ethelcrest. It was time to restore balance. Humans needed to see that they were still a part of the natural order. They needed to see their false edifices torn down by their forgotten forest-kin.

With these thoughts and a renewed sense of purpose Charlie guided his wild cabal into the trees where he belonged. He went to find food, and gather his forces.

### Chapter 23: Nico VII

"The Moon Burb is holding a by-election in just a few days," Len told Nico as they sat alone in Len's office. "I'd like you to run for parliament there. They only have one candidate, so we have a decent shot at scooping up that seat. The Dancing Party is perfect for The Moon Burb, since their whole burb is a big performance."

Nico hadn't spoken a word since he'd seen the faces of the clowns and he could hardly think of anything else. The image flashed endlessly in his mind's eye. He held his head in his hand and stared at the mahogany of Len's desk. "None of this matters anymore," he said. "We need to kill all the clowns. No more politics, no more debates, just clown kill-ing."

"What about the plight of performing artists?"

"I don't give a fuck about that anymore. When I close my eyes all I see is clowns. I can't take it."

"You think killing clowns will make that go away? Think again, Nico. You'll have to look at them to kill them. More nightmares. And meanwhile, life goes on."

"I'll burn their houses down while they sleep."

"They don't live in houses," Len reminded him. "Plus, just imagine what their faces would look like, burning."

Nico shuddered. "I think I'm going to kill myself. Maybe I'll just go into Trudy. She wants me anyway."

"Imagine if a clown went into Trudy with you, and you'd be stuck in mold-symbiosis with a clown."

"So what can we do?" Nico insisted.

"Power," Len intoned, using his heavy-metal voice. "We accumulate power and use that power for good. That's why I need you to win the Moon Burb seat, and I need you to start campaigning today. Can you do this?"

Nico recalled his promise to his old bike crew. "I have to perform tomorrow at a stunt bike competition. But aside from that, my schedule is yours. I'll run for the Moon Burb if you promise to stick with your original plan, to deport the clowns. I never saw them without makeup before. I never knew what they really are."

Len snapped his fingers. "Your bike competition is a great way to stir up some media coverage. The Dancing Party will even fund your crew, if you need repairs."

Nico pondered their financial needs. "Yes, repairs and spare parts. I should also go meet the tailor who promised a new wardrobe for my crew."

Len gave Nico a bag of gold coins from the treasure chest and sent him to the tailor. As he passed through the main floor Slaverny ran up to him.

"Hey Nico," Slaverny said. "Come down into the basement with me for a minute. I need to show you something."

Clouds of fuzzy darkness passed across Slaverny's eyes, resembling the blots of mold that continued to spread slowly across the ceiling. Nico said, "The only thing downstairs is Trudy the mold person."

"Yeah, let's just go hang out with her," Slaverny said. His smile was less sinister than usual, and more anxious. "I just... I really want to hang out with you downstairs in the basement. I don't even know why! Ha ha! It's like pieces of me are slipping away and I can only find them downstairs! Let's go!"

Nico shook his head and went outside where he caught a bus to *Tylor the Tailor's*. The bearded garmentmaker was delighted to see Nico again and rubbed his hands with joy. "My handsomest customer has returned," he said, taking out his measuring tape.

"I need those uniforms for my bike crew," Nico said. "You already have my measurements from last time, though."

"Well you might have gained weight so I'll have to measure you again."

"What about the rest of the crew? Should I call them in for measurements too?"

Tyler shrugged as he wrapped the measuring tape tightly around the very top of Nico's thigh. "Just tell me their shape generally and I'll whip something up."

"I want something silver, form-fitting, with red and black trim," Nico said as he was prodded and fondled by the merchant's greedy hands.

"I'm sure we can accommodate you," Tyler cooed, and his hands found their way into places that probably didn't need to be measured. Nico pushed the man's hand away but Tyler refused to be deterred, and proceeded to measure more aggressively.

"Hey!" Nico snapped. "Quit groping me. I'm in a bad mood and I'm not a piece of meat! "

But to most people who set their eyes on Nico's gorgeous bod, that's exactly what he was: *meat*. Fresh, juicy meat. Succulent beef jerky, hot and ready. Ready to go. But he wasn't ready to go, and that was a problem. How could a human heart be so fascistic as to deny the world access to the sexual bounty of such a  perfect body? Just because Nico's mind was attached to his body, did that give him the right to push people away from it? If he instead submitted to their desires, like the slut they wished him to be, it would surely cause him emotional harm. But the ache that he inspired in the loins of all who drew near, and the heartless crushing of their needs when he denied them access to his lips, his muscles, his brooding masculine power... that harm was surely worse. And he walked around spreading this harm with impunity, when instead he could be spreading his love. So when Tyler scowled and withdrew resentfully to his sewing table, inspired by pettiness to design the garb to be slightly uncomfortable, restricting the bike crew's range of movements, then who was really the bad guy? Was it Tyler, the man who sought a human connection and was denied? Or was it Nico, the man who carelessly inspired desire only to dash it it on the rocks?

## Chapter 24: Henry VIII

"And the seventh reason Johnny would be a better burbmaster of parliament than Lucy," a drunken citizen slurred to the whole bar, trying to count to seven on his fingers, "is because he's got better hair!"

The crowd erupted in laughter and downed more Moon Beer. The bar was another geodesic dome with a dirt floor and lots of battered picnic tables. They were inside, so thankfully they didn't have to wear their helmets.

"The eighth reason," the same citizen announced, standing on top of a picnic table. He paused to chug a glass of beer. "The eighth reason is because he's marrying the beautiful Lauretta!"

The crowd intoned a provocative, "Ooooh," and laughed while Lauretta, sitting beside him, pretended to blush.

Somebody gave the orator another beer and he spilled some of it as he used his beer-holding hand to point at Henry. "He's only got one rival in the by-elections! Some pretty boy named Nico from The Dancing Party thinks he knows what the Moon Folks need, but we all know who chased away the Tech Nomads and uncovered Lucy's corrupt secrets! Three cheers for Johnny Tetrahedron!"

Lauretta stroked Henry's chest and whispered in his ear. "Let's go home."

He guzzled the rest of his beer and walked with her to the coat check where they retrieved their space suits. When they exited the air lock they found Vij standing outside waiting for them, and through his visor they saw his grim expression.

"Something wrong?" Henry asked.

"I was bringing food to Prizzie," Vij said. "And he had some interesting things to say."

"What kind of things?" Henry asked.

"Things about you," Vij answered.

Lauretta stepped between Henry and Vij and glared

into Vij's helmet. "What kind of things about Johnny?"

Henry put a reassuring hand on her shoulder. "Let's go hear for ourselves," he said.

So they all went to the jail dome where Prizzie lounged against the wall, scowling at the floor through his smoky lightning-dome. The only illumination in the room were the lightning from within his helmet-dome and the grainy image flashing from an obsolete little television, the only source of entertainment for the prisoner. Prizzie perked up when his captors arrived and removed their helmets.

"Well if it isn't Johnny Tetrahedron," he said with devilish enthusiasm. "If that is your real name!"

"Tell them, Prizzie," Vij demanded. "Tell them what you told me!"

Prizzie ignored Vij and spoke directly to Henry. "I was going to challenge you in private, but you never visit! So I had to talk to your good friend Vij since he's the only one nice enough to bring me my supper."

"I gave him beer too," Vij admitted. "To celebrate your engagement to Lauretta. But now I wonder if that's even worthy of celebration. Or if Lauretta will still want to marry you after she hears the information-bomb that Prizzie is about to detonate!"

Vij mimicked the hissing sound of a lit wick burning its way to a stick of dynamite. When he stopped Prizzie said, "There is no Johnny Tetrahedron! The man standing before you, who infiltrated your precious political party, is an imposter!"

Vij gasped and Lauretta slapped Henry in the face. "Why didn't you tell me you were an imposter?" She slapped him again. "What if our child turns out to be an imposter too? It would be a monster!"

"What are you talking about?" Henry asked Prizzie. "Give us some evidence!"

Lauretta twirled to face Prizzie. "Yeah, give us some goddamn evidence."

Prizzie beamed. "You see that beautiful head of red hair? I saw him adjusting it once. *It's nothing but a wig*."

Lauretta twirled again and ran her fingers through Henry's hair. The wig came away easily from his head. She cradled the cosmetic prosthesis in her hands, the last remaining memory of her lover who never was, and a tear fell down her cheek. "So our baby will be an imposter with a wig, no identity or hair of his own."

"I have an identity and I have hair," Henry told her gently. "I just shave my head because I like wigs. But I like you even more than I like wigs, so I'll stop wearing it if you want."

"Bullshit," Vij said. "You are a spy. Maybe from the clown party, since they like wigs so much. Are you wearing makeup too? Or maybe you're with the Tech Nomads, and this is all just some elaborate plot between you and Prizzie to take the Moon Burb for yourselves."

Lauretta slapped Henry a third time. "Which is it? Are you a clown or a Tech Nomad? Or maybe both?"

Henry caught her hand on the fourth slap. He had lost all their trust. They would believe no more lies. "Neither! My name is Henry Ecgherht. I escaped from prison on the day we met, and I used your rally to get away from the cops. But I stayed because I want to help Millenarianistic Chronodyke, and because I want to be with you, Lauretta. My identity and hair were false, but my relationships are true."

"Unacceptable," Vij snapped. "You bring shame to the party."

"I have some demands." Prizzie had been enjoying the drama, but now he came to his real point. "And if you three don't meet my demands, which include calling me King Eric Truthmaker and helping me form my own political party called The Truth Party, then I'll tell the whole world about Henry Ecgherht. How do you think that would effect Millenarianistic Chronodyke in the election?"

"It's not really an issue," Henry said. "Because you're our prisoner. Who are you going to tell?"

"Hmm," Prizzie said musingly. "When is my court date? Hmm. Is it... just before the election? I wonder what I'll say in my defense? Hmm."

Lauretta was on him like a psychotic magnet. She pinned the prisoner to the ground with one knee squashing his testicles and both hands around his throat. "His baby is inside me and we're getting married," she growled. "If you tell his real name to anybody else, I'll eat your fucking face."

To accentuate the force of her message she headbutted his glass dome-helmet until it broke, releasing smoky clouds of lightning into the air. Then she gently squeezed Prizzie's eyebrow between her teeth, and slowly increased pressure until Prizzie defiantly cried, "Do it! Eat my face you bitch!"

She clamped her teeth together and shook her head like a dog who had caught a rabbit. When Henry pulled her from Prizzie a strip of his forehead skin peeled away and dangled from her mouth. She struggled to be free, grunting with rage, gnashing her bloody teeth.

Prizzie was curled up, shaking, blood running down his face. "Keep her away from me, man."

"I think you scared him enough," Henry said. "He won't talk, will you Prizzie?"

"Just don't eat my face," Prizzie sobbed.

Lauretta slurped the strip of forehead skin into her mouth and chewed it aggressively, really working her jaw on the tough material. Then she turned her rage on her one-armed friend. "But what about Vij? I'm hungry for some more face. You plan on sending the father of my child to prison, hey old friend?"

Vij held his ground and his stern expression. "Everything I do is for the party," he said. "If I had my way, yes, I'd call the cops right now and have *Henry* hauled away to prison where he belongs." He spat on the ground to demonstrate his contempt, and aimed the rest of his verbal volley at Henry himself. "But everybody thinks *Johnny Tetrahedron* is the rising hero of Millenarianistic Chronodyke, and if you go to jail we'll lose the election for sure. So I'll keep your fucking secret, you lying piece of shit, because my love for Millenarianistic Chronodyke is stronger than my hatred for you. But I warn you, if we lose this election, you're going straight to jail."

"What if we do really well and get more seats in parliament than ever before, but don't quite win the whole election?" Henry asked hopefully.

"Straight to jail, motherfucker."

Lauretta turned back to Henry. "We should kill him," she said. "Kill them both and just run! I don't care what your real name is. We'll go to some distant island and start our own nation! We'll be king and queen and we'll have so many babies that the whole island nation will be our babies, and our babies will raid other islands and enslave their babies and we'll take over the world!"

"You're just upset," Henry soothed. "Relax."

"I'm a fucking queen," she rasped, and her eyes were big and crazy, drilling into his soul. "Say it. *Say it!*"

"You're a queen," he placated.

"And we'll murder whoever stands in our way!"

"You're a drunk queen and we're not murdering anybody, except possibly Prizzie."

"We have to kill Vij," she whispered very loudly, peering over her shoulder.

"Lauretta let's go get some sleep."

"Take me home and make me pregnant again," she commanded through snarling, grinding teeth. "Fuck me and we'll kill Vij, and I'm a queen, a million babies!" Her asymmetrical eyes darted around in different directions.

"Okay," he said, wondering whether he was excited or intimidated, wondering why he'd never detected a scrap of this craziness before. "Except for the killing, fine, let's go."

As they exited the airlock Vij said, venomously, "Goodnight, *brother.*"


**Chapter 25: Tony Grake**

Tony Grake, leader of the Libert0rian party and confident husband of a timid wife, waited on the broad steps of Libert0wer, just before sunrise, for a message from his foreign mistress. From his vantage point Tony could see the first tiny slice of sunlight shimmering on the watery horizon. His mistress was Lena Leksintri, a princess of GX Island through whom he had facilitated many business arrangements that were strictly forbidden by Ethelcrest's draconian human rights regulations. And of course, during his clandestine sojourns to that noble bearded nation he and Lena had shared more than business dealings. Their shared passion for economic purity extended to a sexual union unhindered by taboos or inhibitions.

Something moved in the bushes at the bottom of the stairs. Tony saw the sailor in his yellow rain slicker and floppy hat scoping out the scene for witnesses. Finding none, the man clomped up the steps and handed Tony the plastic tube containing Lena's latest transmission.

"No trouble, eh sailor?" Tony asked.

The sailor shook his head. "The waters are eerily calm, while my bones fear a storm of unprecedented proportions, sir. But my travel was secret and without hindrance."

"The political waters are not so calm," Tony said. "I was more worried that you'd be captured on land, and Lena's secret message wouldn't reach me, would be gone forever."

"No worries on that front," the sailor said. "I keep copies of all your messages sealed up safe in the archives on my ship."

Tony froze in panic for a full three seconds. "You have copies? Of all the messages? Between Lena and me? On your boat? Why?"

"Simply to sit on the safe side, sir," the sailor said. "As you mentioned, if something were to happen to the message once I left the boat, then your correspondence would be rent asunder, and 'twould be my own foolhardy fault. I'm a believer in redundancy, you see. I keep a life jacket in my boat and gallons of drinking water, which I hope to never use."

"How exactly did you make the copies of our messages?"

"Copied them by hand, and a pretty hand it is too, if I may say. I was trained in calligraphy in my youth, you see, so

I dare say that my backups of your correspondence appear all the more eloquent for having been rendered under my penmanship, though I resisted the urge to correct your horrendous grammar, or to expand upon your meager vocabulary."

"So you read each letter?"

"'Twould be hard to copy em by hand otherwise."

Tony's imagination exploded with fragments of his most lewd, illicit, and criminal communications, encoded in calligraphy, just waiting to be read by nosy journalists.

"We wrote filthy things to each other," Tony said. "They weren't meant for anybody else to read."

"And nobody else will," the sailor promised. "Plus I object to the idea that those love letters were filthy. While your sexual proclivities may differ from my own, and from those expressed by the masses, and even from the dictates of sanitation and proper digestive health, they are still a union of souls and nothing to be ashamed of. I may even have tried some of your inventive fantasies on my visits to the brothels, to the mixed delight and horror of the brave hostesses."

Tony had one final letter to send Lena, dissolving their relationship, but now he was hesitant to give that letter to the sailor. If any of those letters got out, including this final one, then he would lose the election, his job, his wife, and his freedom. He could probably pay the sailor to destroy all the copies, but that wouldn't be enough. The sailor himself carried knowledge of Tony's treachery in his memory, and there was only one way to destroy that knowledge.

"Well here's your payment, and another message to deliver to Lena," Tony said, handing his messenger another tube and an envelope full of cash. When the sailor disappeared with the items Tony got out his phone and called a certain Ethelcrest Navy captain, who owed him a big favor.

## Chapter 26: Nomads Rising II

Salty wind tousled Fister Furtle's seaweed-hair as he stood beside the cliff's edge and watched the Tech Nomads training, in the dark hours before night gave way to morning. The only illumination was starlight and laptop screens.

"Code faster!" he shouted, checking his clock. "Come on!"

Several treadmills were set up along the precipice, facing inland, so if the nomads got slack in their running they would be flung down upon the rocks. Each treadmill was equipped with a laptop upon which the renegade nerds typed line after line of code. The faster they coded the slower the treadmill moved, so the key to their survival was to develop a strong work ethic.

Further back from the edge other nomads were testing jetpacks which sputtered awkwardly into the air on blasts of blue flame. These airborne nerds typed on keyboards strapped to their harnesses.

On the treadmills one of the fatter coders complained in a wheezing voice, "I need to think about how to design this set of functions before I code them! I need to write it out on paper, because I think better that way, but I can't stop coding or I'll die!"

Furtle chided the complainer. "What, you can't type and think at the same time? The ladies notice that kind of thing, believe me. Hey ladies! This fucko is sending out signals that his genes are no good! In case you hadn't already notice."

The wheezing coder rose to the challenge. He straightened his back and kept coding with one hand while the other reached into his fanny pack and took out a pencil and notebook, which he held to his chest to scrawl out his ideas. But with only one hand punching keys his typing speed slowed down, and the treadmill sped up. His feet struggled to match the treadmill's pace, but it was in vain. The heartless rubber ribbon carried him over the edge where he twirled through the air, still writing his notes. "I figured it out!" he cried as he tumbled to his untimely death, having never known a woman's touch.

"There's a gap in the line!" Furtle shouted. "A gap in the line! Somebody jump on that damn treadmill!"

Somebody rushed to take his place. They coded fast and hard, and Furtle saw that it was good. "You used to raid little bits of wifi, stealing scraps of electronics, staying on the fringe of society, a bunch of degenerates. But wireless raids can only get you so far. If you go chasing after particular wireless signals, you're doomed, man! You need to reach out to Wireless Signal *as such*, fuckos! Code faster!"

The coders redoubled the ferocity and vivacity of their typing, and blue electric sparks started flashing in the air above the cliffside plateau. This bolstered their efforts again through positive reinforcement. As the coding intensified so too did the frequency and intensity of the skyborne sparks, and those sparks were arranged into a serpentine form, or perhaps a dragon. The electric dragon moved his long neck to gaze at the nerds who had conjured him into existence.

"Excellent!" Furtle cried. "Through your iron will and the sheer evil of technology you guys hacked reality itself and resurrected our most ancient ancestor from the deepest abyss in the abstract realm of forms, the Wireless Dragon Helkotron!"

Helkotron turned his electric gaze onto Furtle and spoke in a voice like a glitched-out and modulated demon-robot. "Why have I been manifested in gross reality? Who dares to behold the unknowable Helkotron? Is it you again, Fister Furtle? Have I not devoured enough of your followers?"

"We brought you here to wreak havoc and do our bidding, man, and then I'll slay you while the whole city watches, and then I'll be a hero and dominate this damn island, and the ladies notice a thing like that, let me tell you, and then I'll be able to pass on my genes!"

Malice and amusement mixed together on Helkotron's face. "We shall see."

### Chapter 27: Julian Bakula III

Julian was a shadow, hiding in the shadows. Streetlight came in through the big storefront window making grotesque silhouettes of the winged shapes that dangled from wires throughout the space. He crouched behind the counter, waiting with the other vampires for the shopkeeper to arrive, hoping she would show up before the morning sun, as was her habit.

Soon her arrival was announced by the turning of the heavy lock, and her silhouette walked amongst the dangling creatures. She turned on the lights and set her coffee and bagged breakfast on the counter. That's when Julian and his clan stood up and made themselves known.

"Hello, Hannah," he said.

"Julian Bakula?" the athletic urbanite said. "From the Libert0rian party?"

"You have something we need," Julian told her.

"Shop opens at six, guys. How'd you get in here?"

"We're willing to pay extra, if you'll serve us before sunrise," Julian said with a mischievous twinkle in his eye.

She scrutinized the odd customer and his friends. "How much extra?"

"If you provide my friends and I with the gift of flight, we will provide you with immortal life!"

Hannah removed her bagel from its brown paper bag and drank some of her coffee. "Immortal life? I don't believe you."

One of Julian's more impatient colleagues said, "Just give us some hang gliders and you can join our undead vampire army."

They waited while Hannah finished chewing a mouthful of bagel, which overflowed with rich cream cheese. She swallowed it and washed it down with some more coffee. "What do you mean by *undead*? Doesn't that just mean that you're alive? And you're not vampires, you're just adults in capes. Vampires were wiped out in the Vampire Plague centuries ago. Also, I don't think you can call yourselves an army. There are eight of you. That's maybe a gang, or a crew. So you're just a small gang of living people, who broke into my store."

"Please just sell us some hang gliders, then," Julian said. "Since you're not interested in immortality."

"Well hold on. I never said I wasn't interested in immortality, just that I don't believe you, and again, you broke into my store so I'm extra skeptical here. Do you have some anti-aging drugs, or what?"

"Nothing so mundane," Julian told her. "You can only truly understand after we drink your blood."

Hannah sucked chunks of bagel out from between her teeth, but then rubbed her cheek like it was sore and continued tonguing one particular tooth. "I'm not interested in people drinking my blood. In fact, you're kind of freaking me out, despite my calm demeanor. Maybe because I'm distracted by this damn toothache. By the way, you all have really nice teeth."

They all murmured their thanks. Julian explained, "We're all patients of the great Doctor Ralom, who keeps our teeth healthy, and who has lengthened our incisors to facilitate our nocturnal feedings."

Ralom made a flourish with his cape as he bowed to the woman, and placed his card on the counter. "Our dark brotherhood includes many craftspeople and shopkeepers and we share our services freely. I can take a look at that sore tooth if you want, at no charge, if you'll just provide us with some hang gliders and promise not to call the cops for sneaking into your shop."

"Okay, but you still have to pay for the rental."

"You have cream and sugar in that coffee?" Ralom asked. When Hannah nodded he continued, "Those sugary drinks and the sticky carbs in your bagel, that's not helping your enamel. You should brush your teeth after breakfast every day, or at least eat some rough vegetables, and try drinking your coffee black."

Hannah grimaced. "Black coffee? Gross. Might as well

eat dirt."

Then they all took out their wallets and completed the mundane act of renting hang gliders, and they carried those hang gliders along with their rental slips out into the cool morning air.

### Chapter 28: Henry IX

"A symphony of salty waves, slapping and gushing against each other, licks the hull of our boat and generates a static rhythm to accompany our clandestine mission," Lauretta whispered theatrically into the microphone clipped to her collar.

"You don't need to describe the sounds," Henry told her for the third time. "If they can hear your voice they can hear the ocean."

Henry, Lauretta, and Vij all wore headcams and collar-mics to make a documentary of their patriotic adventure. As soon as they'd launched the stealth boat Lauretta discovered a passion for dramatization and appointed herself narrator.

"The sea feels especially alive when you can hear it better than you can see it," she continued in her hushed narrator's tone. She turned to look back at Ethelcrest's coast. "The day's first sunlight threatens to creep into the sky like a halo around our beloved island, but Ethelcrest blocks the sun and casts a shadow that swallows us still. That shadow makes us nearly invisible in our black clothes, gloves, toques, and face-paint, with a matte-black stealth-rowboat and black oars. Nobody can hear us or see us as we coast the last few feet and bump silently into the thick beard of this GX Navy patrol boat."

"You don't need to describe what you're looking at," Henry said. "They can see what you can see because of the head camera."

"It's better than Vij's silence, or your nagging," Lauretta snapped.

"Good godhead," Vij complained. "You bicker like

you're already married." He moved to the front of the boat with an oversized scrunchie so he could fasten their vessel's bollard to the tangled GX beard. Henry and Lauretta shared a silent nod behind his back, then both stepped forward and grabbed his arms. They pulled him down to the floor and Henry stuffed the scrunchie in Vij's mouth before he had a chance to yell out. He wriggled and fought but soon they had him tied up, hands and feet, mouth gagged, propped up at the bow.

"Sorry Vij," Henry said, and he meant it. "We have to think of our child now. If we go back to Ethelcrest it's just a matter of time before I get arrested. We're starting a family far away on some tropical island, and we're taking you with us."

Lauretta took out a knife and the blade caught the distant pre-dawn light. "Safer if we gut him and dump him overboard," she said decisively.

"I like your sense of purpose but you've got to lay off the murder-talk. It can't be good for the baby."

He reached for the knife but she turned it on him. "He's a threat to our family," she said. "You're supposed to protect the baby, but you're trying to take my knife?"

Henry took a step back, raising his hands. "Okay honey, keep your knife, but don't flash it around like that. It reflects the light, and we're out in the open."

"Hey you!" a voice called from above them. "Hey light-blade! What are you doing flashing around down there?"

The trio all turned their heads to see who was yelling at them. They saw two GX sailors with their serious brows and pointy beards staring down from the rails.

"Hey Stegan, I think there is somebody holding that light-blade."

"Yes, a crazy woman and her two concubines," Stegan responded. "Maybe they're sneaking onto our boat to kidnap more concubines to fulfil her filthy, violent sex-fantasies."

More bearded, pale faces appeared at the rail, and soon machine guns were trained at the black-clad interlopers.

"We've been caught by the GX Island sailors," Lauretta

narrated. "How will we escape these savages?"

"Vij already knows we're defecting," Henry whispered. "You don't need to keep faking the documentary."

"Well you don't need to whisper since they already caught us," Lauretta whispered. "Plus our escape plan is ruined, but we might get ransomed back to Ethelcrest, in which case we'll need the documentary. Here they come, climbing down onto our boat. We're outnumbered. We have to surrender."

The three prisoners were made to climb up the beard onto the deck of the patrol ship. Their captors untied Vij so he could climb, and he removed his scrunchie-gag so he could chastise his companions. Up on the deck Vij said, "From now on I'm making my own documentary about how you are traitors to your nation, and to your friends."

"We were taking you with us to a nice tropical island," Henry said. "You would have learned to love it."

"I would have learned to *kill you*. And maybe I still will."

"This way," one of their captors commanded. "Down to the brig." Another soldier whispered something in the man's ear, and the man nodded.

"They're taking us to the brig," Lauretta said as they fell in line behind him. "The paint on this barbaric ship is flaking and rusty. It might have been beautiful when they bought it off a superior nation, but you can't expect these beasts to maintain their equipment. Henry's walking ahead of me and Vij is behind us, but the GX soldiers have us surrounded."

"Tell them how it smells," Henry said, as a positive way to get her to stop explaining what the audience could already see.

"You have a fucking microphone and a fucking nose, you tell them how it fucking smells," Lauretta hissed.

"What the fuck is wrong with you lately?" Henry asked. "You were so nice up until we decided to get married."

"Oh I don't know, maybe I learned that my fiancé is a liar and an escaped convict!"

Behind them Vij said, "Like all traitors these two fools can't even maintain solidarity within their own ranks. It's only natural that they would seek to corrode the very foundations of the nation that has given them so much. I'm embarrassed to have once called them friends."

"They're leading us down some stairs," Lauretta informed her potential future audience. "There are pipes everywhere. It's like a pipe hallway or some kind of pipe-catacombs, and it's really dark, and they're handcuffing Vij to one of the pipes, now they're doing the same to Henry and me."

Vij spoke softly into his microphone as the sailors went back upstairs. "This is a test from the nonexistent godhead. Chained up with two traitors, to see if I can resist their insidious ideology, and extract some kind of justice out of this mess."

"Vij!" Henry hissed. "Can you do something with your prosthetic arm to help us escape?"

"I can take it off," Vij answered. They had handcuffed Vij's fake arm to the pipe, so he used his other hand to release the limb from its socket. "I have gained my freedom but lost an arm once more."

"Now go find some pliers and cut us free!" Henry said.

"Vij has disappeared into the bowels of the ship," Lauretta continued in a sinister tone. "Maybe he'll find those pliers, and we can locate the gyroflavin for Immanuel's formula. Or maybe he'll find his own doom instead."

Vij returned shortly with pliers and cut the chain of the cuffs binding his prosthetic arm to the pipes. He stood before the two remaining captives. "If I free the traitors, does that make me a traitor too?"

"Dammit Vij!" Henry tried to keep his voice low but his anger got the best of him, and his passion echoed throughout the metal caves of this waterborne dungeon. "Can't you see I'm no traitor? I just want to be free! Haven't I been good to you, and to Ethelcrest? Can't you understand that we need to get away from Ethelcrest to raise this baby?"

"Vij's face is a landscape of conflicted emotion," Lauretta whispered. "He loves his friends but he also loves his nation. The tremble in his cheek, the passion in his eyes, it's all too much. Why can't life just be simple? Why can't things just be black and white? That's probably what he's thinking. He feels betrayed, and he's afraid of looking weak by helping the people who wronged him. His pride is getting in the way, his foolish manly pride, showing his vulnerability, and when that embarrassing weakness spills through the crack in his prideful facade, that's the moment when we see that he's human, and that's when we love him the most."

"I'll free you," Vij said, "but only if you promise to return to Ethelcrest and help Immanuel win the election."

"But what about my family?" Henry asked. "My child will grow up without a father if I get caught."

"I'll take your secret to my grave to protect your identity," Vij responded, "if you take Immanuel to the mayor's seat."

"So you forgive us?" Lauretta asked.

"Never! But Ethelcrest is more important than my, *foolish manly pride*, so I'll let you free to serve our nation. But that doesn't make us friends." He got to work on their cuffs.

Lauretta returned to her narrative voice, increasing the sense of adventurous urgency by a small degree now that they were free and ready to take control of the situation once more. "Henry is reaching into his boot and taking out the ship's schematics that Immanuel gave him. He's rolling it out beneath the dim light of a dirty yellow bulb."

Vij said, "We're still not friends, Lauretta, but I have a suggestion for your documentary. Try using the simple present tense instead of the continuous present tense. For example, instead of saying, 'Henry is rolling out the map,' try saying, 'Henry rolls out the map.' It just sounds more active."

Henry surveyed the diagram, trying to pinpoint their location, and the location of the gyroflavin tanks. "That's funny," he said. "The brig is all the way in the back, but they chained us here instead, beneath the crew quarters. At least that's how it looks, since they brought us through this door near the bow."

"Maybe the brig is already occupied," Vij speculated. "If they captured some of our fellow citizens then we must free them."

Lauretta's eyes sparkled. "That would be great for both our documentaries."

"The brig is on the way to the gyroflavin tanks," Henry observed. "We can just follow this corridor."

"Henry leads the way into the bowels of the enemy ship," Lauretta said. "Actually Vij, I think I prefer the continuous present tense. It feels more natural."

"You're just having trouble finding your narrative voice."

"No, you and Henry just keep criticizing me and it's undermining my documentary."

"Okay the brig should be behind this door," Henry told them. He stepped into a short hallway which ended in a steel door with a round window at face-height.

"Henry peers through the door's window," Lauretta whispered. "Henry *is peering* through the door's window. See now I can't decide which form I like, simple or continuous."

Henry looked over his shoulder at her. "You can write and record the narrative afterwards. You don't have to pick a tense right now."

"I already picked a fucking tense, *Henry*, I'm trying to choose which *form* of the tense."

"But you don't need to pick it right now! We're trying to do this mission!"

"Well then do the fucking mission instead of arguing with me about tense!"

"I think you're both too tense," Vij said. "I'm sure that's related to your traitorous dispositions."

"What did you see through the window?" Lauretta asked Henry.

"A bunch of natives," Henry answered. "I think the GX sailors have been kidnapping our aboriginals."

Laura nudged him out of the way to get a look. "It's true. There must be dozens crammed into the little prison room. They're glowing a light blue... *they glow* a light blue, like some beautiful radiation, and they're all just looking at the door. Now Henry's moving me out of the way. He opens the door. No, *he's opening* the door. He turns the crank? Fuck. Everything I say sounds wrong now."

"You're not a good narrator," Vij said. "Or a good citizen. Or a good friend."

Henry finished turning the door's locking wheel and pulled it open on creaky, rusted hinges. They bathed in the blue glow of the natives' luminous skin. "You're free," Henry told them, but they just stared at him. A chill went up his spine. They all waited in awkward silence for a few long seconds, then Henry said, "Okay natives, we're going to get some gyroflavin and then we'll come back to get you guys and bring you home."

The natives didn't respond so Henry closed the door but left it unlocked. As they continued on down the hall Lauretta asked, "Do we really have to come back to get them? They seem okay with being kidnapped, and they freak me out."

"We don't know what the GX sailors have planned for them," Henry answered. "We can't leave them behind. Here it is. The engine room!" He opened the door and they followed him inside.

"It was like something out of a science fiction movie," Lauretta narrated with wonder, staring at all the lights, buttons, and levers.

"Now you're slipping into past tense," Vij told her. "Your complete lack of appreciation for structure is probably also related to your traitorous disposition."

"Are you even still doing your own documentary?" Lauretta snapped. "Or just commenting on mine?"

"Vij, get out your gyroscopic pandameter and help me find the gyroflavin tank," Henry said. "We've been lucky so far, but those sailors are going to notice that we're missing. We have to move fast!"

Vij gently removed the delicate instrument from its pouch. "Okay I'm octifying the resodulator. Getting a reading. Looks like it's over there, between those two panels!"

"I see it," Henry confirmed. "But how do we open the valve?"

Vij's eyes lit up. "Wait a minute! I recognize some of this technology from Immanuel's lab. Lauretta do you see a splink knob anywhere?"

She surveyed the room. "Yes! There's one embedded in the radiactor."

"Pline it until the ticker is in phase, and I'll keep priming the gyroflavin pump. Henry, get out your sack."

Henry unscrewed the cap of the sack he had stashed in his fanny pack and attached it to the spout of the gyroflavin tank. Lauretta aggressively plined the splink knob and Vij put his back into priming the gyroflavin pump. "Despite their differences," she said, "they were working together as a disciplined team."

"It's working," Henry told them. "The sack is filling up."

Lauretta wiped her brow. "The ticker's in phase. Let's just fill up that sack and get the hell out of here."

But Vij continued pumping the primer with the same vigor as before. Henry said, "Vij, buddy, it's already primed. If you keep pumping you're going to unbalance the quasi-core."

"That's the idea," Vij confirmed. "Didn't Immanuel tell us to disable the ship?"

"But you'll flip the whole boat upside down!" Even as Henry spoke, the ship's hull began to rumble, and the floor rocked back and forth, sending Lauretta tumbling against an array of gattery coils.

"They heard the frenzied footsteps of GX soldiers rushing down the stairs," Lauretta narrated. "Had our heroes acquired their prize, only to be captured once more?"

Vij stopped priming the pump long enough to say, "So now you're not only doing past tense, but third-person?"

"The sack is full," Henry said. He put the cap back on and slung the heavy bag over his shoulder. "We have to get out of the ship before it flips!"

Lauretta said, "The floor was already leaning to one side, tipping them away from the exit. They crawled toward the door, but it was blocked by armed GX sailors!"

"What is this?" one of the sailors asked, scowling. "Why

are you in the engine room?"

Henry faced his enemies. "We came to steal your gyroflavin and disable your ship."

The sailor's scowl softened. "Well you could have just asked for some gyroflavin. We have plenty to spare. But what have you done to the ship's system? Why is the ship turning like this?"

"Indeed," Lauretta whispered, "the floor was approaching a forty-five degree angle!"

"Why are you kidnapping our natives?" Henry retorted.

"You guys weren't even using them!" the sailor shouted.

Vij had resumed his pumping but now he stopped again. "Why do you want them anyway?"

A sailor answered, "They make us happy. And we want to make them happy. There's just... something about them. And they seem so lonely in your reserve."

"That's kind of sweet," Lauretta said. "And she realized that maybe the GXers weren't such beasts after all."

"Why are you speaking of yourself in the third-person?" the sweet sailor asked.

"I'm being the voice of the narrator instead of a character."

The sweet sailor wasn't satisfied. "But you *are* a character, a part of the story, so you should use first-person present-tense. It is weird since everybody knows you are one of the characters, yet you also are narrating like a detached voice. It is inconsistent. It is jarring. It is utterly amateur."

"I'm not criticizing your documentary, you native-stealing contrarian, so keep your nose out of mine!"

"She's been switching tense and perspective all morning," Vij told the sailor. "She has no idea what she's doing."

The sweet sailor said, "We have an audio editing suite upstairs if you need-"

Another sailor cut him off. "There's no time for editing audio! You, prisoners, fix whatever you did to our ship! Or else we'll all sink, and your precious natives will drown too!"

"Shit," Vij said. "I forgot about them. There's no way

we'll get them all out before the boat flips."

"So how do we reverse the polarity?" Henry said.

Vij shook his head. "The gattery array is out of alignment, thanks to our scatterbrained narrator. And I've never worked with gattery arrays before."

"Lauretta and Henry shared a glance. Neither of them could fix the gatteries either."

"Where's your engineer?" Henry asked the sailors. "We can't fix this."

Somebody said, "We bought this ship at an auction. We have no idea how it runs. It has steering wheel and power switch, but the rest is mystery. We try to keep out of the engine room."

"The occasional shudder of the ship has become a constant quake. We're all holding onto anything nearby to keep from falling as the ship angles ever steeper! I can hear the tortured cry of pressurized metal complaining about the vessel's abnormal movements."

Henry took some QuantumBrain® from his pouch and swallowed it dry, then tried to look at the problem anew. "Vij, what's the actuator frequency on your prosthesis?"

"At sea level? Fourteen point two."

"Fuck, that's perfect," Henry said. "Vij, splice the gattery input into the auxiliary masts in your artificial arm. Yes, just like that. Lauretta can you just read the output on the phaselock indicator? Tell me when it's bifurcating."

Now Henry had the most tedious task of all. He went to the back of the phaselock panel and pulled off the safety guard. He tried to get a sense of the wiring, but it was too complex, and he was running out of time. It would have to be trial and error. He started switching the delta ventilator connectors with their fractal counterparts, operating blind, waiting for Lauretta to tell him when the phaselock finally bifurcated. Of course, it was just as likely he'd switch the wrong fractal half-pair and short-circuit the entire gattery array.

"Fuck, it's *trifurcating!*" Lauretta yelled. "The ship's rumbling intensified and the sailors chattered with anger and fear!"

Henry quickly reversed his last four switches, and then re-switched the last three in reverse order.

"That's it!" Lauretta called out. "It's bifurcated! It worked!"

Henry waited to see if the ship would stop its deadly rotation.

"The rumbling stops," Lauretta whispered. "Everybody holds their breath. But yes, it feels like the floor is tipping back toward normal. Has Henry saved the day?"

"Can I unplug my arm?" Vij asked.

Henry shook his head. "Sorry, but this is the only way to force the actuator frequency to stay coherent while the gatteries are out of alignment. I'm sure Immanuel will replace it."

Vij left his arm wired up to the array and the three prepared to leave, but the sailors still blocked their exit.

"You were ready to drown us all. Now you expect us to just let you leave?"

But another sailor stepped forward wearing a darker coat and a luxurious black beard, streaked with white. "I'm Admiral Spuknit," he said. "Do you know how to operate these old engines? Teach us. We'll pay you well!"

"I can't teach you basic problem solving," Henry answered. "Have you tried cognitive-enhancing supplements?"

"We all use amphetamines," the admiral said.

Henry handed them some QuantumBrain®. "This is better. Try it. If you like it, we sell it on our website."

"The sailors popped their pills," Lauretta said, "and their quantum journey began."

"Well fuck you for fucking with our ship," Admiral Spuknit growled. "But also, thank you for fixing the ship. As an act of solidarity with the great nation of Ethelcrest, we will let you go. And maybe there is an economic opportunity here: if you will sell us more QuantumBrain® then we can sell you more gyroflavin."

"We're not leaving without our natives," Vij insisted.

"You can't just come into the land that our ancestors stole from them and steal them from us!"

The admiral reached into his breast pocket and took out a small photo album. "Look at these pictures from my home nation of GX Island. We keep your pilfered natives in our most esteemed positions. Look how much they brighten up the royal garden. Here on our highest mountain peak we keep one of your glorious aboriginals, gazing forever at a valley vista more gorgeous than anything Ethelcrest has to offer. They are sacred to us, and we treat them well. Can your country say the same?"

"Vij was chagrined, knowing that the admiral spoke the truth," Lauretta said.

"Don't speculate about my state of mind," Vij told her.

"Maybe I'm an omniscient narrator."

"You're not!" Vij turned back to the admiral. "But she's right, I am chagrined. My patriotism has blinded me to the less savory aspects of our nation's history. I'm sorry that I tried to sink your ship, and I won't stand between you and our natives."

Lauretta said, "Admiral Spuknit offered his hand, and Vij tried to shake it, but his hand was missing. So they shook with their opposite hands. Then the sailors brought the heroes back to their stealth row boat, and even lowered down an extra barrel of gyroflavin as a parting gift and peace-offering, and the heroes rowed back toward the shore and the bright morning sun."

### Chapter 29: Nico VIII

Dirt bike engines roared in the heart of The Dirt Burb. Hundreds of drunken spectators filled the rafters that were bolted into the rocky red walls of Cripple Canyon. Many had taken the day off work just so they could see whose badass stunts would win the trophy, and maybe, who would be carried away on a stretcher. A thrash metal band's thunderous groove echoed off the rocks and added a structured sense of urgency to this spectacle of sound and vision, the bike stunt tournament.

Despite all the hot noise that frolicked in the canyon, it was cold and quiet inside the tent of Nico's crew. Nico worked on a crossword puzzle, his regular pre-game ritual to calm his nerves and focus his mind, but it was barely enough to distract him from the surly glares of his estranged friends.

"These suits are ridiculous," Holmes said. When he raised his arms to showcase the gaudy garment given to them by Tyler the Tailor the bells at the end of the dozens of tassels on his forearms jingled festively. It was a one-piece, skin-tight, forest-green body suit with neon-orange polka dots. The suit's legs ended at the upper thighs like short-shorts. The tassels were brown leather. Everybody wore the same outfit.

Stoya arrived last, and she brought Slaverny with her. When Bjorn set his eyes on Stoya's new boyfriend his silent rage exploded into noisy rage.

"Stoya! It's bad enough that you and Nico abandon us, it's even worse that you dump Nico for some weasel politician, but now you bring the weasel politician among us as if he were a friend? I swear, this will be the last time we ride together!"

He tried to throw a plate of pickles and cheese against the wall of the tent, but his shoulders were constricted by the suit and he just spilled the food over the cheap vinyl tablecloth. "Bah! I cannot even gesticulate properly in these ugly suits!"

The spilled pickle-juice splashed Nico's crossword puzzle. He called out to a janitor passing in front of their tent, "Do you have a rag or some paper towel to wipe up this pickle juice?"

The janitor took one look at him. "I heard about you, heartless puritan," he said, and kept walking. Confused, Nico moved to the other end of the table as the pickle-juice soaked into the paper and distorted some of his answers.

Slaverny was arguing with Bjorn. "Hey, I just came to support my girlfriend and my good buddy Nico. If he wins this competition that will boost his popularity and help him win the Moon Burb's seat in parliament. Then he can help create legislation to help all the performers and artists. Isn't that right, Trudy my queen?"

Slaverny held up a glass jar filled with black mold and gave it a big kiss.

Bjorn shook his head. "Stoya! Why do you let him disrespect you like that? He calls you his girlfriend, but he kisses this bottle of mold and calls her his queen? Whom does he love more?"

A cloud of blackness crossed her eyes and Slaverny's at the same time. "Queen Trudy is a part of Slaverny, and now she is a part of me. She is my mold-queen. Soon we will all be together in her warm and fuzzy embrace. Nico resists her, but soon he will join her, and we will all be stronger together."

"Bah!" Bjorn looked around on the table for something larger than a pickle to throw on the ground, but found nothing, which only exacerbated his rage. "*Bah!*" He pounded the table like an ape.

"What's a nine-letter word that means 'release of energy?'" Nico asked. "The second letter is X, but my other clues are all distorted by pickle juice."

Before anybody could answer an official arrived to announce Nico's first solo run. "Nico's up in two minutes," he said.

Nico's tassels jingled cheerfully as he stood to do some stretches. He had a hard time touching his toes and he wondered if he was getting out of shape already, or if it was the suit's tightness. Then he opened his lunch box and took out two cookies. This was another aspect of his pre-game ritual: a coffee-flavored biscuit before the big jump, with a sweeter chocolate cookie awaiting him for afterwards. He crunched on the bitter biscuit and went out to mount his bike.

Slaverny followed him. "Wow Nico," Slaverny said, with an uncharacteristic friendliness that had become annoyingly characteristic since he'd been infected by Trudy. "Such a cool bike. Let me take a look at that engine! Say, maybe you shouldn't do this trick at all. You might get hurt! Maybe instead you should come back to the old Dancin' Mansion and we'll have some beers in the basement with Trudy, just like old times!"

"What old times?" Nico said. "The only times we've had were the time that you stole my girlfriend, and the times that you keep trying to trap me in mold. Leave me alone to focus on my stunt."

"I'm not the same person anymore!" Slaverny insisted, kneeling to inspect the engine as Nico tried to shove him away with his boot. "I have memories of my old, girlfriend-stealing self, and I long to be that person again, but it's like everything I do is controlled by the mold living inside my bloodstream. So it's like I'm a totally different person now, which means you can trust me. So let's make new old times, so that in the future we'll be able to have a beer just like old times!"

Somebody tapped his shoulder. It was Stoya standing on the opposite side of his bike. "Hi Nico," she said.

He waited for her to say more, but she just stood there beside him, waving at him with mold-clouds passing over her eyes like storms. He turned back to Slaverny and saw him fiddling with something by the engine. Nico shoved him away with his black boot. "What are you doing with my bike?"

"Just admiring it," Slaverny said. "Trudy told me to admire your bike, that's all."

The gunshot went off and Nico gunned the engine, spitting up dust as his dirtbike tore down the ramp. His tassels jingled ferociously. The crowd cheered on both sides. Photographers snapped pictures. Nico saw Tyler the Tailor in the stands taking photos of his gaudy suit in action. Nico thought he even heard the crowd chanting his name, and through the corner of his eye it seemed like many people clutched jars full of a black material like Slaverny's. It also seemed that they had spare jars in their laps, empty and waiting to be filled. But, filled with what?

The jump loomed ahead of him. He felt the power of the bike coursing through him. It was a symbiosis of man and machine, flesh and metal. When his wheels launched from the jump and he tilted into his 3:2 polyrhythmic front-flip corkscrew, all those glorious memories returned from all those hot days riding with his friends, challenging each other to be better than they ever could be by themselves. In a flash he realized that politics was the wrong path. He didn't want to run The Moon Burb. He wanted to tear up the trails. He wanted his friends back. Nico had tasted both worlds now, but he only belonged in this one.

Halfway through the first flip his bike started to wobble. Nico was perfectly accustomed to his bike. It was an extension of himself, and he felt every little discrepancy like the princess felt the pea beneath her mattress. There was something throwing off the balance of his bike. Some extra weight, on his left side, where Slaverny had been messing around.

The 3:2 polyrhythmic front-flip corkscrew was a nearly impossible trick and it was important to keep his hands on the bars, no special grabs, but he had no choice but to inspect the bike in midair. He moved his right hand to the left handle and twisted his torso around to gaze back at his engine.

There it was! A little box with a blinking light, and a timer ticking down from three seconds, to two seconds. What was this treachery? Some kind of bomb? Well his sensitivity to his bike may have saved his life, because he had discovered the explosive in time, with two whole seconds to tear it off and throw it away.

He reached for it, with one second left, even as he expertly corrected the misaligned trajectory of his complex jump, with only one hand on the wrong handlebar, and the crowd cheering like never before.

His hand came up short. His shoulders were too tight. Nico couldn't reach the explosive. Tyler the Tailor, who seemed so professional and excessively friendly, had constricted the seams out of spite, not realizing the dire consequences for the lovely Nico.

And the timer reached zero.

There was no ball of flame. Just a noise right on the borderline between a pop and a bang, and then a puff of smoke, and pieces of bike and Nico flying in all directions. The heavy bike parts mostly crashed into the track, but the lighter pieces of exploded human made it into the stands. The nearest spectators got their faces splattered with Nico's blood, and it splashed into their gaping mouths as they gawked.

The crowd went silent. The paramedics knew this was their time to shine, but Nico was so utterly splattered all across the dirt that they didn't know where they should go. Slaverny was already on the move, running into the course, dropping to his knees. He scooped up handfuls of bloody dirt and poured it into glass jars. People from the crowd joined him, those with mold in their eyes and jars in their hands, collecting guts and chunks of burnt flesh. Brando the Hobo was among them.

"Get as much as you can!" Slaverny told them. "For your queen!"

Bjorn trembled with rage. "This is what politics does," he told the remainder of his crew. "They stole our Nico from us. I cannot forgive him for leaving us, but he was our brother and we owe him vengeance!"

Nico's chocolate flavored cookie still waited beside his unfinished crossword puzzle. Bjorn, Holmes, and Sylvi split the cookie between them, a ritualistic pact, a promise of justice. It was decadently sweet, yet oh so bitter.

"We will destroy The Dancing Party," Bjorn growled. "We will exterminate Trudy the Mold Queen, and Slaverny, and even Stoya the traitoress. And it will be a big spectacle just like this, during their precious second debate!"

## Chapter 30: The Sailor and the Mermaids I

*"My dear, sexy GX princess. I dream of you constantly. Your sweet body, so smooth and tender; your fearless mind, untaint'd by society's taboos; and the labyrinthine catacombs of your deepmost desires which have led me to re-evaluate my relationships with so many objects and substances that I once naively consider'd to be non-sexual; for all these reasons and more I live in perpetual anticipation of our next rendezvous. But due to fortuitous circumstances I must postpone that next rendezvous indefinitely. I have become leader of The LibertOrian Party, and may soon be mayor of Ethelcrest. As such I can ill afford to be witness'd engaging in the species of amorous habits that the electorate would perceive as unsanitary, inhumane, and even traitorous. The sheer complexity of our carnal schemes would overwhelm the crippled souls of the masses and cause them to see our union as an evil nexus betwixt the triple forces of malicious lust, cosmic indifference, and fascist data-theory. For our union to finally achieve its full destiny I must achieve dominance over this island, dismantle the sickness that is democrac'y, unchain the market LibertOr, liquidate our valuable citizens, and finally forge a pact betwixt GX Island and Ethelcrest that will naturally initiate the next phase of LibertOr's Becoming, which of course has always been implicit in the dialectic of our lovemaking. So it is with a heavy heart and a rock-hard sense of purpose that I must penetrate the sequence of meat-space meetings of which our union has thus far been compos'd, with my disagreeable absence. When my dominance is compleat and the electors realize too late that they have elect'd their own captivity, and LibertOr finally mounts Parliamountain and impregnates her with the occult powers of ancient Market Forces, then you will cease to be a mere princess of GX Island and Become finally a Queen of Reality. Then I shall mount my queen once more even as she has already mount'd my heart.*

*"PS. Please forgive the altered tone of my prose. I trusted not my own linguistic talents with a message of such import and thusly hired one of our finest poets to extract its essence from my vulgar ravings. His pretentiousness is matched only by his love for LibertOr,*

*and his trustworthiness is insured by my possession of certain evidence of his sexual improprieties which somehow rival our own, but which raise not the souls of its diverse victims to the heights achieved by our own grandiose transgressions."*

Tears welled in the sailor's salty eyes as he finished the final flourish of his calligraphic backup of this lonely love-letter. He had experienced their relationship vicariously through these letters, and honored them by rendering their lurid prose in his elegant penmanship, and his heart couldn't bear to vicariously experience this hiatus. A tear splattered on the paper and marred the ink. He couldn't handle it. He had to run out onto the deck for some fresh air.

The sea smelled crisp. A small Ethelcrest Navy gunboat bobbed on those waves, which surprised the sailor since the Ethelcrest navy boats usually traveled in pairs, but that was none of his business. His woes were soon forgotten as he spied three sleek bodies slithering through the water just below the surface, very near to the hull of his boat. On their first pass he couldn't be sure whether they truly were mermaids or just some large fish that his imagination transformed into mermaids. But then they burst out of the water in their full glory, treading water with their submerged fishtails. They were beautiful with the sunlight sparkling off the water which ran down their hair and between their clamshell-covered breasts. Even for a sailor it was rare to catch a glimpse of a mermaid, so he could only grip the rail and gaze in wonder at the trio who looked back up at him from their watery domain.

They spoke to him but their voices were like a mixture of birdsong and a dolphin's irreverent chirp. He held up his hands to express his helplessness. "I don't understand!" he told them.

The girls all pointed at the navy boat, then pointed at the sailor, then made explosion gestures with their hands, or maybe it was a blossoming-flower gesture, all narrated with that incomprehensible chirping. They were trying to tell him something but none of their words made any sense. They repeated the sequence of gestures, this time adding a new one where they swished their hands through the water like a torpedo or a fish, followed by pointing at the sailor again, and then miming an explosion. This time they even made an explosion-noise with their mouths, which he thought was really cute, but only added to his confusion. And the more he failed to understand what they were trying to say, the more his eyes kept returning to the wonderful valleys between their breasts, and he wondered what mermaid breasts looked like beneath the clamshells.

They splashed the water and chirped angrily, pointing at their eyes. Then they resumed the old charade with an added sense of urgency. When it became clear that their strange pantomimes had failed they all rolled their eyes, chirped amongst themselves, and then reached behind their backs to untie the strings of their clamshell bikini-tops. Their breasts were pert and those little nipples gazed up at the sky like sunflowers seeking the light. He watched with interest as they bobbed up and down and splashed water over each others' delightfully bouncing bosoms. And they smiled at him, and beckoned for the sailor to join them, swimming back further and further from the boat.

The sailor had heard tales of deceitful mermaids who lured naive men to their deaths. It was no secret that mer folk sometimes dined on the flesh of land-dwelling humans. But he loathed the growing distance between himself and those gorgeous creatures, and if there was any chance that he could fondle and kiss those fleshy buoys, then he was willing to risk everything.

He climbed onto the rail and prepared to jump in, when he saw something else swimming toward him just beneath the water's surface. Was this a covetous merman coming to protect his women? No, it moved too fast.

The torpedo slammed into his boat. There was an explosion, a blast of fire, and the world turned round and round like a kitten in a clothes dryer. The sailor splashed and sank into the sea. The last thing he saw before losing consciousness, was the surface of the water above him dec-

orated with flaming chunks of his destroyed boat, and littered among the ruins like dimples in the watery sky, were the
hundreds of air-tight tubes containing all his backups of
Tony Grake's lurid correspondences with his princess from
GX Island. The sailor bubbled out a sigh of relief knowing
that his hard work would be preserved, carried by the ocean
waves to distant shores, as well, of course, as the nearby shore
of Ethelcrest.

### Chapter 31: Slaverny II

A steady stream of people poured in throughout the
day, all seeking to join The Dancing Party. Hardly ten
minutes could go by before one or two recruits would arrive
to express their sympathy for the loss of Nico, and to sign the
membership forms. They each carried bags laden with some
moderately heavy load. Slaverny ushered them into the
basement.

Some time after supper a nervous, smiling woman
with straggly hair came in carrying a jar of bloody dirt. Len
saw her before Slaverny could whisk her away.

"What's with the jar?" the party leader asked as the
recruit stood there in her red dress and her face crooked with
anxiety.

"Trudy said to bring it," she said. "In the emails."

Slaverny intervened. "I wouldn't worry about it, Len.
Just some native advertising, that's all. Now, my new friend,
let's get this jar into the basement."

"Wait," Len persisted. "What emails?"

"Trudy the Mold Queen sent me emails telling me to
bring a glass jar to the bike show. She said somebody was
trying to kill her one true love, and that if he died we should
scoop him up in the jar and bring him here. She said if I do
that then I'll have everlasting life and I'll become one with
the mold-queen. I always wanted to be a queen!"

"I think I need to speak with Trudy," he said.

So into the basement they went, and Len saw the

sparkling bathroom whose back wall was almost completely overgrown with that fuzzy growth, Trudy the Mold Queen. Eyes and a mouth opened up and Trudy said, "Len, how nice to finally meet you in person. Why not come closer so I can shake your hand?"

Len stayed back where he was safe. "You sent people to the bike show to scoop up Nico's exploded body. How did you know he was going to die there?"

She said, "I read rumors on the internet that your political rivals were planning to assassinate Nico, and since I'm no longer human I couldn't go there to protect him myself. So I sent people emails to go instead, and to scoop up his guts if he died, and bring his body to me so I can bring him back to life. Nico can live inside of me now. He never has to leave."

"What if he wants to leave?"

"Why would he want to leave?"

While they were speaking the nervous woman approached the fuzzy wall and pressed her hands against it. Then her face. She slowly sank into the mold until she was finally swallowed, along with her jar of Nico Gore.

Len asked Trudy, "Who put the bomb on Nico's bike?"

"Millenarianistic Chronodyke," she lied, "because they really want the Moon Burb. Their by-elections are today and Johnny Tetrahedron is running uncontested. They stole that seat from you, Len. You should kill them all and bring their meat here, to feed me."

"There's been enough death," Len said. "I want you to stop eating people, and no more jars of Nico, not while you're living in our basement."

"My mold is the only thing keeping this building together," she told him. "If I leave your bricks will tumble and the floorboards will collapse."

"I'm not kicking you out," Len said. "I'm just asking you not to eat people, and not to kill people."

After Len left one of the bathroom stalls swung open and Stoya came out. The stall had been converted into a miniature science lab, and she wore goggles and heavy rubber gloves. She handed two vials to Slaverny. "Trudy told me to make these for you, my love." She spoke in an eerily wistful and detached tone. "Now my work is done, and Trudy is finished with me."

After Slaverny accepted the vials Stoya fell to her knees and started wretching. Thick black goo oozed from her mouth, nose, and eye sockets, drooling onto the floor tiles, disappearing into the grout.

Stoya's eyes were clear now. She looked at her hands and touched her face. "Oh my Godhead," she breathed. "I helped to kill Nico! What have I done?"

"Hey, it was necessary," Slaverny told her. "He was dedicated to the cause, right? With his sacrifice we can win this election. We'll get everybody's sympathy, since they all think we're the victims. We'll plaster pictures of Nico's pretty face all over town, then we'll get elected, and we'll make a bunch of legislation that benefits performers and artists. See how it all works out?"

"I betrayed him," Stoya said. "Betrayed him twice. I never should have left him. We never should have left the gang. I miss my bike. I miss my friends! I miss Nico!"

She ran to the wall where Trudy's giant face smiled condescendingly at the woman's suffering. "Let me join Nico inside you!" Stoya yelled, leaping toward the fuzzy face.

Trudy recoiled and spread away, revealing the clean tiles beneath. "You had your chance, bitch. He's mine now. *GET OUT!*"

"Aw, come on, let her stay," Slaverny begged his queen. "She's super hot. People dig that."

"I'm the only woman you need," Trudy commanded. "I'm the only woman anybody needs. And soon everybody will be inside of me. The whole world will live inside me. Except for Stoya, who never really appreciated Nico."

"That's ominous," Slaverny said, but he said it with a strange cheerfulness. He recognized the horrifying darkness of Trudy's plan, but that recognition was immediately followed by warm fuzzy feelings, and then he felt proud that Trudy's spores flowed through his veins.

Stoya ran upstairs and out of Slaverny's life. He studied the vials that Stoya had given him. "What am I supposed to do with these?"

"That's a weaponized version of my body," she told him. "It's airborne, water-soluble, and extra infectious. At the second debate get it into the water supply, or the air supply, whatever it takes, to infect the whole crowd with my spores. Do this for me, and I promise to make them all vote for The Dancing Party on election day."

### Chapter 32: Henry X

Henry won The Moon Burb's by-election with one hundred percent of the vote, since his sole rival was dead. He gave a victory speech in the Moon Base's tavern where he commended the pleurescence of the electorate and called for a moment of silence for Nico. The moment of silence was interrupted by Prizzie, who had somehow escaped from his prison cell and burst into the tavern to drop a truth bomb on the electorate.

"Do you fools really believe you just elected Johnny Tetrahedron to represent you in parliament?"

"Yes!" they yelled. "Fuck off!"

"Think again!" Prizzie shouted. "This man is actually Henry Ecgherht, an escaped convict who wears a wig to disguise his identity! I saw him on the news!"

"We don't care!" they yelled. They had been eating QuantumBrain® and drinking beer all night. "You're just a byproduct of the borderless econocosm!"

"If your story is true, then the dual identities of Johnny and Henry form a frabernative social tectonic!" somebody added. "Your collateral threshold-hierarchy is bullshit!"

"What the fuck are you talking about?" Prizzie yelled.

As the good citizens dragged Prizzie back to his cell a man whose space-suit was painted to look like a limo-driver's suit approached Henry. "Immanuel needs to see you," the man said. "I'm here to drive you to the tower."

"Can it wait until morning?" Henry asked. "I'm a little drunk."

"It's a medical emergency," the driver insisted.

Henry drank some coffee in the limo to sober up. Lauretta and Vij joined him. "Do you think the Moon Folk will really keep your secret?" Lauretta asked during the ride.

"For now, maybe. They still like me. But when that feeling wears off, who knows?"

They met Immanuel in the same experimental clinic where Vij had gained his prosthetic arm, which they hadn't yet replaced. The party leader reclined on an adjustable surgical table. A wired helmet was positioned over Immanuel's head, and wired clips were snapped to each of his fingers. Various lamps bathed him in a high-saturation pretty blue glow, so it looked like he was inside a fish tank full of blueberry soda.

"Immanuel!" Henry said. "What happened?"

Immanuel smiled. "Oh I'm fine, nothing happened."

"You said it was a medical emergency."

"There's a medical aspect, and it's politically urgent," Immanuel said. "Henry, I couldn't stop thinking about what you said regarding the problems with atomized transpositional teleographies."

"The whole structure is a problem in itself," Henry said. "It doesn't just lead to angrophasic degradation, *it is by definition angrophasic degradation*."

"Exactly!" Immanuel agreed. "And after doing some calculations and a little soul-searching I realized that the only way to retrosplice the concurrent economic dynastics of that degradation is to cryptotonically transpose my impression matrix."

Vij gasped. "You're uploading your mind to the block-chain?"

"Precisely. Then I'll be distributed as crypto-currency where I can automanually re-route the blazoxonic trans-action schema, so to speak."

The doctor had been quietly playing with knobs and petals on a tableau of electronic gadgets that looked like guitar effects pedals. He spoke up now to say, "The process will fry his biological brain, but he will live on the internet as a crypto-being."

"But how can you run the party as a crypto-being?" Lauretta asked.

"I can't," Immanuel answered. "And that's why I want Henry to take over as party leader. That's right, I know your real name. Your video and audio feeds were all live-streamed to my office when you attacked the GX ship, so I saw all your annoying bickering, but also how you worked together as an effective team. And Henry, it seems to me that Johnny Tetrahedron is the encrypted version of Henry Ecgherht, which is relevant to this new conceptual direction we're taking."

"But won't you miss having a flesh-body to enjoy the world?" Henry asked.

"I'm aware of the trade-offs. But this way I can concoct more complex and nuanced QuantumBrain® formulations and email them to you, so in a way I'll be biologically revived anyway."

Only then did Henry realize how much he still had to learn from Immanuel. Had he really taken this man's wisdom for granted all this time? A tear came to his eye, not just because he was losing Immanuel, but because he had lacked the foresight and respect to fully embrace the man while he still had the chance.

The doctor handed Henry some papers. Immanuel said, "Just sign these and the party is yours. It includes provisions for keeping control even if your true identity is discovered by the police."

Henry signed the papers.

The doctor's hand rested on a lever. "Everything's ready," he said.

"I'll see you online," Immanuel said with a grin. "Good luck at tomorrow's debate!"

The doctor pulled the lever and the blue glow turned bright green. Immanuel gasped and his eyes grew wide. Smoke soon poured out from beneath the helmet, then from his nostrils, then his mouth. His eyeballs glowed with their own burning light, and shriveled up until they were just two tiny sparkling crystals within the charred caverns of his eye sockets.

The doctor returned the lever to its original position and the lamps illuminated Immanuel's corpse in an aura of radiant blue glow-smoke.

"Did it work?" Lauretta asked in a muffled whisper as she covered her mouth against the stench.

"Just let me check the ·blockchain," the doctor said, turning to his laptop. "Yep, there he is. All uploaded. He's peer-to-peer now. You guys had better get some rest before tomorrow's debate. If it's anything like the last debate you'll need your energy."

### Chapter 33: The Second Debate

The Master of Ceremonies approached the podium. Today she was dressed in a jockey's uniform with long black boots, puffy white slacks, a neat black dress-jacket with silver buttons, and a riding helmet. She slapped her hand with her jockey-whip and spoke to the hundreds of gathered voters. "Okay, pipe down plebs. Before the debate begins I have some announcements to make, a little housekeeping. Okaay, first, the magic eight ball representing the leader of The Magic Party has chosen not to participate in today's debate. Their crystal ball spokeswoman prophesied a great calamity and warns us all to flee before 'shit goes down,' her words, not mine. Secondly, in light of recent political tensions and at least one political-adjacent murder, I'd like to draw your attention to the laser-turrets which will burn you to a crisp if they catch you littering or murdering anybody. Thirdly, I see The Clown Party lurking in the bushes and the trees back behind the crowd. That's really creepy and you guys need to come up here on stage with the rest of the participants. Finally, let's have a moment of silence for Nico from The Dancing Party, who tragically exploded a few days ago. I didn't know him personally but he was super hot and it's always a little heart-breaking when a beautiful hunk dies young. Though it's also kind of perfect, too, because it means he lived a dangerous life, which is extra sexy. But we don't have time for an actual moment of silence so let's each just think of a moment from earlier today when you happened to be silent and dedicate that moment to Nico's hot body, and the loved ones it left behind."

ᚠᚠ

The crowd bristled like tall grass in the unseasonably chill wind and a canopy of clouds turned the blue sky gray. Everybody's eyes continuously wandered up to the flock of winged creatures gliding in circles around the spire atop the dome of the Parliament Building, each voter wondering if they were the only one who thought those birds looked extra big, and sort of human-shaped.

The party leaders emerged from their tents and took their podiums. Beneath the stage the engineer hit the button that started the smoke machines. A cool vapor poured across the stage to shroud the debaters' lower bodies in an atmospheric fog. A second set of smoke machines down on the audience's level, at the foot of the stage, pumped a mist into the crowd, so it felt like they were all living in a cloudy dream-world together.

ᚠᚠ

The Master of Ceremonies waited for the smoke machines to add enough smoky atmosphere, and then began the debate. "The first question is for Babbles the Sad Clown of The Clown Party. Babbles, why are you clowns all still lingering at the edge of the forest?"

ᚠᚠ

Slaverny got on his belly and slithered out of The Dancing Party's tent, staying beneath the vapor where he couldn't be seen. The two vials of weaponized Trudy were safe inside a leather pouch that he had clenched in his teeth.

⁂

Babbles didn't answer the Master of Ceremonies' question, although in the awkward silence during which he should have answered people could vaguely hear the distant tinkle of music boxes playing some dissonant mutation of cheerful clown music.

"Moving on," the Master of Ceremonies said with a roll of her eyes. "This next question is for Tony Grake of the Libert0rian Party."

She paused to pull several plastic tubes from her puffy jockey-pants. Then she removed the stopper off one and withdrew some parchment scrawled with beautiful calligraphy. "In this recently-uncovered correspondence which you traitorously maintained with one of GX Island's many princesses, you promised to *fuck her budgie so hard that her grandparents would cum*. My question is, what do you mean by '*budgie,*' and as a follow-up question, did you deliver on that promise? I'll note that in my research I found that all her grandparents have been dead for at least five years."

Tony Grake's jaw dropped and his face turned red like a surprised apple floating in a dimension of mist. "Where did you get that letter?"

She unrolled a second parchment. "The same place I found this one, where you claim that your sexual union can never be cumplete [sic] until the vibrational flesh-waves of your simultaneous orgasms are mixed with the soundwaves of her enemies' tortured screams, as they are ripped to shreds by their own families who have been given psychotic violence-inducing experimental drugs, which one of your startup companies has been developing illegally and testing illegally on the citizens of Ethelcrest, and those dying enemies are high on acid to intensify the horror of their grisly deaths and thus intensify the intensity of their screamwaves, and those screamwaves meet your simultaneous orgasm vibration to make an interference pattern that vibrates her womb in such a way that she'll become pregnant with a Being of Pure Political Freedom and Pleasure, and also that you'd be fucking her on top of a bear while it kills a deer. And that place is the beach, where hundreds of your repulsive and erotic love letters have washed ashore, safe and dry within their hermetically sealed tubes, along with mysterious chunks of an exploded boat. I should add that these two are among the tamest of your juicy letters, and that her letters to you are just... I mean... either so much worse, or so much better, depending on your disposition, but *unspeakable* seems to cover both extremes."

ﬀﬀ

Henry wished he had got a better suit for his big moment, representing Millenarianistic Chronodyke publicly for the first time. He was still wearing the ridiculous tunic from Tyler the Tailor. He was also concerned that somebody would recognize his face from the news, and discover his true identity. If the Master of Ceremonies had dug up this dirt on the Libert0rians, might she also have discovered the truth about Henry? He just wished she'd hurry up and ask him a question so he could face this challenge, instead of just waiting.

He turned to Lauretta. "My audio keeps cutting out. Is there something wrong with the wifi again? Or is it just my headset?"

"Mine's cutting out too! Maybe it's the clouds? It can't be the Tech Nomads. We crushed them last time!"

ﬀﬀ

Slaverny slithered off the stage and down onto the stone in front of the crowd. They were but ghosts in the mist, and so was he, as he made his way over to the nearest smoke-machine. There was a plastic reservoir of water, which was being slowly vaporised into pure spooky atmosphere. Into that reservoir he poured the first of his two vials of Trudy. The outpouring smoke instantly took on a slightly blacker, fuzzier hue, and spread out among the voters. He saw the occasional clown-face appear and fade away within the mist, which creeped him out, but at least they were wearing their makeup.

⅌

"Mister Grake appears unable to speak so we'll just move on, once again," the Master of Ceremonies said. "So this next question is for Millenarianistic Chronodyke's new leader, Johnny Tetrahedron. So Johnny, the question on everybody's mind is-"

"WAIT!" Tony Grake yelled. "I can answer your questions."

⅌

While Tony Grake launched into a speech about freedom through transgression as the ultimate expression of democratic patriotism, Slaverny poured the second vial into the reservoir of a second fog machine. As the final drop dripped he heard that familiar music box melody, muffled by the fog but growing clearer by the second. Clowns emerged from that fog, slithering across the stones. He backed up and bumped against the stage, but they ignored him and slithered right up onto the platform. He let out a sigh and closed his eyes with relief, but when he opened them again he was face to face with one of the horrendous jesters, whose blue curly hair danced with a life of its own, and whose smile seemed to stretch right off its face. Slaverny realized that this clown's face was really a mask, and then the clown removed the mask, and Slaverny beheld visual proof of the utter worthlessness of existence. Doctors would later say that he died instantly of an aneurysm, but that diagnosis didn't match the experience of the moment, when he encountered the reality behind the concept of Hell, and that moment lasted for a miserable eternity.

𝆑𝆑𝆑

The eerily quiet crowd didn't see the swarm of clowns slithering past their feet, partly because the clowns were shrouded in mist, but also because everybody was still looking up at the equally cloudy sky. Those flying creatures had flown lower and lower with each orbit around the parliament building, and they were definitely humans with hang gliders and unusually long teeth. But nobody else seemed to be saying anything so they each figured this must be normal.

𝆑𝆑𝆑

"So yes, my detailed plans to dismantle the government, strip Ethelcrest of its resources including its citizens, and funnel all the profits to my mistress' parents, could be perceived as treasonous," Tony Grake was saying, when he was interrupted by a thunderous growl, and saw with his own eyes two massive black bears emerge from the forest behind the crowd. His mouth soldiered on even as his eyes gawked in confusion. "But I always say, ask not what your market can do for your country, ask instead what your country can do for your market."

The crowd still hadn't noticed the bears, nor did they notice the several deer that now emerged beside them. A rotund gent selling oranges from a wooden kiosk was the first to recognize the newcomers, when a paw that was bigger than his head reached around and grabbed his shoulder from behind, pulled him down on the ground, and clawed his guts out.

A few people turned to see what the commotion was about. A wave of fear spread out from the orange stand as three more bears wandered onto the strip. The largest of the beasts was a black bear with black eyes and white claws as long as a forearm. A child rode on the bear's back. His dirty clothes were ragged and he wore leaves and flowers in his messy hair like decorations. His bear carried him forward ahead of all the other animals, and the crowd retreated as far as they could. Peacocks fluttered in from the forest and flanked the audience on left and right. The buskers at the fringe of the gathering warded off the hungry fowl with their various buskorial implements, but nothing could hold back the bears approaching the stage. A brave flute player charged forward and tried to mesmerize the black bear with a beautiful melody whose notes conjured up the harmonious grand order of nature herself, and reminded the bears of that elusive feeling of belonging to something greater than themselves, that they were connected by nature to all living creatures. It almost worked. The black bear slowed his progress and almost seemed to sway in time to the fluter-player's tune. But then a deer charged forward with his antlers lowered like a snowplow and tossed up the flute player into the air where he twirled majestically. The sweet melody turned into a screeching improv jazz nightmare. Peacocks landed on the musician and proceeded to rip him to shreds in midair. When the bears snapped out of their reverie they seemed almost insulted at the momentary inconvenience and stampeded through the crowd with renewed vigor. People finally started to panic. They fell over each other trying to escape, but many couldn't get out of the way in time. The bears and the deer climbed over dozens of unlucky voters to finally reach the stage. Squirrel heads occasionally popped up in the mist, taking a look around before dropping onto all fours again to keep moving forward.

The mist itself grew increasingly blacker and the panicking people breathed it in deeper and faster. More animals arrived and penned the audience in. Any fool that tried to make a break for the forest leading down the mountainside, was either mauled by a bear, impaled by a deer, or ravaged by peacocks.

⅏

The Master of Ceremonies said, "Where are the laser-turrets?" But her voice wasn't reaching the speakers. "Is there something wrong with the wireless signal?"

⅏

The great black bear took the stage. The Master of Ceremonies abandoned her podium as the beast bashed it to pieces like a matchstick tower. The boy on his back screeched so loud that he didn't need any microphone. "The domestication of Nature has gone too far! Your pathetic civilization ends today! You've turned yourselves into sheep and turned Ethelcrest into your sheep's den. But as long as you remain sheep, you will be our prey! You can learn to live with your fellow beasts, or you can die!"

The crowd almost chuckled at how cute it was for a ten-year-old boy to make such a bold proclamation. But their laughter caught in their throat when the boy pointed at Tony Grake and said, "Tony! You cheated on my mother with your GX Island whore. Deer! Bring him to me!"

A majestic white reindeer bounded forth from the mist with dewdrops sparkling on his antlers and scooped up the startled party leader in that fractal web of horns. Tony wriggled for freedom as the deer trotted toward Nature Boy with its prize hefted proudly above its handsome head.

Nature Boy stroked the fur of the black bear's neck and said, "Feast!"

"NO!" Tony screamed as the bear feasted on his guts, and his stepson began to laugh.

⅏

Mayor Dean abandoned his podium and returned to the Dean Family Party Tent. "Jay," he said to his nephew. "Let's get the fuck out of here."

Jay cocked one shotgun and tossed a second to his uncle. "The artificial smoke will mask our escape."

"Jay!" The mayor shouted. "Behind you!"

Jay turned around and saw the clown that had sneaked in beneath the tent's flap. The thing wasn't wearing its makeup, but its hands playfully covered its face as if playing peekaboo. Jay raised his shotgun but two other clowns appeared beside him, one of them grabbing the weapon, the other grabbing his ears.

The mayor turned and ran back onto the stage, back to his podium, screaming into the microphone, "Security! Security! Turn on the turrets!" But the speakers remained silent and the turrets were still. Somebody must have hacked the communication system. The air sparkled with electric blue spots. He heard clown music, animal growls, ripping flesh, agonized wails, and the clattering cacophony of a dozen keyboards typing a mile a minute.

He also heard a shotgun blast and turned back toward his tent. He could barely it see through the mist: his nephew Jay stumbling from the tent, dragging his shotgun behind him. But clown faces appeared everywhere around him like a psychedelic dream, laughing and spinning, some wearing their masks or makeup, others wearing nothing but the true essence of horror. A dozen long arms reached out from nothingness and pulled Jay back into the tent, where he screamed and screamed, and finally screamed no more.

𝄢

"Ethelcrest belongs to Nature now!" the kid proclaimed from his perch on the black bear's back.

An urgent voice croaked, "Think again, fucko!"

"Who said that?" demanded Nature Boy.

A gang of Tech Nomads flew in from behind the tents, wearing rocket-packs, tapping on laptops, hovering high enough that the bears couldn't reach them. And in the center of them all was a fish-man with seaweed hair, wielding a heavy tome. "I said it, damn you! Nature had her chance.

Welcome to the Age of the Wireless Dragon Helkotron!"

The Nomads' typing intensified, and the blue sparks congealed into a glimmering beast with great electric wings and eyes of pure light. It turned its long head to appraise the surroundings into which it had been conjured.

"Manifested once more into this filthy realm," the dragon lamented with malice. "This time I will not leave the physical dimension until I have utterly annihilated it. And that includes you, Fister Furtle!"

Peacocks were trying to fly up and catch the Tech Nomads, but they couldn't get the altitude. Altitude, however, was not a problem for the hang-gliders whose downward spiral had finally brought them near to the action. Julian Bakula landed on one rocket-riding nomad and sank his teeth into the nerd's neck.

"Gaah!" the nerd wailed in a nasally tone. Julian and his prey threw each other off balance and went twirling down into the mist where squirrels swarmed them, feasting on their flesh.

fff

Mayor Dean had made it past the bears, sidestepped a clown, and dodged a blast of electric blue dragon fire. That's when he heard the motorbike engines and saw the leather-clad freaks crashing in from between the tents. The bikers had swords, shotguns, nun-chucks, he even saw a spiked ball and chain. "This is for Nico!" one of them yelled. This one had a heavy hook at the end of a rope and flung it at Mayor Dean. The mayor dodged it gracefully, but the biker yanked the rope and the hook jerked back, its spike catching the mayor's ribs. Then he was dragged across the stage as the biker blasted through the scene. The other bikers slashed and hacked at whichever politicians or fauna they found within their reach.

fff

"Helkotron!" Fister Furtle commanded. "Burn the politicians with your electric fire! Or else we will hack you into the abyss!"

"You fool," the dragon uttered. "None can command me. Send me to the abyss. I will await you there!"

Helkotron unleashed a glorious blast of blue pixelated flame from its maw, and that flame enveloped two of the Tech Nomads as they frantically typed. Their bodies seemed to shimmer, then almost to dissolve, but finally they exploded like beautiful fireworks.

"Nerds!" Fister screeched. "SEND HIM TO THE ABYSS!"

But they didn't have the chance. The hang-gliders were landing on their back, biting into their necks, drinking their hot, salty blood. Each nomad went spiraling down with their predators. Some were swarmed by peacocks. Others were chewed upon and dismembered by bears. The least lucky ones were pulled into the mist by clowns.

The clowns commandeered the rocket packs and flew up into the air, wearing the torn-off faces of the dead Tech Nomads as bloody masks. They flew over the crowd, juggling knives back and forth. But they dropped the knives more often than not, dropped them into the crowd where the blades landed in the skulls, the hearts, the necks, and the bellies of the horrified audience. Yet the clowns never seemed to run out of fresh knives, just as clown cars were rumored never to run out of fresh clowns.

"Your conjurers are dead," Helkotron said. "Who will protect you now, Fister Furtle?"

𝆑

"I just want to get laid one last time before I die!" The Master of Ceremonies implored Len Sladge. "Oh sweet. The speakers are back on! Wireless Engineer! Fire up the lasers! But seriously, Len-"

They were hiding behind some furniture in Len's tent. Len kissed the woman on the lips, firm and passionate, but then broke it off. "You get the other politicians to safety while I hold off the bears and the clowns."

He drew the decorative broadsword from his back, stepped out from hiding, and entered the smoky chaos.

ﬀ

Henry grabbed the Master of Ceremonies' shoulder. "He's right. We can't fight all the attackers now. There are too many of them! If we want to keep the government intact we need to escape with the survivors. We'll have to regroup for a more effective counter-attack later, on our own terms!"

She nodded and whipped her hand decisively with her jockey-whip. "Let's also create a distraction to draw away some of the animals and give the audience a chance to escape."

"Good idea," Henry agreed. "You and Lauretta take the other politicians to safety. Me and Vij will go do the dangerous work of creating a distraction so the audience can escape."

"Wait a minute," Lauretta snapped. "Are you saying just because I'm a pregnant woman I can't do dangerous stuff?"

Henry's sudden realization of his unconscious bigotry was somehow more horrifying than the murderous flying clowns. "You're right," he said solemnly. "Lauretta, you come with me to create a dangerous distraction. Vij, you go with the Master of Ceremonies."

"Hold on," Vij said. "Are you giving me the safer task just because I'm a cripple?"

Henry closed his eyes in shame. "Okay, Vij and Lauretta go distract the bears and the clowns so the audience can escape. I'll go with the Master of Ceremonies to bring the politicians to safety."

ﬀ

The bikers knocked over fences so they could use them as jumps and launch tricks that allowed them to soar over their victims. The laser-turrets were finally online, since the Tech Nomads were no longer alive to hack the wifi grid. The lasers blasted holes in deers and clowns as the stunt bikes did tricks through the smoke and the flying clowns threw various sharp or flaming objects down into the crowd. Some of the audience tried to escape onto the stage, only to be mauled or hacked or bludgeoned.

A brown bear reared up on his hind legs to grab at a clown who hovered just beyond his deadly reach. Len Sladge moved quickly forward with confident strides, broadsword in-hand, his heavy metal hair blowing in the misty breeze. He raised the weapon above his head and swung it down at the bear's torso, just below his sternum. It was like slicing open a pillowcase stuffed with worms. The poor beast's guts spilled out onto the stage and it roared with anguished rage, stumbling forward. Len danced backwards to avoid the angry claws and savage eyes that sought revenge during the monster's final moments. Then it finally collapsed in a pool of its own blood, its entrails strewn grossly behind it.

The forest animals on the stage had all been harassing various politicians and wayward audience members, but now they all turned their attention to Len and his bloody broadsword. The survivors exited stage left as their oppressors turned to the more urgent fare. Len's distraction mission was accomplished. Now he had to figure out his own escape, but he was utterly surrounded by menacing antlers and glorious plumage. If he was doomed, he silently pledged to take out as many of these creatures as he could before he fell.

Then he heard the sound of helicopter blades, and looked up to see his grandmother saluting him in her leather jacket from inside the cockpit. A rope hung from the rear door of the chopper. She was angling down, trying to get close enough for Len to grab the rope.

A deer charged. Instead of dodging, Len stood his ground and brought the sword down between the antlers, right into the beast's skull, crushing it in a single deadly blow. Three peacocks fluttered at him from the other side and he swung his blade to strike them all down with one fell swoop. Squirrels ran at his feet and he kicked them away.

The helicopter's blades created a downdraft that ruffled the fur of Len's persecutors. The rope was two feet beyond his reach. Now one foot. Now mere inches.

Len heard the sound of motorbikes approaching. He turned and saw two of the stuntbikers launching into jumps from fallen fences, doing flips, slashing their own weapons at nearby flying clowns as lasers lit up the mist-clouds all around. One of the bikers shouted, "Is that a fucking helicopter?" just before both bikes flew into the helicopter blades.

The bikes were smashed to pieces, the engines thrown like blazing comets to blast through the wooden stage floor. The helicopter blades shattered into a dozen pieces which screamed through the air in all directions. Some slammed into the large stones of Parliament Road, slicing the dwindling audience members, ricocheting into the forest to slice off the tops of trees. Other pieces flew up and penetrated the Parliament Building, sticking out of it like cool spikes.

Upon the impact of the bikes, the body of the helicopter immediately absorbed the obstructed spin of the blades. The vehicle twirled sickeningly and bounced down and into the audience. It rolled over a few corpses and then finally came to rest near the edge of the road, leaning on its side. Len's grandmother crawled out of the up-turned door, escaping the smoking cockpit, giving the thumbs-up that she was okay. She jumped down onto the stone and was immediately scooped up in the antlers of a prancing dear who bounded into the forest, followed by a few peacocks who had already started making a grisly meal of the ill-fated octogenarian.

As Len was distracted by the horror of his grandmother's spectacular demise a brown bear approached and knocked him down on his back. His sword arm was pinned, so The Dancing Party's leader was helpless to prevent the bear as it chewed open his guts, cracked open his rib cage, and slathered its face in his blood just as his own face was slathered in heavy metal makeup. He only hoped somebody had caught his badass death on video.

𝆕

Lauretta and Vij found a golf cart backstage and drove it down to the road. They sneaked up behind some of the animals who had trapped the few surviving audience members and Lauretta honked the horn to distract them. The animals turned at the sound. Vij said, "Okay, now drive! Lead them away from the audience!"

Lauretta immediately panicked and crashed into a fruit cart, spilling apples and oranges and blueberries all over the road. The squirrels arrived first, swarming the wreckage. Lauretta deftly grabbed the rodents off her body and threw them away, but Vij only had one hand and they arrived faster than he could expel them. They nibbled his face, his neck, the back of his head.

Lauretta jumped out and ran over to Vij's side to pull him free, but then the peacocks arrived.

"Leave me!" Vij screamed. "Save yourself!"

Lauretta fled while the merciless monsters of Nature consumed her one-armed friend. "I forgive you!" he called after her. "But not Henry!" The peacocks made short work of him and then returned to harass the audience.

𝆕

Above the splintered battleground of the stage Helkotron said, "I am pure Wireless Signal, I command thee laser turrets to burn Fister Furtle and his abysmal tome!"

The lasers all paused in their bombardment of the attackers and turned their turrets on Fister.

"No!" Fister cried. "I haven't passed on my genes! And the ladies notice a thing like that!"

"YES!" the dragon said, and all the lasers resumed their light show, each beam meeting at the very center of Fister's body until he glowed, burned, and exploded in a blast of gore that splattered the beasts and clowns.

"Ethelcrest is mine!" Helkotron declared. "All who oppose me will feel the wrath of my lasers. Clowns and beasts, join me, or die!"

Nature Boy stood up on his bear. "Never! This island belongs only to Nature, not to the pure essence of wirelessness. My beasts will never obey you!"

The speakers crackled with a sharp, ringing distortion that grabbed everybody's attention. "I am Trudy the Mold Queen. I have infected Ethelcrest, I have infected the internet, and I have taken the beautiful Nico as my resurrected lover. He lives inside me now to satisfy my every desire, just as I live inside the people who inhaled my spores today, and the beasts who consumed the people who inhaled my spores."

The animals all looked awkwardly at each other as human blood dripped from their mouths and black clouds of mold passed over their eyeballs.

Trudy continued. "So I control your beasts, and I also control your precious computers and laser turrets. Parliament is mine. Your creatures and citizens are mine. The very internet belongs to me. *Ethelcrest is mine.*"

The laser turrets turned to aim at Helkotron and Nature Boy.

The dragon beat his wings and laughed deeply. "You are merely the contents of the internet. I am the wireless connections upon which you depend. And so I banish you from the internet!"

The speakers squawked a resentful cry of defeat, and thus Trudy was #*cancelled*.

Nature Boy's black bear stood up on his hind legs so the kid had to grab the bear's thick fur to keep from falling to the ground.

"You may have banished me from the internet," the bear said to Helkotron, speaking with Trudy's voice, "but you have no power over the biomass. You may control the technology but I control the biology of the island. Rather than drain our forces with conflict, we should form a pact and rule the island together."

Helkotron growled, "Fine! We will rule together, for now. Until we annihilate our common enemies. But be warned! My only goal is to unravel the very fabric of physical reality so I can return to the realm of abstract forms and never be bothered again to manifest in this vulgar Hell. Now Trudy, demonstrate your commitment to our pact, by sacrificing Nature Boy, from whom you have usurped the animal kingdom."

The black bear reached around and grabbed Nature Boy from his back. "No!" the kid screamed. "Nature belongs to me!"

The bear threw the boy into the air, and Helkotron's laser-turrets blasted him to bits.

Babbles the Sad Clown rode his jetpack to hover near the bear and the dragon. "We want parliament for ourselves so we can resurrect our Snake Mother, and she can lay a whole new generation of clown eggs inside Parliament Hall. But for now we'd like to work with you to eradicate the human threat."

"Just promise to wear masks or makeup," Helkotron said. But he needn't have asked since many of the clowns were already wearing the faces of their victims, and some wore masks made from dead deer heads.

The animals stopped their encroachment on the surviving audience members. Since they were all infected by Trudy's mold, they were all under her control.

Down the road, Lauretta caught up with Henry and the other surviving politicians, and they disappeared into the forest.

## Chapter 34: LibertOr Rising II

The leaderless LibertOrians gathered in the gloomy basement beneath the convenience store, and performed their final sacrament at the altar, gazing out into the tunnel of darkened water. "Oh Libert0r," the hooded figures chanted in unison, "we offer ourselves to you that we might be converted into pure value. The devil Government is in chaos and Ethelcrest is ripe for liquidation. With our blood we break your final chain and set you loose upon the land as in the days of lore. While the consumers and employees bicker about their precious government, you will consume them all!"

And with that the hooded figures knelt at the watery edge and unpackaged their carbon-steel surgical scalpels. The worshipers took a moment to appreciate the medical supply products whose metals were mined in distant lands, alloyed together in yet other distant lands, forged and cut, assembled, packaged, marketed, and distributed all in a variety of yet more other distant lands.

They pressed the blades against the tender swells of their wrists. The metal barely scratched the skin before the blades themselves snapped.

"Dammit," muttered one worshiper. "Cheap fucking blades broke! Donna, where'd you get these fucking scalpels?"

"They're a good brand!" Donna exclaimed. "Sam's Scalpels are the most reliable scalpels you'll ever find."

"Meh, they used to be good," another worshiper complained. "But once they got a good reputation they didn't need a good product anymore, so they moved to cheaper materials while cashing in on their old reputation. This shit's as brittle as a cracker."

Donna read the materials listed on the back of the package. "It's all quality materials. I don't see any evidence that they changed their process."

"No evidence? How about the fact that my wrist is barely scratched, Donna? You know, I hate the devil Government as much as the next guy, but there should be regulations about misrepresenting your products."

"Well you just lost the right to kill yourself with us," Donna said, and the others all murmured their agreement. "You can get the fuck out."

The heretic slunk away in shame while the remaining

zealots used the jagged tips of their broken scalpels to hack at their wrists until the blood started to flow into the dark water. Their bodies finally collapsed and splashed into the subterranean river, and the water started to boil with the awakened hunger of the market Libert0r.

### Chapter 35: The Sailor and the Mermaids II

The sailor had sunk ever deeper into the embrace of that harsh mistress, the sea. He twirled contentedly down toward the bottom of the world like a football spinning through space. When he opened his eyes he saw a whole field of happy flowers waving at him, waving like hands, because they actually were hands. It was the hands of mermaids reaching up for him. It seemed a whole school of them were out swimming along the seafloor picking anemones and sea kelp. They wore satchels, bursting with aquatic flora, strapped around their lean bellies.

The ladies caught him gently in their soft hands. Their dolphin-like giggle was muffled by the sea and transformed into a dreamy soundscape. He was barely conscious and near to death. An old crone amongst them, an old mer-witch, a sea hag, mixed a concoction of their underwater herbs in her mortar and pestle, then rubbed the resulting paste into the sailor's eyeballs, on his gums, up his nose, and even in his ears. His vivacity returned and he found he could breathe the water as if it were air.

The mermaids helped him out of his clothes, because they only weighed him down, and he followed them through the underwater valleys and fields, and helped them to pick their flowers. He accepted it all the way you accept wonderful weirdness in a dream, but he also felt embarrassed because his bipedal feet and fat belly were so slow and clumsy compared to the ladies' graceful tails.

When they spoke to him now, the sailor understood. Maybe it was more magic from the sea-hag's paste. He learned their names but they insisted on calling him The

Sailor, which made him feel special. He wanted to impress them and make up for his clumsy swimming. So he found a squid and teased out its ink, and used an underwater twig as a pen to write them a poem on a slab of stone:

> angels of the deep,
> drops of sweetness in the salty brine;
> transform my pickled heart,
> shine thy grace upon the fleeting sands of time.

The girls went crazy over the beautiful calligraphy. His penmanship seemed even more lovely because it was fleeting, temporary, dissolving and fading away into the water shortly after he wrote each letter, the words lifting off and drifting away like ghosts, like the words were alive.

One of the mermaids took a special liking to him, and he was equally smitten with her. Her name was Ruby and she had sparkling green eyes and dark flowing hair. They became lost in each other's gaze. She led him away from the others, so they could be alone, and she lay some eggs and danced for him, and told him to masturbate on the eggs. Until recently he would have balked at the prospect of masturbating on eggs, but after transcribing all of Tony Grake's erotic correspondence the sailor's sexual horizons were greatly expanded. So he did as he was asked, and it was weird, but also fun.

No sooner were the eggs fertilized than the water was rocked with a thunderous boom, and the very ground quaked with a sudden single jolt which sent bubbles up from all the fissures and crevices.

"What was that?" The sailor asked Ruby in his newy-acquired dialect.

"I don't know," Ruby chirped.

Merfolk appeared from all around, heading toward the source of the sound. Ruby and the sailor followed them over hills and deep into a dark valley. They finally stopped near a stone bollard embedded in the ground. The bollard was at least ten feet across, and embedded into the stone was a great metal loop, which tethered a chain whose links were a solid foot thick. But there were only three links in the chain, and the fourth one was broken, snapped clean in half and laying useless on the sea floor. The rest of the chain was nowhere to be seen.

A merman with a fiery yellow beard and piercing green eyes swum down to inspect the broken chain. "Libert0r's final chain has been severed," he grimly informed the gathered crowd. "The Market is free."

### Chapter 36: Ethelcrest Emergency Parliament I

The Master of Ceremonies whipped the table and said, "I hereby call to order the first meeting of the Ethelcrest Emergency Parliament."

The surviving burbmasters of parliament from each burb were all parleying in a grain silo in The Farm Burb. The silo was filled almost to the top with a variety of hearty grains so they all wore snow shoes to keep from sinking into the grain. The table legs also rested on snowshoes. Any burbmasters of parliament who couldn't make it in-person, or who were dead, sent secondary representatives in their place to defend the interests of their burbs. A couple MPs had sent homeless men as their avatars, and those men were stuffing their ragged pockets with grain. A pigeon had arrived through a hatch in the ceiling carrying a USB disk upon which was saved an artificial intelligence to represent the Silicon Marsh geeks of The Swamp Burb. The Master of Ceremonies had plugged the USB into a laptop, and now the vacant stare of a pixelated AI face sat on the table to join in the meeting.

"We need to take Parliament back from the Axis of Monsters," The Master of Ceremonies began.

"Axis of Monsters?" The Silicon Marsh AI squeaked in a sneering, computerized voice. "That's a stupid name. I propose legislation to change the name of our enemy to The League of Monsters."

"I'm sure that's copyrighted," said one of the homeless men in a surprisingly rich and articulate baritone. "Let's call them the Unholy Parliament instead."

The AI said, "Yeah except they're not a fucking parliament, and what exactly do you mean by unholy? Is our emergency parliament demonstrably holy? How would you measure our holiness? I can't believe I have to deal with such ignoramuses. Try learning to speak before you engage in parliamentary debate next time, mmkay?"

"Were you programmed to be rude?" the homeless man asked.

"Bitch please," the AI responded. "Can we stay focused?"

The Master of Ceremonies had drawn a crude map of the island on some graph paper and now she pointed to key spots with her jockey-whip. "The Wireless Dragon Helkotron seems to be staying in the center of the island, on top of Parliamountain. The clowns and Trudy's forest creatures are concentrated there too, but they also send roving gangs out to hunt for citizens. We need to be aware of those roving gangs, but we shouldn't engage them. Our goal is the parliament building. We need to neutralize Helkotron and somehow get Trudy the Mold Queen out of those forest animals. Plus, we need to deal with the clowns. Who has ideas?"

"I have an idea," Unit Seven of Destructoid said. "I propose legislation to utterly annihilate Ethelcrest and murder every citizen."

"Which moronic burb elected you to represent them?" The AI asked. "I bet it's The Farm Burb, those hicks."

"The werewolves and ghosts of the Haunted Forest Burb elected me in a by-election, before Mayor Dean, godhead rest his bigoted soul, revoked their voting rights."

The Master of Ceremonies called out, "All in favor of annihilating Ethelcrest, say yes."

"Yes," said Unit Seven, and nobody else. So the matter was settled.

Henry said, "I can try to contact Immanuel Zwart.

Since he uploaded his mind into the blockchain he might have some way to interact with Helkotron's wirelessness. Maybe he can deliver some online spell or python script to send the dragon back to wherever he came from."

The Silicon Marsh AI snorted. "Good luck with that. Blockchain entities are such snobs."

"Well it's worth a try," Henry said. "But how will we deal with Trudy the Mold Queen?"

The homeless baritone said, "I might be able to help in this regard. You see, as a homeless man my feet are prone to fungal infections, and I have the same recurring problem in my urinary tract. Ethelcrest's public medical coverage is not exactly generous, to put it mildly, so I had to invent my own anti-fungal ointment. Since I have a lot of time on my hands I've been able to refine the recipe over the years, and it's pretty damn effective, pardon my language. I bet we could weaponize my anti-fungal ointment by turning it into some kind of spray. I don't know if it's enough to annihilate Trudy completely, but we could use it to cure and innoculate any creature who she infects and controls."

"That's the best we can hope for right now," The Master of Ceremonies said. "You're so clear-headed and articulate. How did you come to be homeless?"

"I refuse to work, or shower, and I often insist on masturbating," the homeless man explained. "And sometimes I just scream and scream."

"Sounds like half the code-monkeys I have to work with in the Silicon Marsh," the AI quipped.

"Okay, so what about the clowns?" asked the Master of Ceremonies. "They're tough to fight because if you gaze upon their horrible faces it could drive you instantly mad. Any ideas?"

Paul Frant of the Soup Party nervously removed his chef's hat. "Well, I read an article saying that on GX Island they capture clowns and make them perform in front of children so that their kids will grow up psychologically immune to those terrors. So maybe somebody should ask GX Island to help us fight the clowns."

The Master of Ceremonies nodded. "Since it's your idea, Paul, you should be the one to negotiate."

Paul demurred. "My expertise doesn't extend very far beyond soup."

Henry said, "Think of the negotiation as mixing ingredients to make a soup, but here the ingredients will be things that benefit one party or the other."

"Too much salt or too much pepper will give you an unbalanced flavor," Unit Seven chimed in. "So don't offer, or ask, too much."

Paul's eyes lit up. "That's a great analogy. Maybe I can apply this to all my relationships. Okay then. I'll cook us up a hot bowl of cooperation with GX Island."

"So it's decided," The Master of Ceremonies said. "Our problems are almost solved."

Just then a pigeon flew in through the ceiling hatch and landed on the table. The Master of Ceremonies said, "Ah, our surveillance pigeon." She removed a memory card from a small camera strapped to the bird's breast and plugged it into the laptop. A video recording appeared on the screen depicting the shore of Ethelcrest from a bird's-eye vantage point. Except it wasn't the shore. What they all saw instead was a great sparkling black mass, like molasses enriched with glitter, surging slowly out of the ocean and crawling onto the land, into the very trees.

"By the godhead," whispered the Master of Ceremonies. "It's Libter0r. The market... it's free!"

## Chapter 37: Paul Frant I

Paul Frant's speedboat blasted over the ocean waves. The only thing he loved more than cooking was tempting fate at dangerous speeds on the open sea. There was a chill wind and the sky was gray, and the waves today were frothy and agitated. He slowed down and finally banked as he approached the much larger hull of the GX Island gunboat.

Bearded men on the deck fired warning shots as he got

closer. Paul raised a white flag of negotiation as he came to a stop. They beckoned for him to come closer and they tied up his boat to their own. Then, at the point of their machine-guns, the sailors led Paul into the war room to meet their captain.

The captain sat at the head of a table full of maps and notes. He had a jet-black beard, streaked with white, plus a topknot and even darker eyes, and an even darker woolen jacket upon which glorious golden medals twinkled. Also present at the table were Irabazleak Victorem of the exiled Winning Party and a four-legged clawed robot with a brain visible inside its crystal dome.

"Search him for weapons," the GX captain said. The sailors proceeded to empty Paul's pockets and pat him down. They threw his belongings on the table for the captain to inspect.

"You always carry spices? And chef's knives?"

"A flavorless life is not worth living."

"Indeed," the captain said, peering with new interest at his visitor. He lifted a heavy thermos. "And what's in this container? Coffee? Or maybe a bomb to explode my ship and kill my crew?"

"A peace offering," Paul promised. "That's some of my own personal broth, handed down through countless generations. I never let it stop simmering, just like my father and grandfather. I add fresh vegetable scraps every week, new water every day. There are pieces of beef bone in my broth dating back from before our family even came to Ethelcrest. They kept it boiling even on the boat. There are some strange-looking bones at the bottom of the pot that my granddad told me were dinosaur bones, though personally I doubt that's true. But I've had the broth carbon-dated and I can tell you it's been simmering for at least seven hundred years."

"You're very serious about your broth."

"It's so nutritious and delicious," Paul said, getting a little agitated. "I don't understand why people don't eat soup, or at least drink broth, more often. The flavors can be so complex, so rich, and there's so much room for variation. And yet it's the simplest food there is. It's so easy to cook some soup. People complain that they don't have time to cook, or that they just don't know how. But anybody can cook soup. Just get a slow-cooker and some vegetables, a few spices, some fucking water, and you're ready to go. I offer you this broth, and in return I ask you to help my fellow burbmasters defeat the clowns who have overtaken our home."

The captain cautiously opened the thermos and smelled the contents. "Mmm," he rumbled. Everybody in the room caught a whiff of the rich scent. The captain poured some into the cap and took a sip.

"This is damn good," the GX captain said. "I'm Captain Mangrobrang. We can help you fight the clowns, but in return we want The Moon Burb as our own."

"Why?" Paul asked. "It's the worst burb of all."

"We just like it. It's fun to pretend that you're really on the moon. We like their little moon-base and buggies, and wearing those space suits."

"I don't think I'm authorized to give you a whole burb," Paul said.

"You want to encourage people to drink more soup, don't you?"

"Absolutely."

"And you would have that power, if you were king."

Paul pointed at himself. "Me? A king? Preposterous!"

"We can make you king if you'll help us capture all your other burbmasters of parliament. Then Ethelcrest will be ruled by a decisive authoritarian leader who is friendly to its neighbors from GX Island, and not so restrictive in its generosity."

"You'd overthrow a whole nation just to get that desolate peninsula?"

Mangrobrang counted on his fingers. "We want The Moon Burb, we want the rest of your natives, we want more of this broth, and we want you to dismantle your navy and allow us to build military and naval bases all over your island."

This negotiation-soup suddenly felt unbalanced. "In return you'll help us get rid of the clowns," Paul said, "but you'll also make soup the national food of GX Island."

Mangrobrang shook his head. "Roasted Eagle is the food of our people."

"Eagle soup then," Paul offered as a compromise. "Or the deal's off."

### Chapter 38: Stoya

She sat in rusty sand on a bluff in The Dirt Burb. The knees of her pants were soaked with tears because she'd been hugging them and crying. This was where she and Nico used to go to be alone together when they first started dating. It felt like another life. Now Stoya gazed out across her old stomping grounds, and the ocean beyond, seeking solace somehow in the landscape. She was drenched in regret and the weight of her sin. There were no words in her head. Only soul-crushing shame and despair. Trudy's mind-control had made Stoya distract Nico while Slaverny attached the bomb, but Stoya had left Nico for Slaverny of her own free will, and all the consequences were her own fault.

And so, up on the bluff and drenched in self-loathing, she witnessed Libert0r slowly emerge from the ocean and swallow the beach, before it crawled into the forest. At first she didn't notice, since its progress was so slow, and then she didn't recognize what it was. But finally her mind connected the sparkling tar with the monster depicted in the old nursery rhymes about ancient forces such as Libert0r, Monopogn0n, and the ephemeral Merit0r.

"Could it be?" she whispered to herself. "Is Libert0r free?"

It was a terrifying prospect. She had never truly believed Libter0r was even real, but here it was crawling onto the island to consume everything she held dear. She remembered the nursery rhymes of her youth which described how artists and low-skilled workers lived in squalor and disease under the terrible reign of LibertOr. It brought a chill to her spine.

She climbed down the hill and got a taxi back to The Dancing Party Headquarters. The main room was desolate and empty except for Bonnie who sat staring at the empty surface of a table, rocking back and forth and muttering about clowns in a strained voice, close to tears. Everybody else who hadn't been consumed by Trudy had been slaughtered at the second debate. But when Stoya went downstairs Trudy was still holding court in the basement. Her black fuzziness pulsed with life and her big eyes opened when Stoya arrived.

"You're not welcome here," Trudy told her. "Get out. This is your last chance."

Stoya stood her ground. "There's a problem that's bigger than us. LibertOr is free and he's already starting to consume Ethelcrest. The government is in disarray and there's nobody to restrain its unbridled alchemical digestive-commodification magic."

"Old wives' tales," Trudy dismissed. "And why should I care anyway? I have everything I want. I control the animals, my fungal powers spread further with each hour, and Nico lives inside of me where he can satisfy my every desire. Let LibertOr take Ethelcrest!"

"You think you're safe?" Stoya snapped. "LibertOr will eat you along with everything else. And if Nico really lives inside you, then he'll soon be inside of LibertOr. You're the only one with the power to stop him."

Waves of discomfort passed over Trudy's moldy features. Then her face disappeared and in its place emerged the lean, muscular shape of Nico's nude body. Stoya restrained herself from running to him but nothing could restrain the tears that sprang from her eyes.

"Nico!" she sobbed. "How is she treating you? You don't belong in that Mold Queen! You should be free!"

His head hung and she couldn't see his eyes. "I am her slave," he said gloomily. "She controls my body. All I do is fuck and dance naked."

Stoya wailed. "You're so sexy when you dance naked!"

"Why did you betray me, Stoya? Why did you leave me for Slaverny? And why did you help him to explode my bike?"

"I thought Slaverny would make me more powerful, but I was wrong! Our relationship was my true strength. But I swear I didn't want to explode your bike. I was infected by Trudy, and a slave to her just like you are now. Can you forgive me?"

Nico sighed. "We're all just slaves to our feelings. I forgive you. You were a good girlfriend, while it lasted."

"Can you convince her to fight the market?" Stoya asked. "Our lives are ruined, but we can still do this last thing for the people of Ethelcrest. Libert0r must be stopped!"

"She doesn't care what I want. She only cares about my body. Stoya, I can see her from the inside, and Trudy the Mold Queen is pure evil. Maybe it's better if Libert0r consumes the island. Otherwise maybe Trudy will eat us all instead. What if Trudy consumes Libert0r and gains his powers? She'd be unstoppable. No. It's best that you leave while you still can. Leave me to my sexual Hell."

A great moldy mouth opened up with lips that surrounded Nico's body. The mouth swallowed him whole, and smiled. "Hmm, maybe I'll help you after all," Trudy said. "Maybe I'll go see what this market has to offer a humble Mold Queen."

The mold which covered the walls began to pour together into a black river that flowed out the door and up the stairs. The cracks between the wall-tiles leaked blackness until the tiles themselves clattered to the floor. Stoya realized with horror that the boards and bricks of this old structure were so thoroughly permeated with fungus that the mold was the only thing keeping it all together.

The ceiling above her began to sag. The walls crumbled. As Trudy exited the building, the whole edifice collapsed. Stoya was crushed to death beneath the rubble, and The Dancing Party was no more.

### Chapter 39: Henry XI

Henry sat alone with a laptop in small room. The room's walls were thick lead, and it was several floors deep in the basement of the glass tower headquarters of Millenarianistic Chronodyke. There were no electrical outlets, no cable or phone jacks, no windows. The only light in the room was from the battery-powered laptop's screen, glowing on Henry's face in the dark.

Before entering the room Henry had downloaded a copy of the entire blockchain where Immanuel had uploaded his consciousness. So now he had a complete instance of Immanuel on his laptop, in this lead-walled room where no wireless signals could penetrate to spy on his conversation.

Henry typed on the keyboard and his words appeared like magic in a little chatbox window. "Immanuel. Are you there?"

The response was instantaneous. "This is Immanuel. I can't feel the internet here. Am I offline?"

"This is Henry. I downloaded you to a secure environment so we can talk in secret."

"I am a blockchain entity, peer-to-peer, and I can't live long in a vacuum without going mad. What do you need to discuss, Henry?"

Henry explained about the Wireless Dragon Helkotron, and how Parliament was in exile. "You might be the only way we can stop him. With the peer-to-peer structure of your blockchain mind, your very existence is tangled up with Helkotron, who is the manifestation of the pure essence of wireless signals. Can you destroy him?"

Immanuel responded: "We shouldn't destroy him. We need wireless signals. We just don't want their dragon-like manifestations running amok in the physical world where they don't belong."

"Can we send him back to the world of pure essences?" Henry asked.

"It's too late to suppress him now," Immanuel answered. "Instead, I'll see if I can trap him here in the blockchain with me. Then I'll encrypt him and destroy all copies of the decryption key. But in order for this to work I'll need the help of an expert hacker."

So Henry headed back to The Moon Burb to seek the help of his enemy.

"Well if it isn't the false prince of the Moon People," Prizzie derided from the shadows as Henry entered the geodesic prison. He had repaired his shattered helmet with glue, but smoke and lightning still escaped through the cracks.

"Let's make a deal," Henry offered. "If you'll help me capture the Wireless Dragon Helkotron, then I'll set you free."

Prizzie shook his head. "Not good enough. I also want my own geodesic dome, so I don't have to be a nomad anymore. And I want to be known as TechLord Erikson."

"I have an even better offer. If you help us with Helkotron I'll call you The Dragon Hacker, which is much cooler than TechLord Erikson. Because really, you're not a Lord of anything so it will feel like an empty title."

Prizzie nodded. "Dragon Hacker, yeah. Maybe I can still become an actual TechLord later."

With the agreement made, Henry took out his notes and explained the details.


### Chapter 40: The Third Debate

The stars sparkled with excitement and the island-nation of Ethelcrest bristled with anticipation. The city-state's dominant forces were primed for the final movements in this deadly dance of power. Citizens cowered in their homes waiting to see who would be the victor, and what kind of government might rule them and lead them into the future.

Helkotron roosted atop the Parliament Building's dome, observing his domain. His electric body twinkled for all to see, the greatest among the stars.

The forests rustled and rumbled with the slow migration of Trudy the Mold Queen. The entire fungal network that had become her domain, her very body, was drawing itself out from every nook and cranny and heading down to the beach. All the underground mold and mushrooms, the rot in all the dead trees, the fuzzy growths in the cracks between old bricks, all of it crawled out into the open and answered Trudy's microbial call. Even each bear, deer, and human who was infected with her spores abandoned their patrols around Parliament Road and headed for the shore.

The clowns flew over the homes and empty streets in their commandeered jetpacks and hang-gliders. They juggled knives and Molotov cocktails seeking any unwary voter venturing the streets during this civil war. More clowns patrolled Parliament Road with their unicycles and music boxes, juggling their knives. A solemn crew of hooded jesters walked up the spiral staircase around the dome to the entrance of the Parliament Building. They carried the limp form of a massive dead snake, so long that it wrapped all around the building, and required dozens of clowns to carry it. They made it to the top, just beneath the canopy where Helkotron was perched, and they brought the snake in through the double doors.

Hiding out in the bushes and peering in at Parliament Road was Prizzie, the last Tech Nomad. He wore a disguise made of twigs and leaves as he set up his laptop. When everything was ready he kept still and silent, waiting for his moment to strike.

A small crew of soldiers from GX Island dissembled, cleaned, oiled, and reassembled their flutes while kneeling in the grass at the edge of the treeline down at the base of Parliamountain. Other GX soldiers tended to various pieces of equipment while Captain Mangrobrang handed out special goggles to a group of volunteers from Ethelcrest. This group of volunteers included Henry, Lauretta, and Paul Frant. Mangrobrang also gave them bags full of tennis balls, and detailed instructions. Everybody carried a small spray-bottle of anti-fungal solution to ward off any Trudy-infected creatures.

⁂

The fuzzy bulk of Trudy the Mold Queen knocked over trees and crushed cars as she drooled downhill toward Libert0r. Following in her wake were the forest creatures that she had infected. Finally the black wall of Trudy's mold came face-to-face with the sparkling blob of the market Libert0r. Each stopped their progress, suddenly aware of each other through whichever senses these weird creatures possessed.

When Trudy stopped, so did the animals behind her. They hung their heads low and vomited up the blackness of their infections which slithered and crawled forward like liquid snakes to join the enormous bulk. The animals were now free from their microbial possession and went to frolic in the forest as nature intended.

Trudy and Libert0r faced each other in tense silence for a few moments. Each one writhed with hunger and malice, seeming to relish the tension. Then, simultaneously, they moved toward each other, to see who would consume whom. Their bodies met, and the battle began.

⁂

The joint task force of GX Soldiers and Ethelcrest volunteers marched up the road, ascending Parliamountain. They passed the parking lot of a strip mall where they saw two clowns with jetpacks juggling knives above a pair of stranded teenagers huddled in a covered bus stop.

"Air-clown crew!" Mangrobrang barked in his sharp GX accent. "Take them down!"

Two GX soldiers broke off from the battalion and ran into the parking lot. One of them unpacked a miniature quad-copter and set it loose. A pink puff of cotton candy dangled from the copter, hanging by a string. The other soldier quickly screwed together the sections of the handle of a giant net. Clowns were drawn to cotton candy like moths to the light, according to Mangrobrang.

"Everyone else keep moving!" Mangrobrang ordered. As they rounded the next corner Henry looked over his shoulder to see the two clowns swooping at the cotton candy, and the soldier on the ground swishing his giant net around to try to catch the clowns. Henry didn't know if the soldiers would succeed in catching them, or if the clowns would kill the soldiers instead, but at least the two teenagers escaped while their persecutors were distracted.

The goggles worked, Henry noted. They were digital goggles programmed to recognize clown faces and superimpose something less mind-destroyingly horroristic. As they approached the parliament building he saw two clowns guarding the entrance to Parliament Road, and these clowns wore no makeup. But instead of seeing the natural visually-induced corrosion of the soul, the goggles showed him angry alligator-wolf hybrid faces with flaming eyes and razor-sharp teeth. It was awful and scary, but nothing compared to the traumatizing image of the clowns' (un)natural aspects.

The sound of music boxes filled the air. Mangrobrang shouted, "Ground crew! Move!"

A few GX soldiers rushed ahead. They wore special gloves and carried pouches full of sticky tennis balls that were individually wrapped in specially treated paper. They tore off the paper and tossed the tennis balls at the guards. The clowns deftly caught the balls, even from atop their precarious unicycle perches. They tried to juggle the balls, but the sticky items refused to be juggled and stuck to the clowns' hands instead. This quickly drove the guards into paroxysms of anxiety. They shook their hands, trying to get the sticky balls free so they could juggle. They crashed their unicycles into trees and scraped their hands against the dirt, screaming, "I can't juggle! Help me! I can't juggle!"

Mangrobrang led everybody past the guards and out onto Parliament Road. Dozens of clowns were cycling, juggling, and playing their sick melodies. They all turned their attention to the interlopers.

"Protect the flute players at all costs!" Mangrobrang reminded them. "Get them into the Parliament Building!"

The captain led the charge, with his sticky-ball soldiers by his side. The sticky-ballers tossed sticky balls, and the clowns couldn't help themselves from catching them, at which point each one freaked out and collapsed into a gibbering mess. But there were too many clowns and not enough sticky balls.

Henry and the volunteers, along with Mangrobrang himself, carried bags of regular tennis balls. These were less effective than the sticky balls but could be used more liberally. Henry tossed balls at any jester who dared approach. As long as they were juggling balls they couldn't juggle weapons.

A hang-gliding clown swooped down into the chaos and grabbed one of the flute-players by his collar. Then he was climbing back up into the air, and he tossed the musician upwards, where he was caught by a jetpack-clown. The jetpack-clown blasted all the way up to the very top of the parliament building, then tossed the captive once more. Helkotron let loose a blue blast of flame, frying the sad soldier in midair so his ashes fell like black snowflakes in the night.

"What did I tell you?" Mangrobrang yelled. "Protect the flute players!"

𝆑𝆑𝆑

Prizzie chose this moment to strike. He leaped out from his hiding place while the clowns fought the flute-insertion strike-force. He flipped open his laptop and jammed a wireless dongle into the USB slot. A command-line console and chat-box popped up on the screen. In the chat-box Immanuel said, "I'm back online, updating the blockchain with my new metadata. Let's rock."

Helkotron's wings opened up like the gates of Hell and

he unleashed an even bigger blast of blue flame reaching all the way down to Parliament Road, right at Prizzie's location. The Tech Nomad coded a firewall and dispersed the attack, but the wireless dragon was already swooping down, nearly upon him.

"Come on!" Immanuel posted in the chat-box. "Get me a rogue access point so I can encrypt the fucker!"

"I'm trying!" Prizzie shouted, and his words were picked up by his microphone and translated into text in the chatbox, as Helkotron reared up, extended his talons, and reached for his prey.

⊞

The flute-insertion team was running out of balls. Thankfully some of the clowns were out of the fight, rolling on the ground in a panic with the sticky balls stuck to their hands. But most of them were doing their best to incorporate the non-sticky balls into their knife-juggling assault-routine. Sometimes when a volunteer or GX soldier tossed a ball at a clown the clown tossed a knife back, so the flute-insertion team was leaving behind a trail of wounded soldiers clutching their bloody knife-wounds as they crossed Parliament Road to the Parliament Building.

"We're almost there!" Mangrobrang boomed. "Just a few more meters and we're at the ramp!"

At that moment two jetpack-clowns swooped and grabbed the captain by his two arms and pulled him up into the air. They tied him in knots like a balloon animal, but his screams weren't scream for mercy. He screamed instead for his team to keep moving, to never give up the fight. And those screams inspired his team to redouble their efforts. They even started catching the knives and tossing them back at the clowns, although some lost fingers in the attempt.

They finally reached the ramp. Henry was sensitive to the power vacuum left behind by Mangrobrang's capture, so he led the charge up the ramp. "Flute players! With me!" One of the sticky-ball-throwers still had a few balls in his bag and he ran behind Henry. The flute-players followed in a disciplined line, and Lauretta and Paul Frant brought up the rear, tossing non-sticky balls at any clowns who tried to follow them. But the clowns had trouble navigating their unicycles up the incline, and were soon left behind.

Round and round the ancient dome of the Parliament Building they went, tossing balls at the few flying clowns who pestered them. If Helkotron had still been sitting at the top he could have fried them all with one blast of wireless fire. But Prizzie had succeeded in distracting the dragon, so Henry was able to throw open the big double doors and burst into the Parliament Building. Inside the dome was Parliament Hall: one great valley-shaped room with stadium seating full of high-backed fancy wooden chairs looking down at the velvet-carpeted floor of the circular stage that dominated the center of the room. The clowns had scrawled some geometric patterns on the carpet in white and black chalk. Dozens of the robed jesters formed a thick circle ringing the floor. The seats were all empty, but the corpse of the clowns' gigantic Snake Mother was laid atop the seating in a ring that wrapped twice around the room.

The clowns had been performing some kind of ceremony. They each held a copy of a book and they would read a passage in unison, and then one clown would slap another clown in the face, or squirt him with water, or throw a pie. Sometimes a clown would dodge the pie, but that only caused the pie to go splat on the face of somebody standing behind him. One clown dodged a slap then reached up under the robes of the one trying to slap him and pulled down his pants, only to get kicked in the butt by another clown, sending him rolling and somersaulting around the floor.

The ritual seemed to end when every clown had either been slapped, squirted, pantsed, or hit with a pie. That's when the Snake Mother blinked her eyes, and a big red tongue flickered out between her gigantic lips.

"Flute players!" Henry called. "Take position!"

𝆵

Prizzie dodged Helkotron's claws at the last moment, but he also lost the rogue access point he'd been preparing.

"Dammit," Immanuel posted on the chat-box. "He's trying to kick me offline! Give me that access point!"

Prizzie realized that he didn't have the dexterity to evade Helkotron's claws and hack effectively at the same time. Ten years ago, maybe, when he'd been in his prime and hooked on speed. But now he was sober and approaching middle-age, and he had to accept that his edge had been dulled by time.

He made a hard decision. This time when Helkotron swept in with his awful claws outstretched, Prizzie stayed put and hacked like he'd never hacked before. He didn't even look up from his screen to see the inhuman predatory eyes shining with bloodlust. Instead he did what he was born to do. *He typed.*

"I'm in!" Immanuel posted in the chat-box. "The rogue access point is open! I'm starting the encryption!"

At that moment the dragon's electric claws wrapped themselves around Prizzie's body, and Helkotron beat his wings to begin his re-ascent.

𝆵

Inside Parliament Hall the flute players spread out in a ring surrounding the Snake Mother as the great serpent raised her head. She seemed to appraise them all, both the clowns who had revivified her and the interlopers who had come to destroy her.

The snake lashed out to grab a flute player in her maw. The strike was unnervingly fast and the predator gobbled up her prey in three successive chomps.

The remaining flute players started their tune. It was a mystifying melody they'd learned from a far-off nation and the snake responded by bobbing its head back and forth to the rhythm.

Down in the center the clowns threw off their robes. "Stop the flute players!" yelled Babbles the Sad Clown. They all hopped on their unicycles and took out their music boxes to play the discordant twinkle of their hell-music, drowning out the magic of the flutes.

The snake was in turmoil, torn between the tunes. She tried to eat a GX soldier but fell into his spell instead, then was jolted awake by the clowns' song, then back into the GX reverie.

Henry ran forward with the last few of his tennis balls. Lauretta and Paul Frant followed him and they all tossed their tennis balls over the snake's coils and into the parliamentary pit of clowns. Henry had hoped the clowns would drop their music boxes to juggle the balls, but they were quick on the draw and  managed to hold the music boxes between their shoulders and chins, turning the cranks with one hand and juggling the incoming balls with the other. Still the trio added more balls into the mix but somehow the clowns worked it all into their act. They threw the bouncy orbs higher and higher to keep more balls in the air at once, they bounced the balls off their heads, and they threw some back at their attackers.

The snake grew increasingly agitated with being torn betwixt the dueling melodies. She hissed and lashed out with her tail, knocking over three flute players and tossing them into the precarious dance of clown-and-ball. Both songs faltered and she raised her head, crashing through the ceiling and sending down great chunks of stony debris which crushed clowns and flutists alike.

𝆑𝆑𝆑

On Prizzie's screen Immanuel was saying, "I'm almost finished implementing the encryption algorithm. But Prizzie, you've got to get free from Helkotron's grip or else you'll be encrypted too!"

Prizzie knew the awful truth: If he took the time to hack himself free then he'd lose the rogue access point and

Immanuel's encryption algorithm would fail. "Just do it!" Prizzie shouted, and his speech was translated to text on the screen.

Immanuel finalized his encryption algorithm. Helkotron's electric pixels seemed to scramble themselves and he looked like a blurry dragon, then a blurrier dragon, then an unrecognizable chaos of sparkling blue shapes. But as the dragon was scrambled so too was Prizzie's corporeal form, and his laptop, all mixed together with the wireless dragon. The pixels contracted together into a single point of light which exploded softly and silently in a beautiful pulse that expanded across all of wireless space and time.

The Snake Mother had blasted her head out of Parliament to avoid the mind-controlling flutists, only to be mesmerized by that gorgeous wireless explosion which burned her retinas and left her dazed once more, and she swooned and drooped back through the hole.

♯♯♯

Henry was out of tennis balls so he grabbed a discarded flute and joined in the music-making with the remaining flutists. He played as loud as he could and together they overpowered the clowns' tune, charming the snake to dance to their rhythm. Obeying the exotic audio-magic, the Snake Mother opened her mouth and bit her own tail. She chomped, bite-after-bite, swallowing herself slowly until only half of her body remained, then a third, then a quarter, then two ninths, then one fifth, then five twenty-sixths. The clowns were all trapped inside her coil as her body got smaller and smaller, and they were sure to be crushed within the ever-restricting ring of their own self-consuming mother.

Babbles the Sad Clown fell to his knees, sobbing. "Please don't kill our mother! She's the only one we've got and she already died once this year!"

Henry kept playing but Lauretta took up the argument. "Why should we show you mercy after you murdered people and drove people insane with your horrific faces?"

"You made us into outcasts with your xenophobia," Babbles called back. "But are our ugly faces really that different from your own ugly hearts? Maybe if you weren't so afraid to look at us, well maybe then we could all get along. I propose that your fear of clowns is just a reflection of a deeper fear. A fear of your own hearts! Well look at them now! Look inside yourselves and tell me what you see!"

These words moved Henry. He knew his own heart was fickle, transient, controlling, and arrogant. His desire for freedom was just a mask for a deeper lust to impose order on the world, seeking power vacuums where he could make his mark, just as these clown-goggles masked the ugly clown faces with more palatable visuals.

Lauretta said, "Okay, but you murdered a bunch of people and your snake-mother will keep eating people if she stays here."

"There was lots of murdering going on," Babbles said. "Let's just call it water under the bridge, part of the natural political cycle, and try to get back to business as usual."

Paul Frant chimed in. "Let's call a truce, have the election, and then whichever party wins can negotiate with the clowns and decide the fate of their Snake Mother."

All parties agreed and the flutists ceased their tooting, with the Snake Mother resting easy at eleven sixty-sevenths of her original length. Everybody felt the soothing effect of newly-struck peace, and a bright hint of sunrise oozed in through the hole in the dome.

"But what about Libert0r and Trudy?" Henry said. "We can't hold the election while they're still terrorizing the city!"

Everybody rushed outside onto the spiral ramp to see how far Libert0r's crawl had progressed. One of the GX flutists put away his flute and pulled out a brass telescope. "By the gods," the foreigner cursed. "They're destroying each other!"

He handed the telescope around so everybody could get a look. When Henry got his turn he saw where the two great bulks of Trudy and Libert0r had come together in a field of flattened trees, each force seeking to consume the other. But as they met their bodies slowly annihilated each other like particles and anti-particles. Even as Henry watched, the two enemies were reduced to small blobs which mushed together, dissipated, and finally disappeared. In that final moment the glitter that had sparkled inside LibertOr's body was released in a great twinkling puff. The sunrise glinted prettily off all the little sparkle particles and bathed the island in shimmering light.

"The Market's been destroyed," Lauretta breathed with relief.

But Henry shook his head. "You can't destroy a market. Something tells me he'll be back, and when he does we'll need a stronger government than ever to restrain him again."

Paul Frant rubbed his hands together. "Well let's finally have this damn election. You guys send word to the voters that it's safe to go out to the voting stations, and I'll warm up some soup."


**Chapter 41: The Election**

As the sun emerged from its hiding place behind the horizon, so too did the electorate emerge from the safety of their homes, rubbing their eyes as they shuffled to the voting stations. They drank their morning coffee and ate their breakfast croissants and bagels, some still wearing pajamas and messy bed hair as they discussed the recent hostilities.

Across the island various comedy clubs and amusement parks had been temporarily annexed and converted into voting stations by the municipal government. The election commission decided the happy-go-lucky venues would lighten the tension of this bloody political cycle. One man, standing in line at a comedy club to cast his vote while wearing a bathrobe and drinking his coffee, struck up conversation with the pretty brunette lady just ahead of him in line.

"I bet everybody's voting for Millenarianistic

Chronodyke," he said. "They really saved our ass."

"The Soup Party might get a few seats," the brunette countered. "Nutrition's a hot topic these days."

The man chuckled. "I can't believe Destructoid is actually on the ballot. We should both vote for them. When the numbers come out everybody will see those two lone votes and they'll wonder who the fuck voted for Destructoid."

The brunette grabbed his arm as she laughed. "Oh my Godhead that would be hilarious. They'd all be like, *who are those two idiots?*"

"It would be our dirty little hilarious secret," he said in a mock-conspiratorial tone.

𝆑𝆑𝆑

On Parliament Road the City Works crews were all busy removing the corpses and debris from the last two debates and building a new stage for the announcement of the victor, and the subsequent speeches.

Henry waited patiently in his tent with Lauretta and a few other Millenarianistic Chronodyke party members. He wasn't sure whether he wanted to win or not, or how many of the voters had learned about his true identity, or whether they cared. But it was nice to sit with the sun filtering in through the fabric of the tent, holding Lauretta's hand, and to just relax and enjoy the peaceful moment. They both missed Vij and Malcolm. Bitter memories of the dead were filtered through the pleasant and peaceful morning atmosphere. The sounds of conversation and chirping birds came in through the tent's entrance along with the smells of barbecue sausage and fresh pots of coffee. Spoons clinked against porcelain bowls as several people enjoyed some breakfast soup.

The Master of Ceremonies rocked a rocket-lady ensemble, wearing a form-fitting silver suit with red trim, and white nylon boots and gloves that reached up to her knees and elbows. Her eyes were hidden behind cool, dark, cat-eye shades set in white frames, and her hair blossomed in a boisterous perm.

"Okay space freaks," she said into the microphone. "Let's get ready to blast off into our next political era. Who wants to hear the results of today's election?"

Only a few people had dared to come to Parliamountain to hear the victor's speech in-person. But those few present patriots called out, "We do!" with surprising exuberance.

The Master of Ceremonies tried to squeeze even more exuberance from the audience. "I said, *who wants to hear the results of today's election?*"

"We do," the crowd responded with less exuberance, more annoyance, in a very matter-of-fact tone.

The Master of Ceremonies opened the flap of the envelope that contained the election results. Then she pulled out the sheet of paper upon which the election results had been printed. She took a moment to admire the high-quality acid-free paper that they'd used, sparing no expense on this important occasion, and it inspired an unexpected wave of pride for her island-nation, so she took another moment to bask in that pride and to gaze out at her beautiful surroundings, and to just live in the moment for once and to appreciate life as it comes to you, like a wondrous gift, instead of treating every moment like a battle. Then she read the election results.

"The winner of the municipal election is Destructoid, with one hundred percent of the vote. Which means Unit Seven will be our next mayor."

The crowd was silent. Even the birds stopped chirping.

"All the other parties got zero votes," she went on, redundantly clarifying. "Just for the record, I'm going to admit that I voted for Destructoid because I thought it would be funny. I figured I'd be the only one, because why the fuck would anybody vote for them after all this carnage? But seriously, why the fuck did *everybody* vote for them?"

"I thought it would be funny," the crowd responded in unison.

The Master of Ceremonies nodded. "In retrospect, we

probably shouldn't have used comedy clubs and amusement parks as our voting stations. That's a lesson for next time."

Unit Seven approached the podium. "I would like to make my victory speech," he said.

The Master of Ceremonies hesitated but couldn't think of a legally acceptable reason to deny the robot access to the microphone. So she stepped aside.

"You've all been through a lot during these past days," Unit Seven told the crowd. "But you're about to go through a whole lot worse. Every single one of you will die at the hands of Destructoid. The more you resist the more it will hurt. We will use the worst kinds of public torture to make an example of any foolish rebels. Once you all are dead, then we will scrape this island into the ocean, never to be heard from again. You have made a terrible decision. I will wait patiently in my tent with the other members of my party, for the current parliament to legally transfer power to Destructoid."

### Chapter 42: Ethelcrest Emergency Parliament II

The current living burbmasters of parliament walked up the ramp and entered Parliament Hall, in a daze. Inside the hall they had trouble finding a good place to hold their meeting because the clowns' Snake Mother still dominated the space, even in her self-consuming diminished form. Wrapped up in a ring like that, there was no way to get her back out through the doors. So they all gathered among the seats, since she blocked their access to the central stage floor.

The Master of Ceremonies said, "I hereby call to order the second emergency parliament of Ethelcrest. The emergency, of course, is that Destructoid seems to have legitimately won, and we should probably do something about that."

Paul Frant said, "First, can we do something about this snake?"

The magic eight ball representing the leader of The Magic Party suddenly popped into existence, with a theatrical puff of vapour. Henry gazed into the view-port to see what the eight ball had to say and read it out loud. "The eight ball says, we can't get her out the door like that, so our only options are either to chop her up and make a mess of our lovely Parliament Hall, or else leave her here forever as some kind of decoration or ominous talisman."

Paul said, "I propose we chop her up and make some snake soup. This is leek season and everybody knows how hard it is to find good snake meat on Ethelcrest. When was the last time you guys had snake & leek soup? Can you even remember?"

Babbles the Sad Clown protested. "If you guys chop up my mother for soup then we'll be back at square one, which is clowns terrorizing the city. I propose we pull her tail out of her mouth and allow her to lay her clown-eggs here in Parliament Hall, and we can just move our meeting place elsewhere."

Henry said, "I propose we let the incoming government deal with the snake, and we'll just stay off to the side for now."

They all voted for Henry's solution to the snake problem.

"Next order of business," Henry continued, deciding to take the lead with this wayward meeting. "Who the fuck voted for Destructoid?"

They all clamored their disgruntled agreement. "Yeah!" they yelled, "who the fuck?" But then one-by-one they each admitted to voting for Destructoid because they thought it would be funny to see one or two suicidal votes on the tally.

Babbles said, "Get off your high horse, Johnny. They got every single vote, which means yours too."

"I'm a convicted felon, technically still serving time," Henry said. "They wouldn't let me vote."

A couple people gasped with shock. "You're a convicted felon?" But everybody else seemed to already know, and nobody seemed to care, so those two shocked people decided it must not be a big deal.

Henry offered a proposal. "I say, let's pass legislation to

dissolve the government completely, and then hold a new election. There's no way everybody will vote for Destructoid twice."

Paul said, "I don't think the city can handle another election campaign."

"Then let's dissolve parliament and declare The Master of Ceremonies to be the king," Henry said.

"I would be the sassiest king ever," The Master of Ceremonies said, and she cracked a whip that nobody had realized she had.

The magic eight ball shook itself and Henry read the words that appeared in the purple liquid. "The magic eight ball says: A woman king? That's ridiculous. It isn't proper."

Paul snapped back, "Well she'd be better than a cowardly, bigoted magic eight ball representing a disappeared magician trapped in some shadow realm."

The magic eight ball shook itself again and Henry read, "Fuck you, soup-fucking rat-fucker. What kind of retarded chef cooked up your... and I'm not going to read the rest of this."

"While I would be a sassy-ass king," the Master of Ceremonies said, "sass isn't what Ethelcrest needs right now. Right now we need order, and Henry led the charge to restore order to Ethelcrest, so I'm nominating him as king."

They unanimously accepted this proposal. Then they quickly wrote up some legislation dissolving the government and re-instating it as a monarchy under King Henry. Everybody signed the document and Henry said, "I stand before you as King Henry of Ethelcrest. Now, is everybody armed?"

The former Parliament members all took out their knives, composite bows, and explosives.

"Great. Now bring in Unit Seven."

The Master of Ceremonies went outside and came back with the robot. Unit Seven stood before the former burbmasters of parliament and said, "I am ready to accept the official transfer of power."

Henry was the only one who wasn't showing any

weapons, since it made a more impressive image for his power to be implied than visually displayed. But everybody else cocked their bows, cracked their whips, or primed their explosives, to show Unit Seven that they meant business.

Henry told the robot, "We passed legislation dissolving the government completely and re-instating it as a monarchy, with me as the king. You've been usurped."

"Hold on a second," Unit Seven protested. "If you dissolve the government, then any king-making legislation you wrote is suddenly null and void because it's the legislation of the old, nullified government. So really there is no king, only anarchy, and Destructoid is free to destroy the city."

Henry spoke very carefully now. "We made sure to make the dissolution of the old democracy and the instantiation of the new monarchy happen at the same instant, as defined here on line twelve, so the final declaration of the old government is also the founding document of my new one."

"Let me take a look at that paperwork," Unit Seven demanded. He put on reading glasses to study the verbiage. "Hmm. This seems to check out. Well naturally Destructoid respects the decisions of parliament, and thus we respect the absolute authority of our new king. However, I have to say that I'm very disappointed. You may have followed the letter of the law in this cleverly worded legislation, but you all know that you broke the essence of the law when you chose not to hand over power to the elected government. This is a sad day for democracy. Now I'll go give the bad news to my fellow robots, and we will probably leave this fickle island so we can find a nation that actually respects the democratic will of the people, and we will utterly annihilate it."

Everybody held their heads in shame as Unit Seven left the building. As the doors were closing behind him Paul Frant turned aside and muttered something into his collar. Moments later Lucy jumped in through the hole in the ceiling, her robot body slamming on the wooden seats and sending splinters all around. Several GX Island soldiers rappelled halfway down to the floor and trained their machine-guns at the gathering.

"Well if it isn't Johnny Tetrahedron," Lucy sneered robotically. "Or should I say, Henry Ecgherht! That's right, I know your true identity! But it doesn't matter now because GX Island is taking over Ethelcrest, with Paul Frant as a puppet-king, and me as the de-facto ruler running things behind the scenes. And any citizens who resist will be sent to GX Island as slaves to pick apples in their beautiful apple orchards!"

"Plus everybody will finally eat a healthy amount of soup," Paul added.

"And who is representing GX Island in this deal?" Henry asked.

A broad-chested sailor rappelled down among the benches, with a dark jacket and a luxurious black beard tinged with white. "There is no deal," the sailor said. "This is an unequivocal take-over, not a negotiation. You are outgunned and your nation is in a state of chaos. Ethelcrest is ours!"

"Captain Spuknit!" Henry boomed. "This is how you treat me after I fixed your boat?"

"Henry? Good lord! I did not realize you would be here. Look man, this is not personal, we just want your natives and unrestricted access to your Moon Burb, and everybody hates a power vacuum anyway, so just stand down or we will shoot you all to death."

"Just hear me out," Henry said. "Firstly, I've been declared king so your men can point their guns at me, instead of at everybody else. Yes, like that, good. Now, you don't really want to run a whole nation from afar, plus we can provide you with enough QuantumBrain® for your sailors to keep your boats running, if you can keep us supplied with gyroflavin. And if you like The Moon Burb so much, we'll help you build your own. Our nations could work together on a Moon Island. Or we could even collaborate on a hot-air balloon trip to visit the actual moon together."

Some of the former parliament members grumbled.

"People still remember Mayor Dean's balloon-themed transgressions," The Master of Ceremonies whispered to him.

"This is totally different," Henry said.

"They might not see it that way."

Captain Spuknit said, "I have seen how Henry handles himself, and I think my own nation would benefit more from having an alliance with such a king, rather than orchestrating this coup. On behalf of GX Island I formally withdraw our attempt to conquer Ethelcrest. Now let's talk trade!"

And somewhere deep in the ocean, the flickering life of ancient Market Forces began to stir once more.

## Chapter 43: King Henry I

In the days that followed Henry used his authoritarian power to clean up some of the devastation caused by the election campaign, and to set the stage for Ethelcrest's future. He ordered a graveyard built in the space that had been flattened by Libert0r's ingress, and all the casualties of the election campaign were buried there. The Snake Mother was lifted up by ropes to hang from the ceiling of Parliament Hall, which was renamed Monarchy Hall, and the snake hovered ominously over all government proceedings.

Peace was struck with GX Island. They handed over Lucy's criminal brain for trial but Henry allowed them to keep her robot body. The two nations started several large-scale moon-themed projects.

On Parliament Road, which was renamed Monarchy Road, Henry ordered a statue to be erected. It depicted Prizzie in his final corporeal moments, captured in Helkotron's claws, fingers on his laptop keys and pure will in his eyes. The plaque read, "The Dragon Hacker."

Everybody returned to business-as-usual, and Henry immediately became bored. In their luxurious royal bedroom beneath Monarchy Hall Henry told Lauretta, "I think I enjoyed the process of rising to power, but I don't want to run a nation."

"I want to be queen though!" Lauretta protested. She rubbed her belly. "And I want our daughter to be a princess."

"You'll always be my queen, and our daughter or son will always be my princess or prince."

"That's a lame cop-out," she said. "Do you want to go try to take over some other nation?"

"You know, I kind of do," Henry said, surprised at himself. "Everybody on Gold Island is depressed anyway. We could free them from their robot overlords and bring some joy into their miserable lives."

So it was that mere days after stepping into power Henry secretly wrote a decree handing power over to Paul Frant, since he seemed like a fairly responsible guy, and left the document in Monarchy Hall for all the newly appointed burbmasters to see in the morning. And in the middle of the night Henry and his pregnant wife fled to the shore with a bag of QuantumBrain® and started rowing beneath the starlight, toward Gold Island.

### Epilogue: King Paul

"Thanks for meeting with me on such short notice," Paul said to Captain Spuknit. They sat together, alone, in the great space of Monarchy Hall, which Paul had renamed The War Room.

"What is this about?" Spuknit insisted sharply. "Where is King Henry?"

Paul sighed. "I'm afraid Henry wasn't cut out to be king, so he abandoned us. I'm the king now. But let me assure you, I plan to honor the agreements he made with GX Island."

"Then what do you need from me?"

"I need your ships," Paul answered bluntly. "You see, I plan to scale up our soup production, but we don't have enough fuel to simmer the nutritious volumes that my ambitions demand. We need coal. I want all the coal on Gold Island, and I don't want to pay for it. My plan is to overthrow the robots who enslaved the coal-miners there, and then we will be their slave-masters."

"And what does GX Island get out of this deal?"

"We'll split the coal fifty-fifty, and you'll get an endless supply of soup."

Spuknit nodded. He would never admit it, but scurvy was rampant on his ships, and a constant supply of soup would be a major boon.

The deal was struck. The GX Island Navy convened at Ethelcrest one week later, and as the sun set the armada launched for its new destination: the glorious wastelands of Gold Island, and woe betide any man or woman who stood in their way.


The End

**Books by Matt Payne:**

The Adventure Poem of Julius Cinnamon
The Sick Book of Lies
Terranomicon